CW00502212

Blood Fiends' Bane:

Book 1 of the Vampire Queen Saga

William Stacey

Published by Bastard Sword Press

E-book cover by Isabel Robalo – IsaDesign.net
Paperback cover by Mirela Barbu Design
Formatting by Polgarus Studio www.polgarusstudio.com
Map by Steam Power Studios www.steampowerstudios.com.au

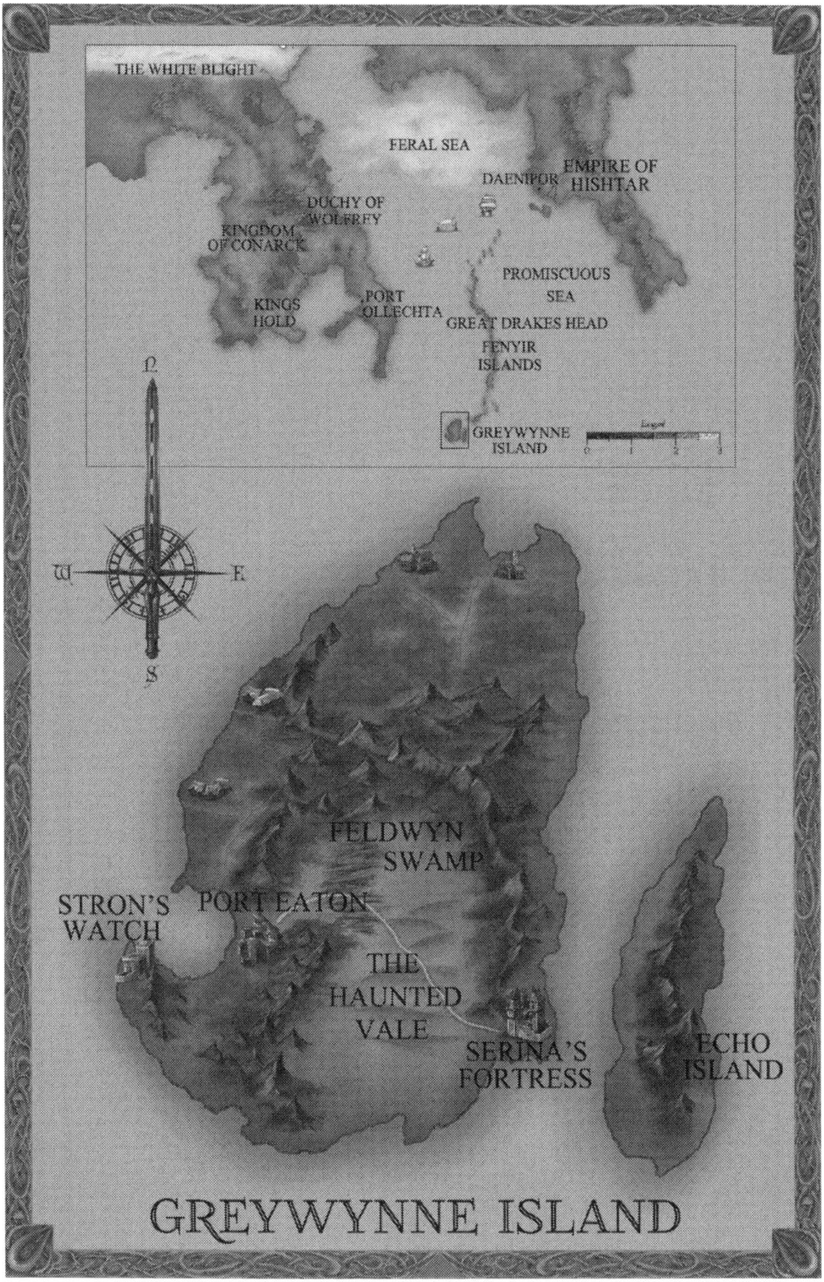
THE WHITE BLIGHT
FERAL SEA
DAENIPOR
EMPIRE OF HISHTAR
DUCHY OF WOLFREY
KINGDOM OF CONARCK
PROMISCUOUS SEA
KINGS HOLD
PORT OLLECHTA
GREAT DRAKES HEAD
FENYIR ISLANDS
GREYWYNNE ISLAND
N
W
E
S
FELDWYN SWAMP
STRON'S WATCH
PORT EATON
THE HAUNTED VALE
SERINA'S FORTRESS
ECHO ISLAND
GREYWYNNE ISLAND

Part One:

A Legend of Death

The Siege of Greywynne Fortress

Auslaug Oar-Arm hesitated only a moment as she stepped over the ring of corpses and dropped down on one knee before the queen. When she had received word that the queen had demanded her presence, she hadn't known what to expect, just that it had been important enough to pull Auslaug from her defense of the fortress as the northerners breached the outer curtain wall. Certainly, she hadn't foreseen the ritual slaughter of her fellow childes—the last of Serina's battle captains—their bodies carefully arrayed upon the rune-marked stones before the throne. She felt no great kinship with them, no regret at their passing—or even real fear for her own safety. In truth, she had already accepted that she was going to die that night. What did bother her, though, was the uncertainty over what had occurred there because whatever it was had been significant—the air within the cavern was still heavy with the residue of eldritch power. Torches set in bronze stands flickered atop the raised stone platform upon which sat the queen in her antler-and-hide-bound throne. The only other servants present, trembling in the shadows, were human.

Am I the last now? she wondered.

Like Auslaug, the queen had girded herself for war, wearing a brightly burnished coat of ringmail. Neither she nor Auslaug carried a weapon—why bother when one's own hands could rip and tear flesh and bone like loaves of bread.

Auslaug's gaze darted upward as the cavern's high ceiling shook. Rocks and dust sifted down upon the coffins and vaults that surrounded them. The Great Crypt was as fitting a locale for the end as any other, although Auslaug had assumed she'd die in battle, killing as many northern dogs as she could before they brought her down.

The queen herself was serenity, her face granite, looking not unlike the statues of her ancestors standing about the Great Crypt. More rocks fell from the ceiling, and the human servants scurried back farther in fear, pointlessly. *A waste of time. Escape is no longer possible.* The invaders would be there soon enough. They were coming with fire and stake and foul-chanting priests—coming to pull down the queen. Auslaug would die herself before that happened, but it would still happen.

"My childe, my brave battle captain," the queen said, filling Auslaug with love despite her melancholy, "lift your heart."

Even then, with the northern invaders almost within the fortress, the queen appeared utterly unconcerned, as if the northern army was nothing more than a hindrance. Her long blond hair was pulled back severely, woven into tight braids and interlaced with bone ornaments, gems, and gold chains. Her blue facial tattoos, intricate arcane runes covering the entire upper half of her face, looked like a mask in the shadows of the cavern. Despite her queen's entreaties, Auslaug's heart remained stone.

This is so bitterly unfair, so crushingly unjust—and all because of Stron and that cursed sword. Why did the Illthori even craft a blade that was so dangerous to our kind?

"My queen," said Auslaug, casting her gaze down again. "I… I have failed you… It is over. They'll be here shortly."

"No, my childe. You have succeeded, given me the time I needed, as have your brothers and sisters—given all."

"My queen, I don't—"

"You don't need to understand, just to trust. Do you, Auslaug? Do you trust me?"

"I… Yes. I love you."

The queen rose from her throne, approached Auslaug, and let her fingers trail through the hair atop Auslaug's head. "I know you do, my general. And I love you, too. That is why you must leave me."

Above them, the cavern once again shook under the impact of the northerners' war machines, dislodging stones and a fog-like curtain of dust.

Chapter 1

Owen

The Duchy of Wolfrey
Forty-eight years after the fall of Greywynne Fortress

Duty is a double-edged sword blade. It can cut the user as easily as the foe. That was what Keep-Captain Brice Awde was always telling Owen Toscovar and the other men-at-arms. Most of the time, he and the other guardsmen would consider it just one more of the Keep-Captain's oh-so-somber life lessons, but right then, Owen was beginning to understand the danger of following one's duty. *Will it cut me as well tonight?*

Owen shifted in his saddle and pulled his otter-skin cloak closer around his neck in a futile effort to keep out the constant patter of rain. His cotton-lined undertunic beneath his ring-mail coat was already damp and had been so since before the sun had set hours earlier.

He glanced at the backs of the others riding ahead of him. Keep-Captain Awde led, with his second-in-command, Keep-Lieutenant Warin Sayer just behind him and Fin Tokke—at twenty-three, only one year older than Owen—riding behind the two officers. For four days, they had been searching the hinterlands for the Ballards. And for four days, they had found nothing but forest, endless summer rain, and a trail long gone cold.

The Ballards were long gone, Owen knew. They wouldn't remain in the north, not with a man like Keep-Captain Awde hunting them—and they had to know that Duke Oskaley would send his best warrior after them. Justice was swift and uncomplicated in the north, and while murder was enough of a crime to earn a hangman's rope, murdering a traveling merchant was bad for trade. If the Ballards stayed in the north, they'd die. They must have known that. Once again, Owen muttered a silent entreaty to Father Craftsman, praying that the Ballards were far away.

As young boys, Owen and Emrys Ballard had been close, spending hours hunting rabbits, squirrels, and fork-tailed wood-hets in the northern woods at the base of Mount Cloven, only a half-day's ride from Wolfredsuntown. Life had been good back then, before his parents died, before his older brother Orin had inherited the stables. Often, he, Orin, and Emrys spent days out in those very woods, camping and fishing, riding recklessly across farmers' fields, swimming in frigid northern lakes, and climbing any rock face that looked dangerous. Like all northern boys, they had been fearless, certain of their immortality. Together, they tackled some of the more dangerous cliffs along the east side of the mountain, risking life and limb while free climbing its rocky surface. In many ways, Emrys had been more of a brother than Orin.

If it came to it, could I kill Emrys?

Could I kill anyone? Could I really hack a man down, end his life? The older guardsmen back at Castle Dain insisted he would, told him that when the moment came, training and self-preservation would guide his arm.

And if not, they said with grins, he'd die.

I'll never forgive Orin for this.

Pushing his steel half-helm back, he ran his fingers over his forehead, raw where the helmet's leather liner rubbed against his skin. At least that night, they'd sleep under a roof, in a real bed instead of on the ground. He smelled the wood fire of the travelers' inn before they came to the southern edge of the forest. From there, he could just make out the dark shape of the inn, seeing the glow of welcoming torchlight through its shuttered windows. His stomach rumbled at the smell of stew.

Just past the forest's edge, Keep-Captain Awde sat upon his mount, looking back at Owen and Fin. Sayer sat his own mount beside him, conversing quietly with the Keep-Captain.

"Toscovar," the Keep-Captain called out, "come here."

As he rode past Fin, the tall, thin young man with a big nose glanced at Owen, met his eye, then shrugged. Owen rode his sorrel up beside the other two men.

"You've been here, the Green Heart Inn?" Keep-Captain Awde asked him.

"I have. Once," Owen replied. "My father sold horses to the innkeeper."

The older man nodded, his stoic gaze locked on Owen's face. "Are the Ballards on foot or on horse?"

Owen paused, considering his response as the two men watched him. Lately, that sort of thing had been happening more often, the Keep-Captain soliciting his opinion, trying to draw more out of Owen. For his first year of service, Owen had put his head down and done as he had been told, quietly learning how to fight, how to get by as a man-at-arms. But several months back, the Keep-Captain had begun to single him out for impromptu discussions on tactics and management. At first, Owen had thought it was because of his expertise with horses, but recently, he wasn't so sure. As the younger son of the local horse-trader, Owen had no particularly impressive future as a soldier, especially since the only reason he was a man-at-arms at all was that the duke had offered him the choice between service or banishment.

"Well?" Awde pressed him.

"They're on foot, I think," Owen said, only realizing his opinion as he gave it. "There were no horses at their farm, but when they were seen at the murder scene along the Forest Way, they ran off on foot into the woods."

That meant, he realized with a heavy heart, the Ballards probably weren't long gone from the Duchy of Wolfrey at all. They could very well have still been about.

"Could have had horses hidden away somewhere," Sayer said.

Owen shook his head. "The stables at their farm hadn't been tended in weeks. I think they must have sold their horses, probably before they took up robbery."

Sayer sneered. "That a fact or an opinion, Horse-boy?"

Owen bit back an angry remark.

"Well, Toscovar," asked Awde, "which is it?"

"Being on foot is an opinion," he said. "But the state of the stables is a fact. There haven't been horses on that farm in weeks. I'm sure of it."

Awde nodded. "I agree. That's what the women told me as well, that the older brothers had sold the horses. Weren't too happy about it, either. So, what sort of welcome do you think we'll find in the inn?"

"None at all," Owen said. "The Ballard farm is close enough to walk from here. They like to drink and fight. This is where they'd do it."

"They're all related hereabouts, anyhow," muttered Sayer.

"Keep going," said Awde, drumming his fingers over his sword hilt. "How do you see things?"

Owen pointed past the inn. "This is as far south as you can go and still be in the north. The King's Road runs along the coast, two days to Port Ollechta."

Awde nodded. "Go on."

"They can walk it if they have to and be gone from the borders of the Duchy of Wolfrey within an hour. Easy for them to vanish."

"And they may already have," said Sayer.

"But they're not from the coast or the south. They know these woods, these lands. They know these people. They'd feel secure here. They can run whenever they want."

Awde gripped Owen's shoulder and squeezed it tightly. "We'll go in quietly. I'll do the talking."

"They won't say anything," Sayer said. "Not to us."

"Not in words," said Awde. "But watch their faces. Watch what they do." He motioned Fin over to join them. "The three of us—me, the Keep-Lieutenant, and you, Tokke—are going to go inside." He glanced at Owen. "You, Toscovar, I want you to hang back on foot. After we've stabled the horses, sneak in close, somewhere you can watch the rear of the inn. If anyone leaves, I want you to stop him and bring him to me. You understand?"

Owen nodded, swallowing.

Awde locked his gaze on Owen. "Use your judgment. If there's more than one, come get us first."

Owen dismounted and handed his reins to Fin.

"I'll save you some beer," Fin said with a grin before following the other two men, leading Owen's horse behind him.

Owen pulled his cloak about him again and slipped away around the side of the inn, keeping his distance from both the inn and the stable. With the rain and cloud cover, the night was dark, but enough light was spilling from the inn for Owen to find his way. As he came around the rear of the building, he found himself breathing too hard, his heart beating wildly. He forced himself to breathe, to calm down. Chances were that nothing would happen and he'd soon be warm and dry, with a bowl of stew. He knelt down, moving his sword belt out of the way, in a spot where he could watch both the rear of the inn and the entrance to the stable.

The others brought their palfreys inside the stable then, a few minutes later, left the stable to approach the inn. Light spilled around the corner of the inn as they opened the door, and Owen heard loud laughter and conversation as the others went inside. In a moment, the noise of the inn's patrons abruptly died. After some moments, the sounds of conversation rose again. The moments stretched on, but nothing happened.

Nothing is going to happen.

He had no desire to fight anyone that night. He was a capable swordsman, one of the best in the garrison, and he was much bigger and stronger than most men—which was one of the reasons they had taken to calling him Horse-boy, his family's stables being the other—but he was no killer, and he knew it. He suspected the other soldiers knew it as well, which was probably why they felt they could get away with ridiculing a big man like him. He had no business being a soldier. He didn't want four more years of being a man-at-arms. It was never what he want—

A shadow darted past the side of the inn, moving in the direction of the stable. Someone was trying to sneak out of the back of the inn after all. In the dark, distracted by his own self-pity, Owen had missed it.

He felt his mouth go dry, followed by a sense of breathlessness. He wondered what to do. If he ran inside the inn and got the others, whoever it was might get away, but he had been distracted and didn't know for sure whether just the one shadow had slipped by. If more than one person was there…

He pictured the sneer on Sayer's face and the disappointment on Keep-Captain Awde's. Grinding his teeth, he flexed his fingers and then made fists. *One person,* he finally decided. *It's probably just one person.*

Drawing his sword, he rose into a crouch. He was a trained man-at-arms. Armed with a castle-forged sword, protected by a ring-mail coat, he was more than a match for any bandit. Moving cautiously, he stalked around the side of the inn and approached the stable's open gateway.

One of the horses whinnied, and he was certain it was his. He inhaled deeply, forced down his fear, and stepped through the stable's entrance. The moment he did, he realized he had been wrong—two people had run past him. Emrys and Trystan Ballard stared openmouthed at Owen, caught in the midst of saddling his horse.

Owen moved first, stepping forward into a fighting stance, his sword held two-handed in front of him, the point threatening the two men. "Don't—"

He sensed rather than heard movement behind him and had just begun to turn when someone tackled him, knocking him down to the straw-covered dirt floor of the stables, hammering the breath from his chest. His sword slid away, and the horses neighed in fear as Trystan and Emrys rushed him. Panic gave him strength as he flipped onto his side, throwing away the man who had knocked him down. However, a moment later, the other two men were on him, pinning him to his back, punching him repeatedly in the face and head. Even for a large man like Owen, three against one was near-impossible odds. He bucked his hips, knocking one man off, but only for a moment. The horses stamped and whinnied in terror.

Will the others inside the inn hear?

Owen tried to yell for help, but a hand covered his mouth, muffling him and restricting his breathing. Desperate, he wrenched one hand free and threw a clumsy, off-balance punch that hit something but didn't have any real effect. Then, his hand was gripped tightly again.

"Hurry," a breathless voice urged. "Stick him!"

He felt a painful jab in his ribs.

They're trying to murder me!

Real terror washed over him. He realized he needed to get to his feet, or he was going to die. He felt another sharp jab in his ribs. That time, one of the men grunted with the effort.

"Not… going in."

"The throat. Saw his throat. Hurry!"

Bright lights burst in his vision, and then he heard a thump, followed by a wheeze. The weight atop him lessened. One fewer man was holding him down.

"Someone else—"

The hand over his mouth disappeared, and Owen sucked in air. Nearby, he heard a squeal followed by the sounds of blows striking flesh, punches. The others must have heard the commotion after all. The walls of the stable shook, and the horses screamed again. Then, only one man still remained atop Owen. Without thinking it through, he jammed his thumbs into the man's face, feeling for the hollow of his eye sockets. When he felt the soft give of the man's eyes, he rammed his thumbs all the way in until they were wet. The man screamed and fell back, freeing Owen.

In a moment, Owen was back on his feet, somehow finding the energy to move despite his exhaustion. He could just make out the forms of two men wrestling on the floor, as well as the writhing and howling figure of the man near his feet, whom Owen had just been fighting. Without pausing to think, Owen drew his dagger, dropped a knee onto the man's chest to hold him in place, and then stabbed him repeatedly. The man's screams changed into a wet, gurgled cry.

Moments later, the pounding of boot steps announced the arrival of others, and torchlight flared through the gateway of the stable as Keep-Captain Awde, Lieutenant Sayer, and Fin rushed in, swords in hand. Behind them, a crowd followed. Somebody grabbed at Owen, but he yelled and threw the person away, his mind still roiling with the need to stay alive.

"Leave him be!" roared the keep-captain.

The terrified horses continued to scream, stamping at the walls of their stables. Some men ran to calm them; others held the arms of a young man with short dark hair. Owen didn't know him, but he must have been the one who saved Owen's life. On the straw-covered floor of the stable lay all three Ballard brothers. One of them, Trystan Ballard, the eldest of the Ballards, writhed and moaned on the ground, clutching at his bloody eyes, the front of his tunic drenched in glistening blood.

Owen glanced at his own hand still gripping the bloody dagger. He stared at it in confusion.

Keep-Captain Awde moved in front of Owen, holding his shoulders and staring into his face. "Toscovar, I asked you if you were okay."

His heart hammered against his chest, and he had to look down at his body, running his hands over his throat and ribs before he realized he wasn't bleeding, hadn't been stabbed after all. He nodded, still gasping for air. "Think… think so."

The keep-captain turned away, leaving Owen.

Sayer knelt down next to the still-writhing Trystan Ballard but then shook his head. "Gut wounds."

"Do it," said the keep-captain.

Do what?

A moment later, Sayer put the point of his sword over Trystan's heart and plunged it deep. Trystan gasped once and then died.

Owen stared in horror. He had done that. Sayer had only finished what he had started, putting the man out of his misery. The veterans had been right. He was capable of killing.

Keep-Captain Awde spun on the young man being held by the inn's patrons. "Who are you?"

The young man was tall, with a swordsman's wide shoulders. His short dark hair was disheveled, with bits of straw stuck in it. His eyebrows were thick, and his nose had clearly been broken before and had healed poorly. He was unshaven, and his tunic and hose were threadbare and dirty, giving him the appearance of having slept in the wild for days.

"Dilan," the young man with the thick eyebrows answered. "Dilan Reese."

Owen edged closer. "Captain, I think he saved my life."

"This true, Dilan Reese?" Keep-Captain Awde asked.

Dilan cocked his head toward the two remaining Ballards, unconscious and still lying on the straw-covered floor, Emrys and his older brother Ralf. "I had no silver for the inn. Thought I'd sleep in a stall, at least get out of the rain. The fight woke me up. Three against one, couldn't do nothing."

Keep-Captain Awde glared at the other patrons. "Sure you could. *They* all did." He sheathed his sword and jammed a finger at the innkeeper and his customers. "The inn is closed for the night. All of you go home. Now!"

A muttering of angry protests rose, mostly from the innkeeper, but the crowd did as ordered. Owen glared at them as they left. They had all known the Ballards were there, probably inside drinking. His face flushed with heat.

"What of them?" Sayer asked, indicating Emrys and Ralf Ballard.

"Clap 'em in chains," said the keep-captain. "We ride back to the castle tonight." He turned to face the innkeeper, still present. "But first, we eat. Free of charge."

The innkeeper's face tightened. "But—"

"Be glad I don't burn your stinking hovel to the ground." The keep-captain turned to address the men holding Dilan Reese. "Let him go. Come, Dilan Reese. Eat with us. As it turns out, you have no need of silver this night."

Chapter 2

Modwyn

The duke's bedchamber in Castle Dain stank of sickness and rot, a nearly palpable miasma so thick it could almost be touched. The only light came from a flickering candle that sat on a table, its melted wax flowing over the holder and hardening on the surface of the wooden table. Modwyn Du'Aig, the twenty-five-year-old physician newly appointed to the noble Dain family, sat beside Duke Oskaley Dain's sickbed, silently watching the sleeping man, with clinical detachment.

A human life is such a fragile thing, he mused.

The old man was close to the end of his life. His bony chest barely moved as his breath rasped in and out. The long hairs within Oskaley's nostrils quivered and danced with each exhalation. Soon, even that sad attempt at breathing would stop altogether. Modwyn's new liege lord, Duke Oskaley, Lord Dain of the northern duchy of Wolfrey in the kingdom of Conarck, was dying.

Modwyn may have graduated from the physicians' university in the capital only three months before, but he recognized the certainty of death. Staring down at his patient, he whispered, "What keeps you going, I wonder? Why do you fight the inevitable?"

The old man didn't answer, nor had Modwyn expected him to. He had been asleep for most of the day since suddenly taking ill the day before.

"What keeps any of us going?" Modwyn answered for him, plucking free a loose thread from his dark-gray physician's robes.

He rubbed his palms over his face and stared at the closed door. Soon, he knew, the Lady Danika Dain, the duke's daughter, would return and once again demand Modwyn do the impossible—save the ailing duke. He sighed, rose, and stood near the open window to feel the summer breeze brush his face as he watched his patient out of the corner of his eye. He didn't have that much longer to wait, Modwyn knew. His charge's breathing was becoming more erratic.

From the window, Modwyn saw the town below, Wolfredsuntown, was nearly dark, as was to be expected at that time of night. The townsfolk would be sleeping, protected by strong walls, surrounded by their fat little children—warm, safe, and happy. In the morning, they would wake with the sun and go about their day. Each day was the same.

What is that like—to be safe, to be happy?

To be loved?

When the bedchamber door softly opened, Modwyn roused himself and forced a smile upon his features. As expected, the Lady Danika Dain slipped inside the bedchamber and then softly closed the door behind her. The only daughter of the duke, and still a maid at twenty-five years of age, she was a vision of loveliness and noble upbringing—the product of a life of privilege and wealth. A small woman, she always seemed… larger somehow, more forceful than one would expect. She had large, clever brown eyes and long dark-brown hair tied up in a bun. As always, Modwyn's pulse quickened at the sight of her.

She nodded once in polite greeting and then sat down on the bed beside her father, her normally impish smile a tight line of worry. "Is he worse? He looks worse."

"The same, my lady."

Her father moaned, his body shuddering.

Her eyes accused Modwyn. "He's in pain."

Modwyn approached, took the old man's hand in his, and measured his pulse, watching Danika out of the corner of his eye. She wore a fine blue gown with wide flowing sleeves and a darker suede corset that accentuated the swell of her breasts—and they were indeed nice breasts, he knew, with fat, rosy nipples that begged to be pinched and sucked—or bitten. A pity she had only allowed him to examine her once since he'd taken service with her family.

Modwyn ran his palm over the old man's forehead, already knowing it would be hot and feverish. "I can give him dream-flower my lady, ease his passing."

"I'd rather you cure him," she snapped, glaring at him. "He's only sixty-four."

Modwyn fought down an irritated impulse to snap back at her. "Sixty-four is not young, my lady. Each of us is called to stand before Father Craftsman in his own time. I'm sorry, but a better world is awaiting your father."

Lady Danika remained silent while Modwyn moved to a nearby table, picked up his mortar and pestle, and ground the petals of the sleeping flower, mixing them with gray marsh fungus to dull the sharp taste.

Once again, the duke's door opened, and a young man, a teenage boy with a mop of unruly blond hair, slipped within the bedchamber—Palin Dain, Danika's only brother, the thirteen-year-old boy who would soon be the new Lord Dain of Wolfrey. *The gods have to be laughing.*

The boy joined his sister and fidgeted nervously beside the bed. The old man muttered in his delirium again, speaking nonsense. Danika patted his cheek, whispering soft words into his ear. The candlelight shone upon her locks of tightly wound hair, creating a nimbus around her head, reminding Modwyn of the stained-glass portraits of the saints in the physician's university in the capital.

Modwyn's pulse quickened, and he thought of a woman who lived in the castle, a widow with five children, who worked in the kitchens and had little prospect for another husband. Desperate to secure a future for her children, she would suffer any indignity. While Modwyn had no intention of marrying some northern goat with five children, he would still visit her later that night, no matter the hour. He would plow her hard from behind, imagining it was Danika.

The boy wore a fine green tunic, the collar and sleeves edged with fox fur. Over his thin shoulders, he wore a short black riding cape fastened with a small silver lion's-head clasp. The hem of the cape was splattered with mud. The boy had been meeting with local landowners earlier, Modwyn knew, and must have rushed back to be by his father's side. The men he had been visiting were influential northerners, men whose support Palin would need in the days to come. He shared his sister's good looks, the same light splatter of freckles across his nose and cheeks, but in truth, he was too young to grow a beard and looked more maid than man. Modwyn himself was clean-shaven, with only a meticulously trimmed goatee and mustache, but that was different. Most physicians needed to carry themselves above rough men.

Lady Danika rose and hugged her brother, burying her head into his thin shoulder. He hesitated and then lightly patted her on the back before meeting Modwyn's gaze. "Well, Doctor?"

Modwyn cocked his head, carefully considering his words. "My Lord Dain, it is as we discussed earlier. Your father's humors are out of alignment, and I fear no medicine will change that."

"But… Doctor, are you sure? Our grandfather lived to eighty-four. Something *must* be wrong. This illness was so sudden."

Wodor help me, he even whines like a maid.

Silence settled over the chamber, interrupted only by the labored, irregular breathing of Oskaley. A storm of emotions flashed across Palin's young face, and Modwyn was certain he was only moments from tears.

"There is nothing anyone can do," Modwyn said. "It is his time."

"How… how long? When should we…?"

"I would send for a priest now, my lord. Before the sun rises."

Palin's face was ashen.

"So soon?" whispered Danika.

Oskaley groaned once more and turned his head to the side.

"Father Craftsman calls to him," Modwyn said.

"Go," Danika told her brother. "I will stay."

Modwyn set the mortar and pestle down on the bed table. "My lady, it will be some hours yet. You should rest, eat something. I will stay with the priest."

"I don't—"

"I will send for you both if he worsens."

Her brother held his hand out, and she reluctantly took it, climbing to her feet. "Just a bit," she mumbled. "I am tired, and we need to wake Father Cotlas."

"What about the new man, this… Father Bowen?" Palin asked.

Danika shook her head. "No. He'd want Father Cotlas. He knows him."

Palin bit his lower lip, staring at his father. As expected, tears swelled in his eyes.

Modwyn took her place, sitting on the edge of the bed. He took the old man's wrist once more. "Go, my lady, my lord. I promise I will send for you if he worsens."

Palin wiped his eyes. "I'll be in my chambers."

The Dain siblings left, leaving Modwyn alone with his patient once again. Modwyn stared at the closed door for some time then rose and tiptoed across the bedchamber before placing his ear against the door. Hearing nothing, he opened it and looked both ways down the empty castle corridor before closing it again.

He stared at his patient. "Well, Oskaley, it's just you and I."

Modwyn eased himself into a chair near the bed and considered the old man's face. His breathing was wet. His lungs were slowly filling with mucus. He'd be dead by sunrise. A fly buzzed through the chamber, landing on the contents of the pain medication that now sat forgotten. The old man moaned again.

Modwyn leaned in closer, putting his lips near the old man's ear. "Just let go, Oskaley," he whispered. "Why fight the inevitable?"

As expected, the old man didn't answer.

Modwyn once again reached to take the old man's pulse, but when Oskaley's hand darted out and gripped Modwyn's wrist, he nearly shat himself.

"I left him," Oskaley said, his voice surprisingly strong. "I left him to *her*."

Modwyn stared at his patient, too surprised to think clearly. Oskaley's eyes were clear, lucid.

How is this possible? He can't be recovering.

"I don't know you," Oskaley said, fear and emotion in his voice. "Are you the new priest? I must confess. I *have* to confess."

Relief flooded through Modwyn—Oskaley wasn't lucid after all, wasn't recovering. Modwyn might have been new in the castle, but he had tended the old man for weeks, and Oskaley knew who he was.

"Please," said the old man, tears forming in his eyes. "I must confess."

Modwyn gripped his hand, leaned in closer, and smiled. "Yes, my son, I am a priest. Confess."

Relief flooded into Oskaley's wet eyes. "Lies, Father. I've been living with lies for so long now, ever since *that* day in the catacombs, in the Great Crypt beneath that cursed fortress."

Modwyn squeezed Oskaley's fingers, causing the old man to wince in pain. He released his grip. "Please, continue, my son," he said. "Confess your sins. Hurry, before it's too late."

"I lied, Father. I lied to everyone. I ran that day. I was so frightened. I left my own brother to that monster." A coughing fit took him then, consuming him for several moments. When he finally could, he continued. "I ran away, Father… a coward."

"No, my lord. You and your brother were heroes. You killed her, saved everyone in the kingdom. You used Sight-Bringer to destroy her. Only you escaped the resulting cataclysm that brought down the ceiling of the Great Crypt when Sight-Bringer shattered within her foul heart."

"No, Father." The old man shook his head. "All lies. She defeated *them*, all of them. I… I hid near the entrance. I saw Belion the battle mage break his own staff—that was what brought down the ceiling, not the destruction of Sight-Bringer. That's when I ran."

Modwyn sat back, stunned, brushing Oskaley's fingers from him. The bedchamber seemed to spin about his head as he struggled to process that revelation. "She… she didn't die?" he finally whispered.

Oskaley, his eyes brimming with tears, nodded. Spit ran from his mouth into his white beard. "Please, Father, others must know. The king must know. I have kept this secret too long."

"She's not dead," Modwyn repeated, as if he couldn't believe the words.

The revelation coursing through Modwyn was like a monstrous wave that swept his world clean. Staring in disbelief at the sad, pathetic shell of a man who had just admitted harboring the greatest secret of all time, Modwyn saw him as he truly was. For almost fifty years, he had lived a lie. Oskaley was no hero.

How did anyone ever believe he was? It was absurd.

Outside the chamber's open window, he heard a red-tailed orkey cry out, its stuttering call echoing through the dark night. Simple folk believed the orkey's cry heralded great events. Modwyn chuckled, shaking his head. *Great things, indeed!*

"Father, please," whined Oskaley, squeezing Modwyn's hand. "I have confessed. I can't go to meet my brother without forgiveness."

Modwyn considered his patient, almost moved by his begging. He leaned in closer, putting his mouth near the old man's ear. "I do forgive you. You have done me the greatest service this night, finally telling the truth, admitting your crime."

Oskaley's eyes widened in confusion as Modwyn stood abruptly, yanking the pillow out from beneath the old man's head.

The orkey's cry echoed in the dark once more.

Chapter 3

Owen

Fin helped Owen put the two Ballards in irons while Keep-Captain Awde, Sayer, and Dilan Reese went inside the inn. Fin sat the Ballard brothers down against the outside wall of the stable. "Go get something to eat," he told Owen," then come take my place."

"Aye, thanks," said Owen.

As Owen was turning away, Emrys Ballard glared at him through sullen eyes, looking more like a savage cornered animal than the boy with whom Owen had spent so much of his youth. Owen glared back at Emrys, rubbing his ribs where one of them—perhaps even Emrys—had repeatedly tried to stab him. In the dark, with Owen wearing his cloak, the Ballards hadn't seen his armor. If they had, he would've been dead.

Owen shuddered as he turned away from Emrys and entered the inn. The captain and Sayer sat at a table, their backs to the wall, facing Dilan Reese, who sat across from them. Owen plopped down beside Dilan just as the barmaid brought bread, cheese, wooden bowls of stew, and mugs of beer.

"I once knew a man named Reese," Keep-Captain Awde said. "Good man. From Shellat's Fief to the east."

Dilan nodded. "Artur, my older brother. You're Brice Awde, aren't you?" Dilan asked.

"I am."

Owen took a sip of his beer and then drank fully half of it in one swallow. He tore off a chunk of brown bread and stuffed it in his mouth, chewing while watching the exchange.

"Then you served with Artur during the Clegg Hills Uprising."

Keep-Captain Awde smiled, his hard eyes softening. "I did. I liked Artur. He always made me laugh."

Dilan sipped his beer and wiped his mouth with the back of his hand, smearing several days' worth of dirt. "Used to make me laugh, too."

"Used to?"

"Artur died. Three months ago."

"I'm sorry. I didn't know that. He saved my life once."

"Yeah, Artur did *that* a lot, too," Dilan said as he pulled his bowl of stew in close and bent over it with his spoon, attacking it.

At the sound of Dilan's noisy slurping, Sayer's eyes tightened. Sayer practically worshiped Brice Awde, Owen knew, following him about like a puppy. Right then, Owen was sure Sayer wanted to knock the bowl of stew out of Dilan's hands and tell him to be more respectful. If the captain was annoyed, though, he didn't show it.

Awde leaned back against the wall, watching Dilan. "Why'd you help us, Dilan? Why not just walk away? The people who drink in this place are friends of the Ballards. They won't love you for this. You can't stay here."

"Nowhere else to go." Dilan raised his hands, palms up. "And no silver. I need work."

"Work? You saved my man's life for work?"

Dilan leaned forward. "It's like this, Captain—"

"*Keep-Captain,*" Sayer said.

Dilan glanced at Sayer and then continued. "It's like this, Keep-Captain. I've known lots of men like the Ballards, predators that would kill anyone for anything—don't care who they hurt, long as they get theirs."

"And you're not like that, Dilan?" Awde asked him.

A heavy silence settled between the two men before Dilan leaned back, pushing his nearly empty bowl of stew away. "Maybe I was afraid that if things kept going the way they were, I'd do just that. Become just like them."

"What is it you want, Dilan?" Awde asked.

"I'm trained. I can fight."

Awde inclined his head. "Yes, we saw that in the stable. Who trained you?"

"I was with Artur in the Mountain Rams before I was discharged."

"The Rams are fighting in the northeast. A border dispute backed by the Lyrians. Why would the Rams discharge you now?"

"They didn't want my service anymore."

Sayer snorted. "You a deserter, Reese?"

Dilan glared at Sayer, and Owen tensed, preparing to throw himself on the young man if necessary. Owen was bigger, probably stronger, but Dilan could handle himself. He'd already demonstrated that.

"No," Dilan replied through clenched teeth. "I'm no deserter. They don't need me anymore, that's all."

"And you think I do?" asked Awde.

"I can fight."

"Wouldn't have been in the Rams if you couldn't."

"Artur saved your life," Dilan said. "You owe me."

"You're not Artur."

"Keep-Captain," Owen said, speaking up for the first time, "I'd be dead if not for him."

"Mind your own damned business, Horse-boy," snapped Sayer.

Without taking his eyes off Dilan, Awde raised his hand to the other man, silencing him. "I've thanked you already, Dilan, and I've warned you about staying here, but you're not telling me everything. There's fighting in the northeast. It's a small war, I admit, putting down rebels, but the Rams would need all the men they can get. If they don't need you at a time like this…"

"I'm not a deserter."

"Not saying you are. Just saying I'm not willing to take a chance."

Dilan ran his hands over his face and looked about himself. "I can't stay here. Not after taking your side."

"No." Awde glanced at the kitchen entrance, where moving shadows were visible. "I wouldn't even stay the night if I were you—not even in the stable."

The color drained from Dilan's face, as did his previous haughty demeanor. He sat forward, looking very young, and ran his hands through his straggly hair. "Please. I have nowhere else to go… nothing."

"Family?"

Dilan shook his head.

"Well, drink up, man," said Awde. He glanced at Sayer. "And there's a reward for helping. Give him ten silver crowns. That'll do you a while, until you find something more permanent."

Dilan exhaled heavily, looking defeated. "Is there no way—"

"No."

Dilan stared at the table as Sayer counted out the silver pieces, placing each one before the young man. That was a good sum of money, Owen knew—more than he made in a month as a man-at-arms. *So why do I feel so sorry for Dilan Reese?*

"How'd Artur die, anyway?" asked Awde.

"Prophet's Bridge."

Sayer paused, his hand holding a silver coin over the others. Owen stared at Dilan. Even that far north, they had already heard the stories—quickly becoming a legend—of how a small company of the Rams, eighty-eight men, had held back a surprise raiding party of Lyrian-backed rebels, over a thousand men. For an entire day, the Rams had fought a defensive battle at Prophet's Bridge, holding the rebels from crossing the river while the residents of a nearby town fled. In the end, the Rams had saved the town's citizens from slaughter, but the victory had come at a staggering cost—every single man defending that bridge had died.

Awde ran a hand back through his short hair, nodding. "I'm not surprised. A man like Artur doesn't go out of this world easily." He raised his mug. "To Artur Reese."

"To Artur Reese," they all toasted, including Dilan.

Awde placed his mug back on the table. "My condolences, Dilan, but here's some free advice. Whatever has gone wrong in your life, fix it! Be the man your brother was. Don't make someone like me hang you from a tree."

Dilan nodded but looked away.

"Thought you said you served with your brother in the Rams," said Sayer. "How come you weren't with him when he died?"

Awde turned to glare at Sayer and opened his mouth, but Dilan spoke first.

"I was."

A log sparked and snapped, crackling in the fire pit as Awde and Dilan stared at one another.

"I heard every single one of those men died," Awde finally said.

"Well," said Dilan, "that would make for a better story, wouldn't it?"

"Aye," said Awde, "it would. Also makes survivors… *inconvenient.*"

"Aye," said Dilan, "it does. Good thing I was the only one."

Awde rubbed his chin with thumb and forefinger. "Sir Hrolf Westgen still commands the Rams, doesn't he?"

"He did when he told me to get the hell out," said Dilan.

Awde snorted. "Once saw him have a man whipped for delivering bad news."

Dilan cocked his head to the side. The corners of his mouth turned up just slightly. "You must have seen him on a good day, then."

Silence stretched out, and the fire crackled again as Awde stared at the young man with the thick eyebrows. "All right, Dilan Reese. I'll give you a job. Don't give me cause to regret it."

#

Much later that night, the four guardsmen, accompanied by the newest recruit in the castle garrison, Dilan Reese, as well as the two surviving Ballard brothers, approached the gatehouse of Castle Dain.

The day's events had drained Owen, and he was glad to see the castle outlined against the stars. He cast a glance at Emrys Ballard, stumbling along behind his brother. Both Ballards looked miserable—for good reason. Duke Oskaley would be unlikely to grant mercy to men who had not only murdered an itinerant merchant but also tried to kill one of his guardsmen. Both Ballards were going to hang. Surprisingly, that didn't bother Owen as much as he had once thought it would.

The faces of the guards on duty at the gatehouse were grave. Each had tied a strip of black cloth around the cross guards of his sword—the traditional sign of mourning in the north. The sergeant of the guard, Mollister Eggers, stepped forward to meet Keep-Captain Awde.

"What's wrong?" Awde asked him. "What's happened?"

Eggers removed his half-helm. "I'm sorry, sir, but the duke died earlier this night. May the Craftsman receive him."

"Died? How?"

"A sickness took him. He went fast."

"The new physician, Modwyn?"

Eggers shook his head. "Was with him but couldn't save him."

Awde swore then dismounted and removed his own helm. He knelt down, muttering a prayer. Owen, Fin, Sayer, and Dilan were quick to follow.

Owen's thoughts were a tempest. Duke Oskaley had presided over his trial for attacking Orin. Duke Oskaley had given him the choice of swearing five years' service or banishment. *What now? Do I now owe four more years of service to a teenaged boy?*

Chapter 4

Danika

Danika followed Palin up the circular tower stairs to the Moon Tower's open-air summit, a round platform surrounded by a shoulder-high crenellated stone wall built simply but solidly—no ornamentation, no statues, no carvings. In the southern duchies of the kingdom of Conarck, especially the capital, castles were built more ornately, with beauty and aesthetics in mind, but in the north, defense and practicality were the only considerations.

Danika faltered when she saw Modwyn waiting for them on the summit. She fought down a momentary flash of distaste at the sight of the effeminate physician. She didn't like him. Nor could she say exactly why. Modwyn had been unable to cure her father, but that wasn't why she disliked him so much—although that certainly didn't help. No, her aversion to the young man had been there the moment he had entered her family's service. Modwyn Du'Aig—tall but thin, with his dark hair slicked back and his painstakingly trimmed goatee—just made her skin crawl. She knew she needed to give him a chance. After all, he was a stranger, and she thought she should be more charitable, but she just couldn't help how she felt. Every time she parted from his company, she felt his slime rubbing off on her.

Forcing down her distaste, she joined Palin. In the courtyard below, she could hear Brice Awde's strong voice as he drilled his soldiers, followed by the clash of wooden sword against shield. The soldiers had been out there all afternoon and into the early evening, well past the point that the garrison soldiers should still be training, but the Dain family's keep-captain was notorious for working his men hard. Since her father's passing, two days before, he had been drilling the men particularly hard, as if they needed to be ready for anything. She appreciated his efforts but knew they were unnecessary. Palin was her father's only son. His claim to the duchy was solid, rock solid—despite the conniving of their cousin, Harold, in the king's court.

Modwyn bowed, a sly smile on his oily face. She forced herself to smile back—she'd treat the man with the respect his station deserved despite her misgivings.

"Master physician," she said, "please tell us what was so important that we had to come all the way up here."

Just for a moment, his eyes darted from Palin's to hers, as if he had been surprised that she would speak before her brother, the male. Modwyn clasped his hands, a solemn look on his face. "My Lord Dain, Duke of Wolfrey, my lady, thank you for seeing me."

The king had yet to bestow that honorific to her brother, but Danika let it go. The man was just trying to be polite.

"Why are we here, Doctor?" she asked again. "There is much yet we must do to prepare for our father's funeral."

"Yes, of course, my lady. Please trust me. It was necessary." Modwyn glanced past her, to the stone stairs leading down, as if making sure they weren't followed by a spy.

"And?" Palin raised his eyebrows.

He's tired and irritable, too. He's too young for all this. So am I.

Modwyn shifted his weight from one foot to the other. "My lord, before he passed, your father… spoke."

Danika's face flushed with heat. "You told us he died without waking," she said. "So quickly that there was no time to find us, to let us say farewell. Was that a lie?"

Modwyn backed away from her, stumbling into the wall behind him. "What? No. That's not what… He did die quickly… It's just… If only there had been a servant about. I yelled for help, but no one came, and I couldn't leave my patient."

Danika closed her eyes and composed herself. *Not his fault. Be calm. Remember who you are.* When she felt capable, she nodded and spoke in a curt tone. "Just… Go on, Doctor. What did he say?"

"I don't understand," said Palin. "He spoke to *you*?"

"Your father did become lucid," Modwyn continued, "but only for a few moments. Then he truly did pass—peacefully. Believe me, my lord, I know my craft."

"Doctor," Danika said, hearing the irritation in her own voice, "*what* did our father say?"

"He… he thought me his priest, and gave me his deathbed confession."

The air atop the tower seemed to go chill. "He confessed… to *you*?" she finally whispered.

Palin glanced nervously at her, stepping closer. "I don't understand," he said. "*You* took our father's confession? You're no priest. You can't absolve his sins."

"My lord, it was not my fault. I wasn't trying to deceive him. I tried to tell him to wait, but he was so near death, his mind was nearly gone. It happens sometimes, so we try to ease our patients' passing."

Danika, her eyes closed, inhaled deeply. "What… what did he say?"

"He spoke of Greywynne Island, my lady. He spoke of… *that day*, all those years ago—in the Great Crypt. He spoke of *her,* of Serina Greywynne."

"My father never spoke of that day," snapped Danika. "Not once."

"My lady, he knew he was dying, that this was his only chance. He needed to talk, to… confess, to meet the Craftsman with a clear conscience."

Palin's lips trembled. "To you?"

"My lord, he mistook me for the new priest, Father Bowen," Modwyn said.

Palin turned away, running his palms over his face.

Danika put her hand on Palin's shoulder while asking the doctor, "And?"

"He spoke of the battle with the blood fiend, of your uncle Stron. My lord, he said… he said he betrayed your uncle, left him to die, buried in the collapse of the entrance to the Great Crypt—while he fled."

Danika advanced on Modwyn, her rage unchecked. "What lies are these?"

Modwyn cast a quick, nervous glance over his shoulder at the courtyard below. "Not lies, my lady. I tell the truth. Your father carried this burden all his life. He said he ran away after Serina was killed. In the confusion of battle, Belion the battle mage broke his staff and caused a magical explosion. *That* was what brought down the ceiling, not the destruction of Sight-Bringer. Your father, realizing he stood to inherit Stron's title and lands, fled, leaving his own brother to be trapped alive."

"Lies!" cried Palin, half drawing his sword.

Danika moved quickly, grabbing his arm. "Palin, no! You will be the duke. You must be calm."

Several tense seconds passed, but then Palin looked away, nodded, and slid his sword back into its sheath. "My… my apologies, Doctor."

"Go on, Doctor," Danika said.

Modwyn, a layer of sweat glistening on his face, continued. "My lord, these are your father's words, not mine. He needed to die with a clear conscience. He needed to admit his crime before meeting his brother again in paradise."

"But that's not what happened," said Palin, shaking his head. "Stron struck down Serina, killing her, but when the holy blade struck her black heart, it shattered. *That's* what brought down the ceiling. It was the Craftsman himself who buried them, all but my father—so he could live to tell others."

Modwyn shook his head. "No, my lord. That isn't true. Sight-Bringer was *not* destroyed. Belion brought down the entrance to the Great Crypt."

Danika swayed in place, trying find balance in her life. *This is all wrong. That wasn't what happened.*

"Your father lived with this shame for forty-eight years," Modwyn said.

Palin's lip trembled. "No, that can't be."

Danika stepped closer to put her hand on Palin's forearm. "Serina?" she asked.

Modwyn's eyes widened. "What? No, of course not, my lady. Serina is dead. Your father confirmed that Stron did indeed kill her with Sight-Bringer—and, after almost fifty years, there's just no way she could still live—but the important thing is that the holy blade didn't shatter after striking Serina down. Your father only said that to forestall attempts to go back, to dig out the entrance."

"But that would mean…" Danika faltered, unable to say the words.

"I'm sorry, but these were your father's own words, his deathbed confession."

Palin bent over, placed his hands against his knees, and breathed deeply, swaying in place. Danika, her hand upon his back, stared at the physician. "Are you… are you sure?"

"My lady," said Modwyn. "I do not know if your father was telling the truth or not, but this is what he told me. I don't believe he would lie, not at the end of his life."

"But our father sealed the entrance to the catacombs after the battle. He said he only just escaped." Her voice was small.

"No, my lady. Your father abandoned his brother and sealed the catacombs so he could become the Duke of Wolfrey. He left Stron there… and the sword. That's why he sealed the catacombs, to hide his betrayal."

"My father was no—"

"Wait," said Palin, rising to his feet. "If what you say is true, then the sword…?"

Modwyn paused, his mouth partially open. "Well… I guess the sword would still be there, my lord, still buried in the catacombs beneath the ruins of Serina's fortress—on an island your family now owns."

Chapter 5

Dilan

Dilan gasped for breath. His shoulders were on fire, and sweat ran into his eyes, stinging him. They had been drilling for hours with wasters, wooden practice swords, and he was tiring. His opponent, Owen, was both skilled and fast, despite his size, and he was giving Dilan a challenge. Dilan forced himself to concentrate, to ignore his discomfort and focus on the swordplay, shifting fluidly between stances, stepping forward on the attack or back and to the sides when parrying.

The light was beginning to fade in the early evening. The entire garrison, more than a hundred men-at-arms, drilled in the large stone courtyard of Castle Dain. Dilan's linen undertunic, beneath his padded leather top and ring-mail coat, was soaked in sweat and chafing. He kept his wooden round shield held high before him while he lashed out with his waster again and again, trying to get past Owen's shield and sword.

"All right, that's enough for now," called out Keep-Captain Awde. "Drop your wasters and plant your asses on the ground."

The men chatted in relief, happy for the break.

"Finally," said Fin, joining Owen and Dilan as they settled themselves on the stones of the courtyard.

Most of the men were still cool to Dilan, but Owen and Fin had accepted him readily enough, likely because of Dilan saving Owen's life. Young boys moved among them, handing out waterskins and apples. Dilan drank deeply and helped himself to an apple, biting into it as the boy moved farther down the line.

"He always drill you like this?" Dilan asked.

Fin snorted. "Aye, but this is more than usual." The young man was tall and rangy, with a big nose and ears, a pleasant enough sort with a sly sense of humor.

"Much cause for fighting around here?" Dilan asked.

Owen shook his head, removed his half-helm, and ran his fingers through his short blond hair. "No, but we can stand together in a fine shield wall… if we ever have to."

"Best hope you never have to," Dilan said and bit into his apple.

Keep-Captain Awde walked down the line of men, his eyes drifting over them. All conversation stopped, and the men watched him expectantly. From all the tales his brother Artur had told him of the legendary Brice Awde, Dilan had expected the man to be eight feet tall and carved from granite, yet he seemed like any other man and younger than Dilan would have expected. Tall and fit, with a swordsman's shoulders, Awde moved confidently before them. As he walked past them, Dilan noticed a large, ugly scar running down the right side of Awde's neck, disappearing beneath the collar of his ring-mail coat.

Awde addressed the men. "Pay attention." He didn't yell, but his voice still rang clearly. "Before we finish for the night, I want to discuss timing and countertiming. Now, before you grumble that you're all a bunch of hardened killers and already know how to fight, hear me out."

A soft chatter of chuckles passed among the men, and they grinned at one another. He had missed that feeling, Dilan realized, the camaraderie of other warriors. *Oh, Artur, why didn't you just let me go and save yourself?*

"Range and timing are everything in warfare," Awde continued. "If you understand range and timing, you can develop an intuitive sense for countertiming." As he spoke, the keep-captain drew his sword and held it above his head with both hands on the hilt, striking out with a downward cut from the high guard to emphasize his point. "What you need is to be able to sense, from an opponent's attack, the exact right moment to move—forward, back, sideways—so that you evade his strike while at the same time counterstriking. To the untrained eye, it looks like you've both struck at the exact same moment, yet your cut hits and his misses—wonderful luck!

"But..." He paused, pointing his sword across their ranks. "There is no such thing as luck—not in battle. What's truly happened is you've anticipated your opponent's attack and moved in such a way that—even without parrying—his strike misses and yours hits. Not luck, not fate—just an understanding of range and timing, but this skill doesn't come easily. You have to develop it over time.

"You develop this understanding by practicing against opponents armed with different weapons. Most men you fight will be carrying spears or axes, rarely ever swords. Make no mistake, while swords are the king of the battlefield—and I have personally seen men cut in two from a single sword blow—most men can't afford swords. Count yourselves lucky you have jobs where we give them to you."

The men laughed at this, rubbing sore arms and shoulders.

"So," continued the keep-captain, motioning to the young boys—who ran forward with bundles of wooden spears, polearms, axes, and daggers in their thin arms and lay them out in piles before the men—"let's go again, but this time, one of you fights with shield and sword while the other uses different weapons. Move slowly. Get a feel for each weapon's reach and speed. Focus on the counterstrike. The very moment your opponent commits to an attack—you attack him, but move in such a way that you evade his blow while yours strikes. Be patient. It's going to take a long, long time to develop."

Dilan and the others climbed to their feet. Owen picked up a spear, its tip blunted, and squared off against Dilan, who held his shield before him, his waster in the middle guard, near his hip, to protect his sword hand behind his shield.

For the next half hour, they drilled. They took turns attacking with different weapons and practicing their countercuts. Dilan had already had some experience at the drill, and he helped Owen. When the keep-captain finally called an end to the training, Dilan was nearly exhausted. The young boys came by again to hand out waterskins, and Dilan clasped Owen on the back as the man drank, causing him to swallow badly and cough.

"That was well done, Owen," he said. "You've some skill."

Owen snorted. "You learn to fight like that in the Ram?"

"My brother as well."

Owen handed him the waterskin. "I'm jealous. You've been places, seen the world. I've never been past the southern border of the duchy. What was it like in the east?"

"I'd rather not—"

"He doesn't want to tell you about it, Horse-boy, cause he's a piece-of-shit coward and a liar," a mocking voice said from behind them.

Dilan felt his face heat. Turning, he saw two of the larger garrison soldiers, Marlin Ornkey and Hooper Tibs. In the days since he had joined the garrison, he had already had the displeasure of meeting both of them, the local big men, the would-be bullies. Marlin, the one who had spoken, was a huge, heavyset man with ruddy cheeks and a thick brown beard at least a hand's length long. He stood there with a shit-eating grin on his ugly face. His friend Hooper, almost as big, stood just behind him. Hooper had a misshapen nose that had been broken too many times and piglike eyes that shone with glee, as if he were having the time of his life.

"This one weren't ever in the Rams," Hooper said. "Never met a man from Shellat's Fief what weren't an ass-raping liar-coward."

Dilan, making sure his balance was evenly distributed, faced the two men. "Which is it, then? Am I a liar, a coward, or an ass rapist? I'm confused."

Hooper's little eyes narrowed in confusion. "Huh?"

Marlin stepped closer, putting his face right in front of Dilan. "That's a big mouth you have, deserter."

Dilan screwed up his face in disgust as he took a step back, waving his hand in front of his mouth. "Craftsman's love, man—your breath! I'm pretty sure it's supposed to be your dick that goes in the sheep's ass, not your tongue."

Marlin's face turned bright scarlet. "What?"

"He's saying," said Owen, moving up beside Dilan, "that you don't need foreplay. The sheep doesn't care. Is that what you mean, Dilan?"

"Well, I don't really know," said Dilan, ready to move. "I don't fuck sheep."

Owen snorted. "I don't know anything about sheep-fucking either, but I imagine you don't really need the foreplay. Just catch 'em first."

Fin joined them then, standing on the other side of Dilan. "Are these two bragging about sheep-fucking again? I just don't see the appeal, but to each his own, I guess."

Marlin's eyes narrowed, and a trace of fear replaced the anger as he glanced from Owen to Dilan to Fin. "You sure you want to do this, Horse-boy?" he asked Owen. "I'm not your brother."

"That true, Marlin?" Fin asked. "You got to catch them first?"

"What? Fuck you!" Marlin spat the words out, turning to glare at Fin.

"I thought you fucked sheep," said Dilan.

"See, here's the thing, Dilan," said Owen. "You don't know about sheep foreplay because you're not an ugly-ass sheep-fucker with shit in his beard and his tiny dick in his hand. And, yeah, Marlin, I'm sure."

Marlin smiled cruelly, shaking his head. "You think you're so clever, but you're nothing more than a coward. Prophet's Bridge, my ass. You probably ran off long before that." Marlin turned and jammed a thick finger in Owen's chest. "And you, Horse-boy, you mark my words, your new girlfriend will run again—probably when we need him most."

"Make your move," said Dilan, blood pounding in his ears. "Make your move or be on your way."

Hooper reached out and grabbed Marlin's shoulder, pulling him back. "Don't. Not here." He smirked at Dilan. "Another time, coward."

"I'm not going anywhere," Dilan said.

"Neither am I," said Owen.

"We," said Fin.

Marlin pointed a thick finger at them. "You're all gonna be sorry." Spit flew from his mouth.

Fin bleated like a sheep, and all three of them laughed as Marlin and Hooper stormed off.

Chapter 6

Danika

Danika paced the wooden floorboards of the castle's modest library, her thoughts a whirlwind. Nearby, his head lowered in concentration, Palin sat at a table, reading by candlelight, occasionally scowling or whispering to himself. Three long rows of wooden bookstands, each filled with hundreds of dust-covered books, sat against the walls. Castle Dain's library boasted the finest collection of books in the north, she knew, but Palin was still not going to find what he wanted.

The yellowed journal he was reading was the official ledger of their uncle Stron's steward, recording the last days of the war against Serina's undead army almost fifty years before. She had read the journal herself years earlier and still remembered what it contained—almost nothing of value. The individual entries within the journal were very detailed, highlighting the shipborne assault upon Greywynne Island; the monsters within Feldwyn Swamp; the siege of Serina's fortress; and finally, the battle in the Great Crypt where Serina herself had finally been defeated—where, according to

Modwyn, their father had abandoned his own brother, leaving him buried alive as the ceiling collapsed.

Palin sat back, closed the weathered journal, and rubbed his eyes. "She was awake, you know. Serina was waiting for them when they went belowground—even though the sun was up. I thought Blood Fiends had to sleep during the day."

Danika shook her head. "Palin… who knows of such things?"

He nodded, softly bobbing his head. "There's nothing more in here, nothing about… *after* she died."

"I told you before, the man who wrote that journal wasn't there, wasn't in the Great Crypt. He was a steward. He wrote what father told him to."

"I thought maybe… maybe there was something, some clue that would help…"

"This all happened long before either of us was even born. Let it go. The past no longer matters."

Palin snorted. "No longer matters? It matters. Do you believe him?" His eyes met hers, beseeching. "Do you think father could do this thing, abandon his own brother?"

"I don't like our new physician," she said. "But he has no reason I can think of to lie to us. He has no connection to the north. And this *new* version of events, father's deathbed confession… It would explain why father never spoke of that day."

"But to abandon his own brother—just to become duke!"

"I don't believe that was the case, no matter what father may have said. Who knows what lies he convinced himself of over the years. But I think… maybe, maybe he did… run away. Maybe he was always carrying this shame."

Palin wiped his eyes. He looked so tired, so worn out. Kneeling down beside him, she placed her hand on his knee. "Palin, our father was a good man. You must know that. We weren't in the Great Crypt with him when he confronted *her*. It must have been terrifying. They say that there was a—I don't know—an unholy aura that surrounded her. They called it the Dread. Many other men ran from her presence. But… abandoning his own brother to become duke? Father was never that ambitious."

He sighed. "You've got the right of that. When I was seven, I saw him confront the elder Lord Wolm, back when the miserable old bastard was still alive. He came to the castle to discuss an incident between our troops." Palin snorted. "*Incident.* Everyone knew his troops had attacked ours, murdering two of them. I was sure father was going to kill him for it."

"I remember that," said Danika. "I'm surprised you do."

"I remember it far too well. I wanted to see father be the great man I knew he must really be. After all, he was the hero who helped kill Serina, the only survivor. So I hid behind one of the doors and spied through the keyhole." Palin's shoulders trembled. "Father was so… so… not what I wanted him to be. Wolm treated him with contempt, insulted him, insulted mother, you… *all of us*. He dared father to fight him, called him craven. He spat in father's face before he left, laughing at him."

She sighed. Placing her head against his, she wrapped her arms around his neck. "Our father was a gentle man, Palin, not a warrior. Why must men be beasts in order to be great?"

"We need to regain our honor. We lost it on that damned island."

"We lost nothing."

He frowned. "You don't—"

"Understand?" She stood up and backed away. "I don't understand honor? Why? Because I'm a woman? Oh no, brother, I understand honor all too well."

"I didn't mean that—"

"Where was the king that day? Where were the Wolms, the other noble families? Stron *and father* saved the Kingdom of Conarck when no one else would, when everyone else was too frightened."

"The other families tried," he said.

"Tried and gave up. Tried and decided her undead army was unstoppable. *We* kept fighting—our family, the Dains—the northern lions. At the end, only we stood against her. Stron beggared our family paying the army. And for what? The king never repaid our debts despite promises he would. Now, our family's wealth is a fraction of what it once was, and so much of our land now belongs to others." She turned away and approached the stained-glass window to put her forehead against it, cool against her skin. "Why?"

"The sword," Palin said softly, getting up and standing behind her. "The king blamed father for losing Sight-Bringer. He still blames our family."

She snorted. "Blood Fiends' Bane, the Sword of Justice—what rubbish. Always just a sword."

"Not to the king, not to the people, not to the other noble families. We lost a holy relic that day, one that the king had only loaned to us to stop Serina. We lost our honor with it."

Turning, she stared at him in challenge. "No, Palin, we didn't. We don't need to prove anything."

He shook his head. "If I can dig out the catacombs, give Sight-Bringer back to the king—"

"Palin, those islanders hate us. They blame us for killing Serina, their queen. The king may have given us Greywynne Island, but those people have only ever been loyal to her and her family. They won't help us."

"I need the sword to be duke. If not, Harold—"

"The king won't favor our idiot cousin. The line of succession is clear. You are the only son of the last Duke of Wolfrey. We don't need some stupid Illthori sword."

He shook his head. "You don't understand what the sword means. You're not a warrior."

She laughed, unkindly perhaps, then regretted it when she saw him blush. "Warriors, Palin? Which warriors? Our king, all those cowards who refused to fight Serina?"

"That was almost a half century ago. They're not the same nobles."

"It's the same king! Now he's just an old fool instead of a young one."

"Old or not, our cousin gains favor at his court while I look like a child here. I need something to solidify my claim."

She shook her head. "No, you don't!"

"I can't take the chance. Besides, think about it… Sight-Bringer? After all these years. How can we not go after it? Just think how grateful the king would be. The Holy Three Illthori artifacts—Crown, Rod, *and Sword*—would be reunited. He might even finally honor our war debts."

She bit her lower lip and stared at him. *He really believes that, doesn't he? Is he right? Am I wrong?* "Palin, if he ever had any intention to, the king would have honored his debts forty-eight years ago." She approached the table and let her fingers drift over the flaking pages of the book. "Besides, this late in the summer, it's too late for sea travel."

"Not if we leave right away."

"Do you really want to risk getting stuck on that stupid island once the weather turns? Do you want to spend an entire winter in that little fort with Wendel Dert? The man is an insufferable ass."

"But a competent one. If nothing else, the Greywynne Islanders provide us with more salted fish than we could ever eat. And our trade with the Histari is profitable."

She shook her head, tugging on a strand of hair. "It's foolishness,

Palin. We can't afford an expedition."

He placed his hand on her shoulder. "We can't afford not to. Please, Danika, I need your help. It's only you and I now. There's no one else I trust. I need to know you'll watch our family's affairs until I'm back."

He's going, she realized. *I should have known as much. It's the pull of that damned sword. He can't resist it.* Sighing, she nodded. *So be it.* "Fine, but I'm coming with you."

"But—"

"I'm coming with you," she insisted. "You'll need me to arrange the sea travel. The shipping guild will take advantage of you."

"It's too—"

She placed her hands on her hips and stared him down. "I'm coming!"

"The estate, our lands?"

"Reeve Holm will run the estate while we're gone, just as he does when we're here."

He opened his mouth to make another protest, but she saw the resignation in his eyes. When she set her mind to something, she usually got her way. She was the elder child, the firstborn. She had practically raised Palin after the death of their mother.

Palin nodded, his excitement shining on his youthful face. "Let's go have an adventure."

She smiled. *Father Craftsman, help me. I hate Greywynne Island.*

Chapter 7

Owen

Looking down from the hilltop above his family's stables, Owen felt his gut tensing. He bit his lower lip and sighed to himself, certain that coming had been a mistake. Sitting back on his palfrey, he watched Keep-Lieutenant Sayer and Dilan ride down the path ahead of him. From there, he could smell hay and horse manure, which brought back too many memories. Tall stalks of grass blew in the breeze, like rolling waves. A handful of young horses ran together, simply for the pure joy of going fast. The stables, large enough to house more than a dozen horses, stood apart from the barn and his family's farmstead—no, Orin's farmstead. It was no longer Owen's home.

He kicked his palfrey's flanks, urging the horse into a trot and quickly catching up to the others. Their visit wasn't going to turn out the way Sayer thought it would. Orin was quick to anger, but he understood all too well the value of silver.

Near the stables, Sayer and Dilan were already dismounting. Gibbs, one of the hired boys, came running to take their mounts. He paused midstep when he saw Owen. Just for a moment, a look of surprise flashed through his eyes, replaced a moment later by a huge grin that exposed a gap between his teeth.

Owen handed Gibbs his reins and then tousled his mass of thick hair. "Is he here?"

"Aye," the boy said, glancing nervously at the farmhouse, his grin vanishing.

"And Tanda?"

"She—"

The boy's head spun about as the farmhouse door banged open. There, standing in the doorway, his face a mask of barely controlled rage, was Owen's older brother Orin. Five years separated them, but the family resemblance was clear. Orin shared Owen's blond hair, a gift of their mother, but Orin's was long and stringy where Owen's was cut short in the military style Keep-Captain Awde demanded. Both brothers were tall, thickly built, with their father's wide shoulders, but Orin was already going soft about the belly. Their eyes met, and Orin grimaced.

Sayer stepped forward, his hand held out. "A good day to you, Horsemaster," he said.

Orin made no move to shake his hand. "He's not welcome here. You should know that. Was your duke what sat in judgment on him."

"He's your brother, man."

Orin hawked and spat on the ground. "Are you here to deal?"

"I am." Sayer cast an uneasy glance at Owen and Dilan before returning his attention to Orin.

Owen sighed. He would have told Sayer, if Sayer would only have listened.

"Then come inside like a civilized man," said Orin. "That one, though—he can wait outside with the pigs."

Owen raised his eyebrows and smiled. "It's good to see you, too, brother."

Sayer shook his head at Owen before putting his hand on Orin's elbow, trying to lead him away. "Your house, your rules, Horsemaster, but I'm here on the duke's business."

"Duke's dead."

"His son, Palin."

Orin scowled and turned away, clumping back up the wooden steps, dragging his left leg behind him.

Sayer paused to address Owen and Dilan. "I won't be long." Then, he followed Orin inside the farmhouse, closing the door.

Owen sighed, glancing at Gibbs. "See to the horses, lad. Some water, some hay."

The boy nodded and secured all three animals to the hitching post before darting off to do as instructed. Owen stared at the stable's entrance. Inside, horses whinnied. He turned to face Dilan, who like Owen, was wearing a ring-mail coat, half-helm, and castle-forged sword.

"Coming?" Owen asked.

Dilan, a bored expression on his face, nodded. "Why not?"

Owen removed his half-helm, ran his fingers through his short blond hair, and set the leather-and-iron helmet atop his saddle. The stable was cooler inside, out of the sun, and the moment he walked inside, the smell of hay and horse manure washed over him, bringing back some happy memories. Fat green flies buzzed about his head, but Owen paid them no mind. That old stable was as much home to him as the farmhouse. Eight horses occupied fewer than half the stalls—palfreys mostly, a few colts, and some mares.

Dilan followed him inside. In the days since joining the Dain garrison, most of the other men had kept their distance from him, the consensus being that Dilan, despite his claims, was either a deserter or a liar. Few—other than Owen and Fin—believed he had actually fought at Prophet's Bridge, let alone been a member of the Rams. For his part, Dilan seemed completely uninterested in the other soldiers' opinions of him, keeping to himself, but Dilan had saved Owen's life, so Dilan had a friend whether he wanted one or not, and any friend of Owen's was a friend of Fin's, so he actually had two friends.

A loud whinny came from one of the far stalls where a large black colt, easily sixteen hands high and well muscled, raised his large head and snorted.

Owen sauntered over, a grin on his face. "Well, hello you." He ran his hand over the colt's large head and down his neck.

The horse wheezed and coughed, a wet, mucous sound.

"Sounds sick," Dilan said from behind him.

"Aye, he does." Owen ran his eyes over the colt.

Big and strong, the animal was also shaking, but so softly that it almost went without notice.

"What's your story, I wonder?"

"I was going to ask you the same." Dilan leaned against one of the wooden support beams. "You don't seem too popular around here."

Owen snorted. "You should talk." He scratched the stubble on his chin and looked about. A large pile of hay lay nearby, and he pulled out several strands and held them to his nose. He dropped the hay and brushed his hands against his pants. Glancing about, he noted the poor state of the stables. "He runs this place like everything else in his life."

"Your brother?" Dilan asked.

Owen grunted.

"You two not close?"

Owen smirked. "You notice his limp?"

"Hard to miss."

"A year ago, about a month after our father died, Orin beat our little sister, Tanda, saying she had misplaced one of his pipes." Owen fought down his anger at the memory, surprised he was still so bitter. "He broke her jaw… so I broke his leg—seemed fair to me. The local magistrate didn't agree. Neither did Duke Oskaley. Gave me a choice: banishment or soldiering for five years. So, here I am—man-at-arms for the Dain garrison. A professional leg-breaker rather than an amateur one."

Dilan laughed, picked up a piece of straw from the floor, and placed it between his teeth.

Owen reached over and yanked it from Dilan's mouth and threw it on the ground, shaking his head.

Dilan's eyes tightened in surprise, but he looked away. "Seems your brother still bears a grudge."

"He'll carry that grudge longer than his limp, and he'll have that for the rest of his life." Owen flashed his teeth at Dilan. "I broke his leg *really* good. Should've heard it crack."

"Don't seem too disturbed."

Owen opened the stall door and slipped in beside the large colt, running his hands over the animal's flank. He placed his ear against the horse's chest and listened, murmuring soft assurances to him. "Orin was always a bully. Used to beat me, too, until I got bigger… a lot bigger."

"So, if your brother hates you so much, why'd Sayer bring you along?"

Owen paused, eyes closed, listening to the colt's heartbeat. It was strong, fast. *Too fast?* After a few moments, he opened his eyes and saw Dilan was still watching him. "Sayer thinks he's clever. Thinks that if he brings me along, Orin will become flustered, angry, and distracted enough to make a bad deal."

"Told you that?" Dilan's large bushy eyebrows rose.

Owen shook his head, closing the stall behind him. "By now, I'm sure you've heard the others call me Horse-boy?"

"Cause you're a big guy, right?"

"Part of it, but mostly cause they figure if I'm this big, I must also be as dumb as a horse."

Dilan shook his head. "I didn't think that at all."

"Well, lots do, including our keep-lieutenant. He doesn't tell dummies like me what he thinks, but it took me about two seconds to figure out why I was coming today."

Dilan rolled his eyes and snorted. "Must be something to Sayer if a warrior like Brice Awde trusts him."

"If you say so."

Both men turned as a young woman with straw-blond hair rushed into the stable and threw herself at Owen. He paused for only a second and then hugged his little sister tightly. She looked good, tired but healthy. That day, she wore a simple blue dress, her long hair free about her shoulders, her cheeks pink with youth. Soon, she'd be married, Owen knew. She was getting to that age. Orin would have to find her a suitable match, or—less likely—approve one of her own.

He stepped back and held her at arm's length. "You shouldn't be here. Orin will be—"

"Busy for some time yet. I don't care. I wanted to see you. I've missed you."

"And I you, little one."

Tears filled her eyes, and she rushed in again, burying her face in his shoulder. "You're going away?"

"Greywynne Island, but we're to be back before the snows come. It'll be an adventure. I could use an adventure. Soldiering is not what people think. Long walks along cold walls."

When Dilan coughed, Owen stepped back. "Tanda, this is my friend Dilan. He saved my life."

Dilan bowed, taking Tanda's hand and kissing it. "My very great pleasure."

Tanda blushed. "We heard all about the Ballards. May Father Craftsman bless you, Dilan." Then she punched Owen in the shoulder, mashing her fingers into his ring mail. "And you, you great oaf, you must be more careful." She rubbed her fingers.

He smiled, raising his hands to ward off further blows. Then he sighed, his eyes moving past her to the stable's entrance. "Now, go back inside… before Orin comes."

Worry tightened her eyes, and she glanced over her shoulder. "Listen, your officer isn't… well, he's not—"

"Sayer's a buffoon," Owen said, "but he's harmless."

"Orin's going to sell him Gale," she whispered, her eyes going to the black colt behind Owen. "But Gale has the heaves. He's not worth the coin. You must warn your officer."

Owen inclined his head, placed his hands on his sister's shoulders, and kissed her forehead. "Thank you, Tanda. Now inside, quickly."

"But—"

"Don't make me break his other leg. I can't take a decade of garrison life."

Her lower lip quivered, and she rushed forward and hugged him fiercely one last time, as if she'd never hold him again. Then she turned and bolted, running for the stable entrance, kicking up a small cloud of dust and straw. Owen watched her back, hating his brother even more at that moment.

"Sayer *will* want the black," Dilan said.

"Aye, he will." Owen returned to the stall with the black colt. "Gale," he whispered. "A good name. Orin isn't as clever as he thinks, never has been."

The colt whinnied, stamped his hoof against the hard ground of his stall, and then farted. Smiling, Owen moved away from the colt and leaned against a beam near the entrance where he could watch the farmhouse. "And what of you, Dilan? You had a brother."

Dilan ran his fingers through his freshly cropped curly dark hair. Sadness flashed through his eyes, and Owen regretted asking.

"Artur and I were closer than you and your brother," Dilan finally said. "Now there was a soldier." He met Owen's eye. "Not like me—a *good* one. Man could fight like a bear."

"I'm sorry for your loss."

Dilan made a noise more like a grunt than a word. "Have you and your brother always been at odds?"

"When we were younger, it was different." Owen stared past Dilan, at the motes of dust dancing in the beams of sunlight coming through several of the ill-fitted slats in the walls. "But people change. Life changes you. Orin became very concerned with money, with his future."

"Most men do."

"It's just money," Owen said softly, almost to himself.

Dilan grunted. "Tell that to someone who doesn't have any."

Owen chewed his lower lip. "As boys, Orin and I used to ride out together on the grasslands, camping for days at a time." He shook his head at the memory. "I'd love to go back to those days, the freedom. Now, everything is duty and drilling, endless boring watches on castle walls."

Dilan was watching him. "That's the life of a soldier, Owen. It's what we do, and it's far better than the killing and dying part."

"Maybe, but I never wanted this. I've always wanted to travel, to see the world, the sea—and that's the worst of it. Orin knew that, but he still asked the Duke to swear me into his service as penance for breaking his leg, claimed I needed a calming hand, a purpose for my violent nature." Owen snorted, staring at his palm. "And now I truly do have blood on my hands."

"The Ballards were trying to kill you, Owen. You had no choice."

Owen nodded. He still remembered the jolt in his arm when he had stabbed Trystan, when the dagger punched through the man's flesh. Sayer might have finished him, but Owen had been the one who really killed him. Owen was still lost in memory when Sayer and Orin walked into the barn.

Orin moved right past Owen, ignoring him, and went straight to the stall with the black colt, Gale. "He's big and only two years old. He'll grow stronger yet, you mark my words."

Sayer stood beside Orin, assessing the colt. As he did, he rubbed his goatee with thumb and forefinger, pulling on it. "He's wheezing a bit."

"It'll pass. He's young yet."

"All right, this one, then, and the other three we've already decided on," said Sayer. "Eighteen silver crowns."

"Twenty-five," said Orin. "And I'll throw in two draft animals."

Dilan stiffened, but Owen met his eye and shook his head. Dilan's eyes narrowed in confusion, but Owen shook his head again, and Dilan said nothing.

"Twenty, and you can keep the draft horses," said Sayer. "We've enough draft animals on the island as it is. We're going to need horses strong enough to carry armored men for scouts. And with the sea voyage, bigger animals can stand to lose the weight better."

"Done," said Orin.

Sayer spat in his palm, and the two men shook hands. Then, Orin glanced at Owen quickly and smirked in triumph. Sayer turned to Owen and Dilan. "Prepare this one and three others the stable boy can show you. Come, Horsemaster, let's count coins."

The two men turned and left the stable.

Dilan raised an eyebrow. "Twenty crowns for a horse that will be dead in a month? Why didn't you say something?"

Owen walked back to Gale's stall, opened the door, and reached down. He stood up again, holding a handful of hay. "Because this big boy doesn't have heaves, Dilan. There's nothing wrong with his lungs. Orin's been saving coin by using shit hay. This lot's rotten with mold."

"You're sure?"

Owen ran his hands down Gale's flank, smiling at what his brother was losing. "I'm sure. This brute—all by himself—is worth thirty coins at least."

Chapter 8

Danika

Danika's eyes flashed open, and she sat up and stared at her door, letting the covers fall from her, exposing her skin to the cold night air. The night was warm, so she had left her window open, but she thought she had heard something, someone moving about in the solar, the sitting room just outside her bedchamber.

Fully awake, she slipped from her bed, her heart pounding. She wore only a short cotton shift that barely reached her knees, but she quickly tiptoed barefoot across the cold wooden floor to her bedroom door. Placing her ear against its surface, she listened carefully, wondering if she had only dreamed of the noise. When she heard a chair softly scraping across the floor of the solar, she knew she hadn't been dreaming. Someone was out there—someone trying, and failing, to move silently.

She scanned her bedchamber, looking for a place to hide. Darkness cloaked the room, the only light coming from a half moon outside her open window—nowhere to hide. She slid back against the doorjamb so that when the door opened, she'd at least be behind it and out of sight.

A moment later, the door cracked open, and a large shape slipped into her bedchamber—a man. Even in the dark, even from behind, she could tell it was a man, and she was sure she knew who it was. From just behind him, she could hear his quick, heavy breathing.

She held her breath, certain he'd hear her heart hammering against her chest. He took a step toward her bed and then another. She had to move before he realized she wasn't in it. She reached for him, but before she could even touch his shoulders, he spun about, quicker than a moonbeam, and grabbed her about the waist with both hands. Pulling her in tight against him, he crushed her breasts against his slablike chest.

How had he known?

Reaching up, she grabbed the sides of his head, felt the stubble on his cheeks, and pulled his face in close to hers, crushing his lips with her own. He moaned and thrust against her, his erection already like rock. Her lips parted, and his tongue was in her mouth, his hand over her breast, squeezing and caressing it. His fingers brushed against her nipple through the fabric of her thin shift, holding it between thumb and index finger. She gasped and pushed against him, wanting him, needing him. The back of his legs collided with the edge of her bed, and entangled, they fell atop it. Breaking free, she pushed against his hips, creating enough space to reach his pants and yank them down. His breath was hot and wet against her neck.

"Now, Brice," she whispered into his ear. "I want you now."

He kicked his boots free, sat against the bed, and yanked his pants all the way off. She pulled his shirt over his head, exposing his chest and his hard stomach. Unable to wait a moment more, she shoved him back onto the bed, hiked her shift up over her hips, and climbed atop him, mounting him in a moment of pure bliss. They both gasped, as if they had just plunged into a cold mountain lake. Then, taking over, she began to ride him, thrusting against him, moving faster and faster—desperate to take all of him. He yanked her shift up over her head, ripping it from her. Then, he gripped her soft breasts with his rough warrior hands, squeezing them and pulling on her nipples. Leaning forward, he placed his mouth over one of them, his breath hot and wet. She pulled his head against her harder. It felt so good, so right. Soon, they were both panting, and then they were both moaning. He strained to push up against her with his hips, trying to drive himself deeper within her, to become part of her, and she pushed herself down on him even harder. A tidal wave of bliss coursed through her, rippling through every muscle of her body, and she cried out at the same time as he did. Breathless, she collapsed atop him, utterly spent.

Drenched in sweat, she lay against his heaving chest. He wrapped one of his powerful arms around her, holding her tightly. "Save me," she whispered into his ear. "I missed you so much."

Panting still, he chuckled and kissed her neck. "We need to be quieter," he whispered. "We're going to get caught someday."

Disentangling himself from her, he rose to his feet and stumbled into her solar to listen at the door to the hallway. He always did that, as if he were a little boy, worried that someone would catch them. She pushed herself up on her elbows and watched him, the moonlight shining upon his muscled back, his strong shoulders, and his perfect, round buttocks.

She lay back, sighing contentedly. "I was expecting you yesterday," she said, hearing the petulant whine in her own voice.

He came back to her, lay down beside her, and trailed his fingers over her abdomen and breasts, playing with a nipple again.

"Stop that." She swatted at his hand.

But instead of letting go, he gripped her entire breast, holding it in place, as if it were his property. He breathed into her neck. "I didn't think it… proper, not after your father just died. But I can't stay away from you, Danika." His voice was husky. "You're the air in my lungs, my reason for living."

"You should have come sooner. I needed you."

He sat up on one elbow, trailing one finger across her face. "I'm so sorry. Your… your father was a good man. I always… liked him."

Liked but not respected. She grabbed his hand, pulled it from her face, and kissed his palm. "*I* needed you."

"I… I thought you'd need some time."

"I needed *you.* I needed this. Never stay away from me again." She let go of his hand and grabbed his chin, forcing him to look at her.

He pulled free and sat up on the edge of the bed, his back to her.

She moved behind him, placing her cheek against his shoulder and hugging him. "What?"

They sat there in silence for some moments. She knew what he was going to say. It never changed. Brice Awde was nothing if not consistent. She couldn't give him what he wanted, but as much as she dreaded it, a part of her needed to hear him say it, needed to hear him ask—as impossible as it was.

He placed his hands atop hers, over his stomach. "Now…" His voice faltered, thick with emotion. "Now that your father has passed… will you come away with me now?"

"Brice, my love," she whispered into his ear. "You know I can't. Palin will need me, now more than ever."

"*I* need you."

"We need to wait. I can't leave him now, not like this."

"If we keep going like this, we're going to get caught. You think your chambermaids don't already whisper about us?"

"Suspecting and having it thrust in front of your face are two different things. If we are discreet, nothing need ever change."

"*Everything* will change. The nature of life is change. When your brother becomes duke, he will find you a husband. Mark my words, more suitors will come sniffing after you and your family's name."

"And I'll send them running, just as I have with all the others. I only want you."

He shook his head. "You're twenty-five, Danika, the only daughter of a great family."

"Once great."

"*Still* great. More men will come. They'll bargain for you and make your brother offers he can't turn down. He'll need to make a deal before you're too old."

She pushed away from him. "Now you insult me."

He turned and grabbed her, pulling her onto his lap, wrapping his arms around her back, and holding her tightly. "Never," he whispered into her breasts. "I'm being realistic. We need to run now, before it's too late."

Trailing her fingers through his hair, she fought down her emotions. "Things will change, my love. You'll see. If we find that stupid sword, he won't even need me any longer."

"He'll *always* need you, with or without Sight-Bringer."

"He needs me now," she said.

"I need you more. Me. I have silver saved up, enough for us both to disappear across the Promiscuous Sea. No one will know us. In the east, perhaps in Xi'ur, we can just be a man and a woman—start fresh."

"You know I can't—and you? Would you forsake your oath?"

"My oath was to your father."

"And my family."

"No, Danika—just your father. I was very careful about that. Besides, Sayer is a good man, capable. He can take my place, and at least one of the men, young Toscovar, has potential, would make a suitable lieutenant for Sayer. We can do this."

"That blond thug? Please. No. I can't leave my brother, not until he has secured his title. He's obsessed with going back to Greywynne Island to dig up those damned catacombs and find that sword. Would you leave Sayer in charge there? Surrounded by those people?"

"Sayer is—"

"*Is not you.* He's not Brice Awde. My brother needs *you*, and he needs me. I can't abandon him, not now."

Silence settled between them. For long moments, they sat thus, her in his lap, her head against his chest.

Finally, he spoke. "You shame me, Danika Dain. It's you who should be duke. What a leader you'd make."

She trailed her fingers over the hair of his chest, twirling it. "We find Sight-Bringer," she said. "Then, the king confirms Palin as duke, and maybe—just maybe—that old fool finally pays Stron's war debts. Then, everything will be different."

"Palin will still marry you off—and I'll die."

She gripped his chin and turned his face to stare into his eyes. "I won't let that happen, not ever." She kissed the scar that ran down his neck. Then, her fingers snaked downward to grip him.

He gasped. "Save me, woman. How young do you think I am?"

"Brice Awde, you're the best man in the north. Isn't that what everyone says?" She stroked him so that despite his objections, his body reacted, becoming hard for her again. "When this is done," she whispered, lying back and pulling him atop her, "once we're back safe, and my brother is secure in his title, then I'll go away with you."

His teeth flashed in the moonlight. "You promise?"

"Yes, you big stupid soldier. I promise."

She cried out as he entered her again.

Chapter 9

Owen

Owen's gaze took in the horses, wagons, and men preparing to march south. The party setting out from Castle Dain to Greywynne Island was considerable, just under a hundred strong. Seventy-five men-at-arms—half the castle's garrison—were being led by Keep-Captain Awde and Keep-Lieutenant Sayer. While most of the men were walking, with the exception of those riding the supply wagons, Owen, Dilan, and Fin had been chosen to ride as scouts because of their superb riding skills. The remainder of the expedition consisted of young Lord Palin and his sister, the Lady Danika, and her pretty blond handmaiden, Wren. Also going was elderly Father Cotlas, as well as the new priest, Father Bowen. A handful of other servants made up the rest of the expedition, including the new physician, Modwyn Du'Aig, for which Owen was thankful. While Keep-Captain Awde had insisted that all the men-at-arms learn how to minister to wounds—to set bones and cover cuts with poultices—without a real physician, any open wounds were likely to fester—and in the wilderness, that would be fatal.

Owen inspected Gale's saddle, making sure it was cinched tightly. He walked about the large horse, running his hands over his muscular flank. In the three days since they had bought the animal, Gale's raspy breathing had all but disappeared. Good feed and a clean stable could work wonders for a horse's health. Owen may not have been the businessman his brother was, but he knew how to care for horses.

They were traveling with supplies enough to last weeks—not only food and weapons, but also tools for excavation and lumber and canvas to build a provisional camp. For what purpose exactly, they still didn't know, but Keep-Captain Awde had told them they were traveling deep into the interior of Greywynne Island, to the ruins of Greywynne Fortress, the ancestral home of the Blood Queen Serina Greywynne and her family, a place of evil tales and dark legends.

Owen couldn't wait.

They planned to follow the Forest Road south once again, that time moving past the Green Heart Inn, along the King's Road to Port Ollechta and the Bay of Glory, and from there into the fabled Promiscuous Sea. In Port Ollechta, they would board a ship and sail south and east, following the Fenyir Islands chain. The islands, named after their occupants, the barbarous Fenyir clans, swung northeast like a fishhook, reaching most of the way to exotic Hishtar. Their final destination, Greywynne Island—gifted by the king to the Dain family and the Duchy of Wolfrey for their part in defeating Serina—sat near the most southern point of the Fenyir Islands. Greywynne Island had the only deep-water port in the Promiscuous Sea and was a major resupply link between Hishtar and Conarck.

Owen turned as Dilan approached, leading his own horse. Dilan wore his ring-mail coat and a sword and carried a long wooden lance, its metal point gleaming in the early-morning sunlight.

Dilan placed the shaft against the ground and leaned on it, watching Owen. "You seem pleased."

Owen smiled as he adjusted his ring mail, letting a flap of it hang over his belt, taking some of the weight off his shoulders. "I am. I've seen nothing of the world."

"It may not be all you hope for."

A horn sounded near the front of the line—the call to get underway. Owen mounted Gale and rode beside Dilan. Women and children waved good-bye as they left the castle. As Owen rode out under its gatehouse, he saw the bodies of the Ballard brothers twisting beneath the gallows. The face of Emrys Ballard, locked in death, seemed to be smiling at Owen.

#

Two days later, as Owen and Fin rode over a ridge of land, far ahead of the others, he saw Port Ollechta, his first-ever real city, and the sparkling waters of the Bay of Glory. He stood in his stirrups to see better, staring in wonder at gleaming white walls surrounding the massive city. The sea was magnificent, like nothing he had ever seen before. The northern mountain lakes, large though some of them were, paled in comparison.

"Hey! You listening?" Fin raised his voice.

"What?" Owen started and realized Fin had been talking to him.

Fin sighed. "I asked if you were coming."

Owen nodded. "Lead on."

They rode down the ridgeline, following the well-kept King's Road, occasionally passing wagons, riders, and travelers on foot. As they approached the tall white walls of the city, Owen saw that, unlike in the north, most of the city's buildings were made of stone, with bright red-and-orange-tiled roofs instead of thatch. Then, the wind shifted, blowing in from the bay. He almost gagged.

"Save me, that's foul." Fin covered his mouth with his hand.

"Thousands of people all living together within the city's walls."

Owen coughed. "Must get used to it, I guess."

"Civilization," said Fin. "Bigger than Wolfredsuntown."

"At the peak of High Summer Festival, I've never seen more than six, maybe seven hundred people gathered together in Wolfredsuntown," said Owen. "Port Ollechta could swallow all of them and still have room to spare."

Fin smirked at Owen. "Must be a lot of women."

"More likely a lot of whores," said Owen.

"And?"

"And when you come down with the serpent's pox and the new physician has to drain the pus from your enlarged stones with a giant needle, you'll regret having visited the brothels—if the Keep-Captain doesn't just have you whipped outright for stupidity."

"Oh, yeah." Fin's face turned white. "There is that, I guess."

"Let's go." Owen nudged Gale's flanks with his heels.

Chapter 10

Fioni

Fioni Ice-Bound, master of *Fen Wolf*—the sleekest, most maneuverable, and by far prettiest serpent ship to ever carry a Fenyir war party—sat atop the stone wall of a landing leading up to one of Port Ollechta's many alehouses. Her sea boots dangled over the wall, her heels striking the stones in a constant cadence as she watched the soldiers ride past below.

"And where are you lot off to, I wonder," she told herself softly.

"What?" asked her first mate, Vory Eel-Gifted, standing just behind her.

Vory, towering over her from behind, scowled at the passing soldiers. With his bushy, unkempt beard, long, scraggly head of bright-red hair, and massive chest covered in the same thick mat of red hair, Vory looked more bear than man. His bare arms, thick, corded with muscle, and covered by a patchwork of old scars and faded clan tattoos, rested atop the haft of his two-handed war axe. Vory didn't like cities, she knew, didn't like all the people in cities, didn't like the smell, and didn't like the thieves. However, to be fair,

Vory didn't really like anyone who wasn't of the Waveborn Clan or—to be brutally honest—most who were, either.

"She's wondering who they are," said Kora.

Kora Far-Sails, her Oar-Master and closest friend in the world, stood farther back behind Vory, leaning against the doorway to the alehouse, picking at her fingernails with her newly purchased Kur'teshi dagger, for which she'd spent twice its value, in Fioni's mind. Unlike most of the other female warriors among *Fen Wolf*'s crew, Kora wasn't particularly large or powerful, but she was fast, skilled, and utterly fearless—and that combination made her very dangerous. Like Fioni, Kora kept her hair short and pleated, which made it far easier to maintain at sea—and less hazardous in battle. Unlike Fioni, Kora's hair was dirty blond, not fiery red. Just below Kora's hairline, along her forehead, were two dolphin tattoos, each facing the other as they leaped from waves. Kora Far-Sails was well name gifted—a master mariner from a long line of master mariners. Her mother had even sailed with Fioni's great-grandfather Serl, perhaps the greatest of the Waveborn's mariners. Unlike most of the crew, who could only afford axes and spears, Kora wore two finely crafted Lyrian swords.

"I know *who* they are," snapped Fioni. "Do you not see the Lion of Wolfrey on their shields? I'm wondering *where* they're going with all the wagons because it looks like they're planning on staying somewhere a while and maybe doing something… interesting."

"Southeast," said Vory, as if it were the simplest answer in the world.

Fioni sighed and bit her lip but said nothing. *Of course they're going southeast.* They were in Port Ollechta after all, trading post between Conarck, Hishtar, and the far east. *The real question is how far they are going.*

Fioni wondered whether she could profit from that knowledge.

Kora snickered, and Fioni glanced over her shoulder to glare at the woman. Kora looked away, at least having the decency to pretend to be sorry. Vory didn't like it when people made fun of him, and despite what many thought—including many of their own clan, who really should have known better—Vory was more than clever enough to figure out when others were laughing at him, which rarely ever ended well for the joker. And Kora, bless her childish heart, just loved goading the bear, driving him to the point of near apoplexy before relenting, then skipping away as if she had done nothing.

One of these days, she's going to push him too far. What will she do then?

Probably marry him.

One of the soldiers, sitting atop a large horse as black as the eye of a shark, caught her attention. He was a young blond man with wide shoulders, his helmet resting atop his saddle horn. *Very handsome,* she thought, with a strong chin covered by several days of blond grizzle. No doubt, there'd be a nice, strong chest beneath that armor, blanketed by that same blond fuzz. She did like them blond, liked to twine her fingers through their chest hairs… through their *other* hairs.

"Ooh." Kora pushed off the door and moved to sit beside Fioni. She gripped Fioni's bicep and squeezed it, staring at the young man. "He's a pretty pony. How'd you like to ride him hard and put him away wet?"

Vory groaned, but Fioni smiled, shook her head. "I think not. A man that big… probably as dumb as a seagull."

Vory coughed.

"You like to screw 'em smart, do you, skipper? Are they better that way?"

"As a matter of fact, yes, Kora." Fioni watched the young man's back as he rode away. "They are better smart. He *is* a pretty one, though, I'll grant you that."

Vory cleared his throat. "Must be a hundred warriors."

"Seventy-five," Fioni said. "With six wagons."

"We could take 'em," Vory said.

"Maybe," said Fioni as she climbed to her feet, adjusting the eel-skin scabbard of her sword so that it hung just right over her ring-mail coat. "But those are northern warriors, not southern dandies. They're bred tough up north. We'd lose too many of the crew, and we're going to need every sword and axe we have once we find the Gilt-Mane."

"He's not here, skipper," said Vory. "We'd have found him by now. And no one's seen Thunder Killer in weeks."

"Slimy piece of whale shit has probably sailed to the Kur'teshi Empire," said Kora. "He'll sell his swords to anyone without enough sense to toss him as the chum he is. We'll never see Galas Gilt-Mane again."

"We'll see my cousin again," said Fioni, a surprising amount of heat in her voice.

Kora grinned, exposing a missing front tooth, then hugged Fioni fiercely, kissing her cheek. "You're right, and when we do, you'll avenge Talin."

Fioni nodded, turning to her first mate. "Those are Wolfrey men, sworn to the Dains. Ask around, Vory. Find out where they're going."

"Greywynne Island belongs to them," said Kora. "That makes the most sense."

"Greywynne Island will *never* belong to them," said Fioni. "The witch's people still hate them, but you're right, that's probably where they're going."

"You still want me to find out?" asked Vory.

"Yes. Make sure. I'd hate to run into them at sea. It'd be embarrassing, what with all those men-at-arms."

“And we might have to kill the pretty one,” Kora said as she drifted past Fioni.

Fioni nodded, her eyebrows rising. “Yes, Vory. I don’t want to kill the pretty one. Do try to be discreet, yes?”

Vory snorted, shaking his large head. “Bloody master spy I am. Ain’t nobody more sneaky in this whoring, piddling anthill.” He turned and stomped down the stairs, forcing a pair of sailors just coming up to jump aside before he barreled through them.

Fioni smiled, feeling as salty that evening as the sea she loved.

Part Two:

The Great Crypt

Chapter 11

Owen

The voyage to Greywynne Island had taken three turbulent days on an old cargo hulk that soon reeked of vomit and horse manure. Unlike most of the Wolfrey men-at-arms, who immediately succumbed to seasickness, Owen vibrated with excitement the entire voyage, barely able to sleep. As they sailed into Port Eaton's wide, natural bay, he had even climbed the rigging in order to see better. The Wolfrey fort, named Stron's Watch in honor of the great warlord, sat on a rocky cliff overlooking the harbor and the small town of Port Eaton.

Two days after arriving on the island, Owen found himself sitting in a half circle with the other soldiers in the hard-packed dirt of the fort's courtyard. An uncovered wagon sat before them, a large box sitting atop its bed, with an old blanket covering that.

Stron's Watch was little more than a tower surrounded by a wall, with some wooden buildings, stables, and storage sheds, as well as the numerous tents of the Wolfrey soldiers set up in the dirt courtyard. Atop the tall tower fluttered a single pennant with the golden lion of

Wolfrey. The fort sat at the far edge of the cliff. In the sea below, the waves smashed against the rocks, throwing cold mist into the air.

Two hard-looking locals—the first of the infamous Greywynne Islanders that Owen had ever seen—stood beside the wagon. The two men, wearing leather and furs, looked like foresters. One, somewhere in his early thirties, was older than the other. Keep-Captain Awde had greeted the man upon arrival, addressing him as Master Idwal. Idwal was of average height but thick in the arms and shoulders. His hair, reddish brown and receding, was long at the back and pulled into a single plait, with pieces of colored string woven into it. The sun had weathered his ruddy face, lining it with deep cracks. His mustache was neatly trimmed, but his red beard was long and braided with wooden beads. On his belt, he wore a short axe and a long skinning knife, as did the other islander, a lad of perhaps seventeen years with the same red hair but also an empty gleam in the eyes that hinted at slowness. Otherwise, the two men looked alike enough to be brothers.

Keep-Captain Awde and Sayer stood beside, but slightly apart from, the two islanders. The new physician, Modwyn Du'Aig, and the Dain family's reeve on the island—a constantly scowling heavyset man by the name of Wendel Dert—stood farther back, talking to one another.

"What's with the islanders?" Fin asked, plopping himself cross-legged between Owen and Dilan.

Owen shook his head, pursing his lips.

"Don't like the way they look," said Fin.

"Just men," Owen said. "No webbed fingers, no gills."

"What do you suppose is under that blanket?" Fin asked.

"I think we're about to find out," said Dilan.

Idwal and the other islander climbed up onto the bed of the wagon. With the blanket still covering it, they carefully lifted the object down. The object clearly had some weight to it, and both men moved very slowly and carefully. As they set the object down on the dirt, an alien screech echoed across the courtyard. Nearby, in the stable, the horses whinnied in fear.

Now Owen understood—a live marsh tick was beneath that tarp.

The soldiers glanced at one another, muttered beneath their breath, and scuttled farther back. Owen knew of no one who had ever seen a live marsh tick, but every child in the north had grown up hearing stories about those monsters from the veterans of Stron's army. Giant, horrific insects that could rip a man's arm free with its pincers, they were said to be nearly invulnerable and frightened only by fire. Idwal stood watching the Wolfrey soldiers, his thumbs stuck into his belt and a smile on his face.

"Quiet down, all of you," Keep-Captain Awde commanded. "His lordship is coming."

The keep-captain turned and faced the stone steps leading up to the tower's entrance, where Lord Palin and his sister had just appeared, approaching the gathered men. The men jumped to their feet, Owen included, lowering their heads in respect.

The young lord was dressed in a fine blue tunic and gray leggings, with a black fox-fur-lined cloak over his thin shoulders, but as impressive as the boy looked, most of the men were watching his sister. Lady Danika glided along beside her brother, holding his arm. She wore a simple green dress with a short red cape, her locks tied up atop her head. Such a beautiful woman was out of place among all those soldiers. The Dain siblings approached the keep-captain. Where young Lord Palin's face clearly reflected his nervousness, Lady Danika's was the picture of serenity.

"My lord, my lady," said Keep-Captain Awde.

"Good day, Captain," answered Lord Palin. "Is everything…?"

Keep-Captain Awde nodded. "We were just waiting for you, my

lord. With your permission?"

The men created a space near the front, allowing servants to place two high-backed wooden chairs before the covered box.

"Not too close," said the keep-captain, and the servants moved the chairs farther back.

Once seated, Lady Danika placed her hands on her lap while her younger brother fidgeted with his sword, thrusting it out of the way before meeting the keep-captain's eyes and nodding.

Keep-Captain Awde glanced to Idwal. "If you would, Master Idwal."

The islander stepped forward, bent over, and grasped the trailing edge of the blanket. In one quick moment, he yanked it free, revealing a metal cage half the height of a man. Inside the cage, as expected, was a marsh tick. At the sight of the insect—the size of a small dog—a wave of revulsion swept through the men. The only place in the world where those creatures lived was that island, deep within Feldwyn Swamp. Its body, bloated and shiny, reminded Owen of a pregnant spider, fat with eggs. Bristles covered its small, pointy head, and it had numerous tiny red eyes and gnashing mandibles. Two stubby translucent wings sat atop its torso, and it had six segmented legs, but only the rear two legs looked large and powerful enough for locomotion, with the others appearing too small to help it move. Still, despite those legs, the veterans had all spoken of how fast the creatures were. A glistening green carapace, highly regarded for its armor-like properties, covered its torso. The marsh tick lifted its head and once again emitted that horrible stuttering cry. As it did, its wings beat so rapidly they seemed to blur into nothing.

"There's little to fear while it's in the cage," said the physician, Modwyn, as he stepped up next to Idwal. "It can't get out, and it's actually quite docile during the day."

"Aye." Idwal nodded at the doctor. "Usually, they sleep during the day." He paused, smiling. "But this one's a bit cranky at being caged. It's also a bit larger than they usually come."

Owen stared at the angry creature. *This is docile?*

The marsh tick settled, becoming less agitated. Idwal watched it for some moments and then actually moved one hand through the bars, letting his fingers trail along its green carapace. It didn't react, didn't move, except for a brief moment when its wings buzzed quickly then stopped.

"Craftsman's blessing," whispered Fin. "He's got balls like a bear."

Idwal pulled his hand free and smiled at them, exposing yellow teeth. "Safe enough now, with the sun overhead, but you should see them at night."

"And we will," said Keep-Captain Awde, stepping closer. "To get to the fortress, we'll need to follow the old road, and it goes straight through the heart of Feldwyn Swamp. Years ago, when the road was still maintained, a man could cross the swamp in a single day. But the islanders consider the interior to be haunted—taboo territory. That's why they call the land on the other side of the swamp the Haunted Vale. The road's fallen into disrepair, and there's no way to get through the swamp before nightfall."

As he spoke, Awde glanced at Idwal, who nodded in agreement.

"Nor," continued the keep-captain, "can we bring the wagons we'll need over the hills surrounding the Vale and the grasslands. We are going to have to spend the night in the swamp, and it's certain we will see these monsters."

Once again, Idwal nodded. "'Tis a sure thing."

"So," said the keep-captain, "Pay close attention to what Doctor Du'Aig and our guest, Master Idwal, have to say. Master Idwal makes his living hunting the ticks. He knows them well, as does the doctor, who studied them at the Royal University in King's Hold. What's more, Master Idwal and his brothers have agreed to travel with us, to show us the way through the swamp."

"They won't be popular for that," Dilan whispered.

Idwal bowed his head. His brother cackled, as if he had just heard a great jest. Idwal glared at him, and the young man stared at his feet.

Marsh tick hunters? Owen watched them both with a newfound respect. *That has to be a hard profession.* Marsh tick carapaces were highly sought after, especially in the east, in the Kur'teshi Empire. If Idwal and his brothers were good at their trade, they likely made a nice living. *So why are they helping us, men they hate? Lord Palin must be paying them a great deal.*

"We've hunted hundreds of these beauties," Idwal said. "But only one at a time. Make no mistake, they're very dangerous, but they have weaknesses—like fire, which I'm sure you've heard—terrified of it, they are."

"It's true," said Modwyn. "Like most animals, they run from fire unless driven by desperation."

Fin raised his hand, and Modwyn paused, raising an eyebrow.

"How do you fight such things?" Fin asked.

"With courage and determination, and by being forearmed with knowledge." Modwyn looked over the men, letting his gaze stop on one, Hrawlgir, a tall, lanky young soldier, a friendly enough man standing near the back, leaning on his spear. Modwyn held his hand out to the young man. "Your spear, if you please."

Hrawlgir hesitated, his eyes going to Keep-Captain Awde, who nodded. Pushing through the crowd, Hrawlgir handed the spear to Modwyn. Modwyn stood above the cage, holding the spear so its steel head hovered over the now-docile marsh tick. After bracing himself, in one quick motion, Modwyn stabbed the spear down into the crate, striking the insect between its small wings atop its carapace. Instantly, the marsh tick erupted in an angry frenzy, its wings a blur as it thrashed about in the cage. It screamed so loudly the horses whinnied in fear again, and several men had to rush away to calm them. When Modwyn pulled the spear out, they saw it hadn't done more than scratch the insect's carapace. The marsh tick, calm once again, settled back in its cage.

"I've dissected one of these creatures at the university," Modwyn said. "They are most remarkable. Their exoskeleton is harder than steel, or very nearly so. I've seen an entire suit of armor made entirely from the chitin. In fact, their carapace is so hard that one would think these things invulnerable." The physician paused and moved around to the front of the cage, where the creature's small head was. "Other parts of its anatomy are also very useful as medical ingredients although not nearly as well understood." He used the spear to point out various parts of its body. "Several of the internal organs can be used to dull pain. Amazing, really."

"You said one would think them invulnerable," Dilan called out. "That means they're not. So where, then?"

Modwyn slowly placed the head of the spear through the bars once more and let its tip dangle over the space just behind the insect's head. "Here," he said softly, "between the head and the prothorax."

"The what?" someone asked.

"The prothorax," repeated Modwyn, almost in a whisper. Then, without warning, he rammed the spear into the insect, right behind its head. The spear point impaled the creature, pinning it to the ground. It shrieked once, thrashed about for a second, and then lay still. Yellow blood pooled about the bottom of the cage, soaking into the ground.

"This spot, just behind the head"—Modwyn kept staring at the dead marsh tick—"is where you'll find a nerve cluster. Strike that cluster, and the insect dies immediately. But strike with care, because you need to let it get close first."

"Not if you put an arrow into it," said Fin.

Modwyn raised his eyebrows. "Indeed." He yanked the spear free, and yellow goo dripped from its point as he handed the weapon back to Hrawlgir.

The young man stared in revulsion at his weapon.

"Best clean that," said Idwal. "Quicker than you'd think, tick blood will rot steel."

"A marsh tick is a fearsome creature, make no mistake," said Modwyn to the soldiers, "but if you know where to strike, as I have just demonstrated, it dies easily enough. We now understand these creatures far better than in your grandfathers' time, when Stron and his army fought their way through the swamp. Now, we know they burrow into the earth and sleep during the day. We know they avoid fire. If we're careful, no one needs to worry about the Feldwyn Swamp."

Idwal snorted. "I wouldn't say that. A smart man always needs be watchful in that swamp… if he wants to come out again."

"Yes, thank you. They see poorly at night as well," continued Modwyn. "Might not even notice you unless you're making a lot of noise."

Dilan leaned closer to Owen. "Like say, seventy-five soldiers with half a dozen wagons, as well as horses, all blundering through the mud?"

Owen snorted in laughter, but Sayer glared at them, so he put on a more serious face.

"There's one more thing you need to remember," said Modwyn. "Almost all of these creatures are males, and they're dangerous enough, but 'ware the females. They're infinitely worse."

"Just like all women," whispered Fin.

Owen elbowed him in the ribs.

"I doubt you'll see a female, but if you do, tell me immediately,"

Modwyn said. "Run and get me if you have to."

"How will we know?" Owen asked.

"You'll know, lad," said Idwal, smiling cruelly.

"The females are larger, bigger than a horse." Modwyn paused. "And they fly."

An uneasy muttering swept through the men. Keep-Captain Awde stepped forward, silencing them with a look. "Get a grip on yourselves. No one ever sees a female," he said. "Or so I've heard."

"It's true," said Idwal. "I've only ever seen a corpse, never a live one, but they're out there. I heard 'em in the night. Nearly shat myself." His face blanched as he glanced at Lady Danika. "Sorry m'lady," he mumbled.

Keep-Captain Awde frowned at Idwal. "Doctor Du'Aig and Master Idwal have offered to remain behind and answer any further questions you may have, but for now, your new liege lord would address you."

The men silenced immediately. Idwal and his brother hurriedly lifted the crate with the dead marsh tick out of the way. Keep-Captain Awde lifted the blanket that had been over the crate earlier and tossed it over the bloody ground, making a clean spot for the young man to stand. As young Lord Palin stood before them, Owen noted that Modwyn and Idwal were off together, separate from the others and engaged in their own private discussion. Lord Palin looked unsure of himself, as if he wanted to be anywhere but there. Addressing a large group of men was a hard thing, Owen knew, especially when they were all considerably older than Lord Palin. The teenaged boy stood in place, like a statue. Someone coughed.

Lord Palin's eyes darted to his sister's, and then he began to speak. "Men, I'm glad you're all here with me—with us. I know this has been… unusual for you, coming all this way without understanding why." He took a deep breath. "You've only been told that we're traveling to the ruins of the witch's fortress, destroyed by Duke Stron and many of your own fathers and grandfathers. What you don't yet know is why."

He paused. A wind picked up, causing the nearby tents to flap and blowing the young man's hair about his face. He pushed the loose strands away. "We have discovered something, something grand." His smile looked forced, and the young man paused once again. Keep-Captain Awde moved closer and whispered something in his ear, and the young man's lips tightened.

"On his deathbed..." Palin glanced quickly at the physician before continuing. "On his deathbed, a... a *spell* that had been placed on my father by the blood fiend and witch Serina Greywynne finally fell away, revealing an important memory, a memory that Father Craftsman wanted my father to reveal to us.

"Sight-Bringer was *not* destroyed in the battle against Serina Greywynne as we've all believed all our lives. It still lies buried—but within our reach—in the catacombs of her fortress, and we're going to find it and return it to the king."

A chill gripped Owen. The men muttered, and some swore. Keep-Captain Awde and Sayer glared at them, and the whispers stopped instantly.

Owen found thinking clearly difficult. The news seemed so impossible, like a minstrel's tale. *Sight-Bringer?* Every child in the kingdom had grown up on tales of the longsword—a remnant of the long-dead Illthori race—that could slay the undead with a single cut. Duke Stron had used it to kill Serina, ending her unholy life in one blow—before it shattered in her chest, the resulting backlash bringing down the ceiling of the Great Crypt, burying her and its broken shards forever.

Sight-Bringer was one of the greatest legends of the north and one of its deepest shames—because the king had only loaned it to Stron to defeat Serina.

"So," continued Lord Palin, "tomorrow, we shall do something no man of the north has done in two generations—we shall return to the ruins of the witch's fortress and reopen the catacombs, and then we will find the Great Crypt and dig out the sword. We will all be heroes."

Keep-Captain Awde was nodding, his face fierce. The elation seemed to sweep through the men as Owen also felt it keenly.

"When we ride out that gate tomorrow morning," the young lord said, his voice rising, "we ride to finish what other men began almost fifty years ago. We have a responsibility to complete the pact Duke Stron and your grandfathers made to the king, to the kingdom. We will bring back the sword!"

The men cheered.

Chapter 12

Palin

Hours after his speech to the men, Palin still felt the heady excitement of success coursing through him. He had done it! He had stood before warriors and convinced them they were part of a great adventure, that he was a man worthy of following—and not just a young boy pretending to be a lord. For the first time in his life, he finally felt like a real leader, not just a young boy.

He stood in front of a table with a large map of the island unfurled on it, surrounded by other men—Keep-Captain Awde, Wendel Dert, Father Cotlas, and his young protégé, Father Bowen. They were going over the final preparations for the expedition, which would set out the following morning.

The expedition would be a grand adventure, the chance to change his family's destiny.

His sister was wrong. The king would pay back their war debts—just as soon as Palin placed Sight-Bringer in his hands again.

As Dert droned on—something to do with the hunters—his attention kept drifting back to the moment when, standing before the men-at-arms, he felt himself becoming the man he had always wanted his father to be. Palin was a man, not just the son of a duke, but a man in his own right.

All his life, he had deferred to his older sister, rarely making a decision without her or—the Craftsman forbid—deciding something *against* her wishes. That would have to change. Danika was no bully, just an older sibling with a very strong personality, but he needed to be his own man.

When he glanced at Brice Awde, Palin's good mood vanished. Awde had always been more of a father to Palin than his own had ever been. Awde had been the one to teach him how to use a sword, to ride properly, to stand tall before other men. All his life, Awde had been teaching Palin.

"Duty is a double-edged sword," Awde had always said.

On that day, that sword was going to cut Palin.

At that moment, Palin noticed Dert was watching him, a look of puzzlement in his eyes.

"My lord," the reeve said, "is everything…"

Awde was also watching him with a tight look. The keep-captain had been jotting down notes, calculating the number of firepots to bring, no doubt concerned they didn't have enough to drive off the marsh ticks—although in truth, they were likely bringing thrice what would be necessary. Awde was always troubled, always worrying, and always insisting Palin worry, too. A man couldn't worry enough, Awde insisted. *"Be prepared or be dead,"* he said. *"Battlefields are littered with the corpses of those who thought* good enough *was a plan."*

"I'm fine, Master Dert," Palin said. "You are quite right. We will watch Master Idwal and his brothers, but these men are my subjects now. We must treat them like men, not dogs—else they will act like dogs."

One corner of Awde's mouth turned up in a smile. Approval was rare from the keep-captain. Once again, Palin felt guilt weigh heavily upon him.

"Yes, my lord," said Dert, wiping his sweaty face, "but you must understand. These… these men aren't like us in the kingdom, good pious men. They still worship evil—"

"These are my subjects, Master Dert. We shall treat them with respect."

"But we will still watch them carefully," Keep-Captain Awde said, still bent over the table.

Palin nodded. "Yes… well, someone once told me: *'Be prepared or be dead.'*"

"Indeed," said Keep-Captain Awde. "Clearly, a very wise man."

Palin was still smiling when the chamber door opened and Danika slipped in. When she saw the small group of advisers around Palin, she frowned. Just for a moment, a spike of uncertainty rushed up Palin's back, but he fought his fear down. *If you're truly a man now, start acting like one—get out from beneath your sister's dress.*

"Did you gentlemen forget to invite me to your council?" Danika asked, her eyes flashing from one to the other and pausing as she glanced at Awde, who grimaced.

"My good lady," said Dert. "I'm afraid this is a matter for—"

"Gentlemen," said Palin. "Please give us the chamber… if you don't mind."

Dert muttered beneath his breath as he joined the others in leaving the room. Father Bowen held Father Cotlas's arm as they left. The elderly priest was going to remain in Stron's Watch. The sea voyage had been worse than he had expected, and he still hadn't fully recovered. Palin noted the look that passed between his sister and the keep-captain as he bade her farewell and followed the others out.

Palin sighed. Father had been so weak, so blind. He must have known about their secret affair but for some reason had let it go on.

Palin knew if he didn't put a stop to it immediately, the relationship would end badly for both of them. A man like Brice Awde deserved better than that. A hero he might have been, but he wasn't noble. He could never be a husband for Danika.

Duty is a sword.

Danika stood before him, waiting.

He inhaled deeply and met her eyes. "You're not going. You'll stay here with Father Cotlas and Dert."

She frowned, looking at him as if he were a particularly stubborn child. "We've already had this discussion. You'll need me."

"Why is that, sister? Will you swing a pick and carry rocks for us? What exactly is it you will do, other than distract me… distract *him*?"

Her eyes tightened, and she looked as if he had just slapped her. "What are you—"

He shook his head, forcing himself to go on. *Hurt her a bit now or a lot later.* He stepped closer and put his hands on her shoulders. He was taller than her and could look down into her eyes. *When did I grow taller than her?* "Danika, I know. *We all know.* This ends today."

Her face drained of color, and he saw fear in her eyes—something he had never seen before on her face. "I don't—"

"You're not going. I love you. I need you, but you have a duty as much as I do. We are going to restore our family's name. *All of us* have a role to play. I won't have you out there in the wilderness, risking your life, getting in the way, and bringing him down as well. This ends now!"

"You don't—"

"I won't talk of it, won't make it real through words! You will stay here. When we return—and I have given Sight-Bringer to the king—you will take a husband, one befitting our family's name."

Her eyes welled with tears, something else he had never seen before, and he realized just how badly he had hurt her, but he couldn't stop, not then. "This thing between the two of you ends today."

She reached up and gripped his hands, pulling them from his shoulders and squeezing them. "Palin, please. You don't understand. I love him."

"You can't love him, Danika. You know that. You never could."

She rushed forward, hugging him. "Please, Palin, don't do this. Just let it go." Her voice cracked with emotion.

Just for a moment, he felt his resolve waver, but he tamped his weakness down, forcing himself to go on. "Danika, you are a Dain, the only daughter of the Duke of Wolfrey, the sister of the man who will be the new duke. There have been kings in our family's past, and there may yet be again—but not if you chase after a man beneath your station."

Her shoulders shuddered, and he heard agony in her voice. "Palin, please… If you love me—"

"It's because I love you." He turned away, stalked to the window, and gazed out at Port Eaton. The sun had already dropped below the horizon, covering the town in a dark, lightless blanket. Simple folk couldn't afford the candles or lamp oil. When the sun went down, they went to bed. The only lights he saw were coming from the town's alehouse, sitting prominently in the village green. The alehouse was the largest building in Port Eaton, with two levels of closely fit stone walls.

"Palin…?"

"You will stay here. When we return, I do not want—do not *ever* want—to speak of… of my keep-captain and you. You shame our family." He turned and faced her. She was looking down, staring at her hands, tears running down her cheeks. She trembled before him, not his sister anymore, but a new person—a timid, broken person.

Is this what I wanted?

"We must all do our duty, Danika. I will be duke. You will marry well, have children."

"Duty," she repeated softly.

He sighed. "Duty is a sword, Danika."

Chapter 13

Idwal

Idwal stood in the shadows next to the alehouse, hidden behind a short wall where he could watch the entrance. He had been in there earlier that night, but his deal with the northerners had angered the others so badly they had nearly come to blows. They weren't happy Idwal and his brothers had agreed to lead the northerners inland. Several of the more vocal men—men whom Idwal had hunted and fished and drank with all his life—promised him that he would regret taking their silver. One of them, the barrel maker Galvin—a man who was as close a friend as any to Idwal—none too subtly promised a reckoning. Idwal had left the alehouse before he did something he couldn't walk away from. He knew he might have to kill Galvin someday—although he would regret doing so—but if he did, it wouldn't be in front of witnesses.

Idwal pulled his hunting knife from its sheath and picked at his fingernails. *How much longer should I wait? What if the northern doctor doesn't come at all? What if this is all a trick of some kind? They know we hate them, would kill every stinking one of them if we could.* Then, he heard a horse's hooves clumping on the dirt road through town. A figure appeared out of the night, highlighted against the night sky, riding a small horse. *So… he kept his word.*

The rider approached the alehouse and dismounted. As he secured his horse to a hitching post, Idwal stepped out of the shadows. "Hsst. Doctor, is that you?"

Modwyn Du'Aig spun about. "Master Hunter, why are you out here? I thought we said inside."

"Whatever business you want with me, Doctor, it's of no matter to others. Besides, you wouldn't be welcomed in there. Now, what is it you want? I've already agreed to take your lord's silver. Trust me, that has caused me difficulty enough already."

Modwyn stared at him for several moments, as if unsure how to begin. Finally, he did. "What do you know of the queen," he asked, "of the legends of Serina Greywynne?"

Idwal grabbed him by the collar and threw him back against the wall, slamming the air from his lungs. Surprise and fear flashed through Modwyn's eyes, and Idwal held him against the wall by one hand, using the other to hold his hunting knife against the man's throat. He leaned in close, putting his lips near the doctor's ear. "Know this, Northerner, her name is not to be spoken—especially by one such as you."

"I'm no northerner," Modwyn squeaked, "but I have much to tell you." The man's eyes betrayed his terror but also a sense of fervor, of righteous indignation.

He's insulted. Why? Idwal removed his knife from the man's throat. "What are you playing at?" Modwyn asked him.

"Have you ever asked yourself why your people consider the Haunted Vale and the ruins of her fortress taboo?" Modwyn asked as he rubbed his throat. "Why do you suppose that is?"

"They've been forbidden all my life," Idwal said. "The land is… cursed."

"Cursed how?" asked Modwyn. "Think, man. What evidence do your people have for believing the lands surrounding her fortress to be cursed?"

"The dreams," said Idwal as Modwyn bobbed his head in agreement. "The nightmares?"

"Yes, exactly," said Modwyn. "But what is the source of the nightmares?"

"The gods," answered Idwal. "It's their curse for failing her."

Modwyn shook his head. "No, the nightmares have nothing to do with the gods, nothing at all."

"But… that's what the priests say—"

"Your priests are wrong."

"I… I don't…"

Modwyn stepped closer to Idwal, his eyes shining in the moonlight. "She isn't dead. She dreams, Master Idwal, and her dreams bleed into the world of men. That's what causes the nightmares. You haven't failed her. She's calling for help."

Chapter 14

Owen

As promised, early the next morning, Idwal and his five brothers returned, riding small, wiry palfreys. Each hunter was clearly kin to Idwal, with the same dour expression, thinning red hair, and weathered skin. Owen stood beside Gale, adjusting his saddle as the hunters rode through the fort's gatehouse. The hunters, in well-worn leather armor, were armed with axes and short hunting bows. Longbows, such as each of the Wolfrey men-at-arms carried, were much more powerful, but Owen had no doubt that any man who hunted marsh ticks for a living would be a deadly shot.

Owen and all the others had been up since before the dawn, eating and preparing. Most of the men would be on foot, with some riding in the wagons, but once again, Owen, Fin, and Dilan had been chosen to ride as scouts. The six wagons, carefully restocked, carried food and water for the men and grain for the horses. They also carried excavation tools and weapons, including bundles of arrows and spears. One of the wagons, carefully kept away from the others, carried clay jars filled with cooking oil—firepots—as well as bundles of pitch and cloth-wrapped torches and hundreds of arrows with a piece of pitch-soaked moss wrapped around each. While the added weight would throw off the aim, a good archer would be able to compensate, especially at short range.

The sergeants—older, more experienced men—began moving down the line, getting everyone ready. Gale snorted, stamping a hoof. Owen checked his saddle straps one last time and mounted the animal. Dilan and Fin rode just ahead of him, sitting atop their own mounts.

Owen edged Gale between them. "Are you both ready for this?"

Dilan nodded without comment, his expression somber. Fin grunted and adjusted his helmet. Keep-Captain Awde rode to the front of the line, where the young Lord Palin sat on his own mount. Father Cotlas stood, leaning on his staff, near the ramparts of the gatehouse, talking with Father Bowen, no doubt some final instructions.

Lady Danika, her face pale, stood near the two priests. She wore a green dress with a dangling satin belt. Her long brunette hair partially obscured her face as she flicked the strands out of the way before saying farewell to her brother.

That day was going to be long—and the night even longer—before the expedition rode free of the Feldwyn Swamp. Sayer and one of the sergeants rode down the line together one last time. Then, Lord Palin, riding next to Keep-Captain Awde, led the way out of the fort and down toward Port Eaton. For the first time in generations, northern warriors were returning to the ruins of Serina's fortress.

Owen kicked Gale's flanks, and the big black colt trotted forward. As they marched, the soldiers chatted and told jokes. Throaty laughter swept through the men, but it felt strained.

They rode down the winding fort trail, past the glittering harbor filled with fishing boats, and into the town. Small rock walls lined the side of the road, rising as high as a man's knees. As they rode through Port Eaton, its residents, surly and angry looking, stopped to watch them. The children ran along, pacing them and making faces. One of the little rats even threw a stone before darting away. Roosters and chickens ran loose, dogs barked, and farmers glared from their fields.

"Little respect for their liege lord," muttered Fin.

"They've never accepted the Dains as their lords," said Dilan.

A small group of women stood beside the communal bakery in the town's center, faces filled with hate. One heavyset matron spat upon the ground.

Owen stared back at them. "Serina's rebellion was a long time ago. You'd think they would be over it by now."

"I don't think they ever will be," Dilan said.

They passed through the town, pretending not to see the hateful glares of its residents. Soon, they were back out in the countryside, traveling along an overgrown trail, all that remained of the road that led through the dark forest. Feldwyn Swamp—home to the marsh ticks—was deep within that forest. Owen shuddered when he thought of the giant tick in the crate.

An old wooden bridge spanned a softly gurgling stream, its banks green and muddy. On the other side of the bridge, the old road led into the woods. Wildly overgrown, the path was just wide enough for the wagons.

The expedition entered the woods, with Owen and the other scouts riding along in front. Squirrels chased along beside them, keeping pace. On occasion, they had to stop to clear brush so the wagons could continue, but they made good time, traveling faster than Owen would have thought. The islanders might have avoided traveling inland, but they clearly still used the path on occasion, likely for logging. The deeper the party went into the forest, though, the more overgrown it became. Around midday, they came across the remains of a crossroads, the other road almost completely reclaimed by the forest. A wooden sign covered with blackened letters and strangled by vines identified the other road as leading to the Greywynne family's once-rich silver mine. They stopped at the crossroads long enough to give the men a chance to wolf down some dried fish, apples, and hard brown bread.

Owen approached the weathered sign and ran his thumb over its letters. "You think there's anything there still?"

Dilan shook his head. "Silver mine ran dry a long time ago."

"How can you be sure? Mines must run deep."

"Do you think Idwal and his brothers would risk their lives hunting marsh ticks if there was silver to be dug out of the earth?"

Owen stared down the overgrown trail leading to the hills and the mine. "Guess not."

After lunch, they remounted and resumed their travel. The trail quickly worsened, and Owen soon found he had to dismount and walk Gale. The men on foot pushed and pulled on the wagons and spent most of their time clearing away the overgrowth. By early afternoon, they were all drenched in sweat and covered in dirt. Mosquitoes assaulted them with every step, and the ground became damp and muddy, sucking at the soles of their hobnailed boots. *We have to be near the edge of the swamp by now,* Owen mused.

By late afternoon, the air chilled and became moist. The pervasive reek of decay blanketed them, stinking of maggoty carcasses and sodden vegetation. Storms of mosquitoes assaulted them. The trees thinned, becoming twisted gray wardens, their skeletal arms grasping outward. A thick layer of fog settled over the wet, grasping mud, swirling about their horses' hooves. Pools of brackish green water, their surface broken by reeds and willows, rose up around them. The road became nothing more than a bridge of higher land, sinking back into the swamp in places. Occasional hillocks, large mounds of rocky terrain, rose out of the swamp waters like islands of refuge.

Owen pushed on, leading Gale, but at some particularly difficult, muddy spots, the strong horse had to pull him along. Above, the sky began to darken, and the shadows lengthened. They would have to stop soon, he knew. They would need to set up camp and establish their defenses before the marsh ticks came out.

As if on cue, the distinctive, stuttering cry of one of the creatures echoed over the swamp. Owen stroked Gale, whispering calming words to the horse. The men looked about themselves nervously. Shortly after, the order to leave the road came down the line.

A particularly large hillock rose out of the waters on their right. The column of men and wagons left the road, marching into muddy water up to their waists and then up onto the dry, rocky hillock. The hill, dotted by large boulders and stunted gray trees, was wide and high, its summit large enough to hold all the wagons and horses. Owen led Gale up the hillock's incline to its summit and secured him with the men detailed to care for the mounts. Removing his traveling cloak, he resigned himself to the miserable task ahead. Trudging back down the hill, he once again entered the dirty marsh waters to help push and pull the wagons across.

The next hour's work was as miserable a task as any he had ever known. While straining against the rear of one of the wagons, he slipped and fell face-first into the cold waters, his hands sinking deep into the muddy bottom. He panicked, swallowing some of the foul waters and flailing about, but then someone grabbed his shoulders and yanked him free. His rescuer was Lord Palin, grinning with muddy water running down his chin.

"Thank… thank you, my lord." Owen gasped and spat out foul water.

The young lord slapped him on the back and moved on to help shove the wagon the rest of the way onto the hillock. Owen shook himself like a wet dog and set off to help again, still wondering at the sight of a nobleman pushing a wagon. He had never seen Duke Oskaley getting his hands dirty. Of course, Oskaley had been an old man.

Shadows grew as the sun dropped out of sight. Several more times, they heard the eerie, stuttering cry of the marsh ticks. *Could they be communicating? No, they're just bugs.*

The sergeants moved among them, sending the men to their defensive positions. Owen recovered his cloak, his longbow, and his weapons and moved to his spot on the line surrounding the hillock, halfway up its length, between Fin and Dilan. Each man understood his role that night. Keep-Captain Awde had thoroughly briefed them before leaving the fort.

Owen set his round shield and spear against the ground and strung his longbow. The damp air was bad for the bowstrings, but they had little choice. Soon, men came by with bundles of replacement torches and fire arrows, as well as the firepots, each twice the size of a man's clenched fist. The pots had been sealed shut with a sticky tar residue. Once thrown, they would burst upon impact, casting flammable oil around.

Owen unrolled his bundle of arrows and examined them: each bundle contained eighty arrows. He pushed each one, point-first, into the spongy ground before him, so that he could easily grab them for use. If the torches didn't stop the marsh ticks, they'd put flaming arrows into the damned things, aiming for the unprotected area just behind their heads. If fire and arrow still didn't keep the creatures back, they'd use the firepots. They'd set the entire base of the hillock on fire if they had to. Men were tasked with keeping the line supplied all night. If fire, arrow, and oil failed to stop the marsh ticks, then they'd fight with spear, sword, and axe.

And probably die.

He set his two torches afire, as did the other men, and set them standing up into the wet soil, one right beside him, the other about twenty yards down the hill, near its base. A double ring of fire surrounded the hillock, giving it an otherworldly appearance as the fog thickened with the night. Each torch created its own glowing halo.

"Just stay away, you damned bugs," Owen whispered to himself, holding an unlit arrow beside his longbow.

He started when another marsh tick cried out, sounding not *that* far away. Owen shuffled in place, his feet wet and freezing. One of the men, Bokke, younger than Owen and half his size, came by with food. Bokke squished as he walked, his face gray and mud streaked. Owen waved at the young man, glad that he wasn't the only one who was miserable. Bokke handed him some cold jerky and black bread before moving farther on down the line.

Owen chewed and swallowed, surprised at how hungry he was. His meal done, Owen pulled the edges of his cloak in tighter around his neck.

Then it began to rain.

Chapter 15

Modwyn

The rain dripped down Modwyn's head, soaking his hair to his scalp. He stood near one of the large bonfires atop the hillock. His sodden clothing stuck to him, the slimy feeling making him even more miserable. Somewhere close by, a marsh tick called out, its staccato cry echoing in the night. He shivered despite the heat from the fire. He didn't like being out there where he had to risk his own life. The horses, corralled together, whinnied in fear, and the soldiers detailed to watch them moved about, trying to calm them.

Idwal stepped up next to Modwyn, hawked, and spat into the fire, his spittle sizzling on the coals. "There's no need to be scared," he said, his voice too soft for any other to hear. "They might come close, come see what all the fuss is about, but this much fire?" He shook his head, water dripping off his nose. "No. They're not going to cause any ruckus this night."

Modwyn glanced about himself. "They will to protect a female. Did you see a good spot to set it?"

Idwal snuffed, wiped his nose with his forearm, and then

motioned down the hill with his chin. "That way. There's a large fallen tree near the base of the hill, waterlogged, too heavy to move. But how will we bring her—"

"I have something that should draw one closer. In Port Ollechta, I found a man, a finder of rare alchemical substances. It was hideously expensive, but if it works, it will be well worth the price." Modwyn patted his chest, where a small glass vial sat inside a pocket sewn within his tunic.

Idwal grunted. "You sure this lot is up to the task? She'll call out to the males. It'll be worse than a squid frenzy."

"We have to take that chance," whispered Modwyn. "Besides, Awde is supposed to be a great warrior. I'm sure he'll keep us safe. It's the least they can do after all the horror his kind have caused."

"I hope you're right."

"It's worth the chance. Worth any chance."

"Unless the old man was senile, his mind gone."

"No," said Modwyn softly. "I have to believe. For so long now, hate is all I've had. Now… now I have hope again."

"Hope," muttered Idwal. "It's been so long since we've had such a wondrous thing."

Modwyn turned and stared down the hill at the rings of torchlight glowing in the fog. "Be ready with your gear. We'll do it soon, while they're still busy worrying about their defenses for the night."

"What if we're seen?"

"I have a plan for that. Think of *her*."

"Aye," whispered Idwal, nodding.

Another marsh tick cried out, and Modwyn shivered once again.

#

Modwyn watched from a distance as Palin and Awde discussed the defensive preparations. A small group of older warriors, sergeants, stood nearby. The boy remained silent while Awde—who was clearly truly in charge—gave pointed instructions to the sergeants. So far, despite the cries, no one had seen a single insect, but they had all heard them. If Idwal was right—and Modwyn had no cause to doubt him—the ring of fire would keep them at bay that night.

But Modwyn needed at least one to come close.

He had been watching Palin and Awde for some time now, waiting to speak to Palin alone. He didn't want Awde interfering. Unfortunately, the sad little boy wouldn't leave the warrior's side. Instead, he had been like a shadow to the older man, no doubt annoying him with his constant hero-worship. *And such as that,* he mused, *is the best the Dains have left.*

When one of the soldiers brought Palin a bowl of stew and some hard bread, Modwyn realized he might finally have his chance. Awde said something to him, no doubt telling him to sit down and eat his food like a good little boy, and then he and the sergeants moved farther on to continue their discussion. Palin was finally left to himself, sitting on a rock and eating his dinner. *Now or never.* Modwyn squared his shoulders and approached the boy.

Palin looked up and smiled. "Doctor, how are you this evening? This isn't like King's Hold, I imagine."

Modwyn flashed his teeth back at him. "Indeed not, my lord, but much more adventurous."

"Yes, yes it is." The boy just sat there, waiting. "Was there… something?"

"My lord, Master Idwal is worried about the marsh ticks. He's not certain there are enough torches to keep the insects at a distance. He'd like your approval to inspect the outer ring of fire, make sure it's adequate to the task."

The smile disappeared. "I don't think that's a good idea."

Modwyn bobbed his head. "Yes, of course, my lord, of course.

Your concern for your subjects is commendable, but I assure you, Master Idwal would be quite safe. No one knows these creatures better than he does. Moreover, our keep-captain is a famous warrior, but Master Idwal is beside himself with fear for *you*, my lord."

The boy's eyes narrowed. "Me? Why?"

"It seems you've already made quite an impression on him, my lord. He's mentioned several times how… different you are from other northerners, especially Wendel Dert."

"Well, that's… that's good, but—"

"I don't like to speak ill of others, my lord, but it doesn't look like your reeve is much loved by these people. Some of the stories Idwal has told me…"

"Doctor, I appreciate your concern, but I'm sure Master Dert has performed his duties with respect for all."

Modwyn raised his palms. "Oh, of course, my lord, I didn't mean to even imply any improprieties, just to repeat Idwal's—no doubt baseless—fears. You know how simple people can be. At any rate, while I don't agree with Master Idwal about Keep-Captain Awde's defenses, prudence dictates Master Idwal should quickly look over the outer ring. It would only take a moment and no doubt set his mind at ease."

"Have you broached this with Keep-Captain Awde?"

Modwyn forced a look of surprise upon his features. "Oh, oh… I see, my lord. It's just that you're the new… That is… of course I should ask the keep-captain. So… it's Keep-Captain Awde then, for all important decisions?"

"Well… we've *both* already inspected the line. Neither of us saw a problem."

Modwyn bobbed his head. "I don't imagine there is a problem, my lord. It would be the work of only moments to let Master Idwal see for himself. At the same time, I guess I could accompany him and speak to the men, inquire as to their physical well-being. But if you can't—I mean, if you'd like, I can ask the keep-captain."

Indecision flashed through Palin's eyes. "You mean you haven't checked on the men yet?"

"No, my lord. I apologize. I've been so busy with other matters. I… could do so now—accompany Master Idwal and kill two squirrels with one arrow."

The boy nodded, put another spoonful of stew in his mouth, and chewed while he spoke. "Yes, Doctor, please go see to the men. Take Master Idwal with you, show him everything is fine. If there's a problem, come and see *me*. Do you understand?"

Modwyn found it hard not to grin, but he managed.

"Perfectly, my lord."

Chapter 16

Owen

Owen peered out into the darkness down the slope of the hillock, seeing nothing but the flickering ring of torches. The night had grown dark, but the rain was only a drizzle, not a downpour. If their torches went out…

He heard footsteps behind him and looked over his shoulder to see two figures approaching, Modwyn and Idwal. The physician slipped, fell on his ass, and slid a bit before Idwal helped him back up.

Those two had seemed to be in each other's company a great deal since leaving Stron's Watch. In the short span of time since Modwyn had entered the Dains' service, Owen hadn't ever seen the young doctor befriending anyone.

Stopping just beside Owen, Modwyn and Idwal stared down the hill. Idwal was carrying a sack over his shoulder, its metal contents clanking when he shifted it.

"Are you well, man?" Modwyn asked, not even looking at Owen. "Does anything ail you?"

"No, sir," said Owen. "Should you be—"

Modwyn started as a tick cried out once more. Then, he stared at Owen, tightness in his eyes. "Have you seen anything… any of the creatures?"

Owen shook his head. "No, but we've been hearing them."

Idwal stepped past Owen, squinting at something farther down the hill. He turned and met the physician's eye then nodded. Modwyn also moved past Owen and peered down the hill. "I don't see it," he said softly.

"No, I told you. I haven't seen anything," said Owen.

"It's there," said Idwal, "just past the torch."

Owen glanced at Dilan, standing several feet away. Dilan shook his head. Just at that moment, someone yelled out from the other side of the hill that he saw something moving. They all turned and stared back up the hill. A moment later, they heard the release of a bowstring, followed by the whistling of an arrow and a trail of fire in the dark night as the flaming missile rose up and then fell from sight. A cheer rose from the men on the other side of the hill. Someone had just seen their first marsh tick and, by the sounds of it, had killed it.

The hunter leaned in closer to the doctor and grabbed his arm. "Now. We need to do it now."

Modwyn nodded then stared at Owen. "Soldier, we need to check something down below. Master Idwal is concerned the insects may be moving about, trying to get around us, and we need to go look. You will stand guard here and yell out if you see anything."

Owen stared at the two men in disbelief. "Doctor, that's a very bad idea. I'll have to check with—"

Modwyn spun on him. "You'll do as you're told, soldier, or I'll see you punished. His lordship himself has sent me to make sure. We'll only be a moment."

On the other side of the hill, more men cried out in warning.

Moments later, Owen heard the release of more arrows. Fire flashed through the night, like falling stars. Another cheer rose.

"But—" Owen began.

"Do as you're told!" Modwyn glared at Owen.

Hating himself for his own weakness, Owen nodded and looked away. Nothing was happening on his side of the hill. If Modwyn and Idwal wanted to take foolish chances, that wasn't his concern. Besides, Keep-Captain Awde was no doubt busy right then and didn't need Owen's interference.

"Go fast," Owen said.

As Modwyn and Idwal trotted down the hillside, the contents of the hunter's bag clinked.

"Are you daft? Why did you let them go?" Fin asked.

Owen sighed, raised his palms as if to ask what else he could have done. Fin shook his head, notched an arrow, and lit it on his torch. Dilan and Owen did the same. The three men stood watching as the doctor and hunter moved past the far line of torches and disappeared into the darkness.

"What are they doing out there?" Dilan asked.

Owen shook his head. "I don't know, but they know these insects the best. Besides, his lordship sent them. He must have cause."

"His lordship is a thirteen-year-old boy," said Dilan. "We should have checked with the keep-captain or even Sayer."

More fire arrows lit up the night, followed by more cries from ticks. "They're busy," said Owen, hating being put in a position where he had to choose between obeying his orders and obeying the physician.

"I can't see them anymore," said Dilan.

"Me neither," said Fin.

"I'm moving down a bit," said Owen. "Watch me."

"Be careful," said Dilan.

Owen snorted derisively as he stepped down the hill, his lit arrow nocked and ready to release. As he approached the lit torch he had set out earlier, he saw the dark shapes of Modwyn and Idwal farther away. Both men were up to their knees in the water at the base of the hillock, next to a huge fallen tree that lay half-submerged. The hunter had wrapped something around the tree's trunk and was moving back, making way for Modwyn. The doctor pulled an object from his clothing, but Owen couldn't see what it was from where he stood.

"Hsst," he hissed at them. "What are you doing?"

Idwal spun, his hand going for the hand axe in his belt, and Owen felt a momentary spike of concern. Modwyn turned, scowling at Owen, but reached out and gripped Idwal's forearm, stopping him.

"Don't come any closer!" Modwyn hissed. "You'll attract the ticks." He put his back to Owen.

Meanwhile, Idwal kept staring at Owen in open hostility.

What in Father Craftsman's name were these two—

A foul stench washed over Owen, so bad it almost made him gag. He took an involuntary step back and almost dropped his lit arrow. A marsh tick cried out, that time very close. Modwyn and Idwal ran past him, back up the hill, as if Old Grim himself were chasing them. Owen stared at their retreating backs and then at the waterlogged tree. *What are these two up to?* He moved closer to the tree. As he did, the stench grew worse. The fire from his arrow glinted off metal wrapped around the tree. *Is that a chain?*

He froze when a marsh tick leapt up on top of the tree from the other side. Its numerous eyes shone red in the light, and its translucent wings beat in a frenzied blur. Owen stumbled back, almost falling. After recovering his balance, Owen drew his arrow back and let it fly directly at the tick. The shot was bad, and the arrow sizzled into the wet bark beside the insect. The fat insect bunched up as it prepared to leap at Owen just as a second fire arrow flashed past

Owen's ear and thudded into the tick—striking deep in the killing spot just behind its head. The insect shrieked and fell into the water.

"Move, idiot!" yelled Fin from behind him.

Owen scrambled back up the hill to where Fin and Dilan waited for him. Owen reached them just as they heard something new—an impossibly loud staccato cry shattered the night, followed by the buzzing of monstrous wings. Dilan hurled a lit torch down the hill. The torch spun through the air, trailing sparks, and then landed on rocks near the tree trunk. It burned weakly but still cast enough light to make out the horror before them. A massive winged form the size of a warhorse dropped out of the fog and landed in the water just before the fallen tree—*a female marsh tick!*

Her massive triangular head darted from side to side as if she were searching for something. Tufts of spiky hair jutted from her segmented carapaces. Her huge wings buzzed, disappearing into a blur so powerful, it cleared away the fog near her.

"Father Craftsman, help us!" said Fin, lowering his bow.

The three men stood frozen in horror, staring wide-eyed at the obscene giant insect. Then, a loud metallic snap rang out, and she cried out again, that time clearly in distress. Something was wrong. Her wings blurred again, and she rose into the air, but the waterlogged tree rose with her. She dropped back onto the ground.

What?

"Kill her quickly, you fools," Idwal cried out from behind them. "She'll bring others."

Someone loosed a flaming arrow at her, but it glanced off her carapace, winging off into the night. Then more arrows struck her. Owen, Dilan, and Fin sprinted back to their positions in the line. As fast as he could, Owen lit and loosed fire arrows at her. Several of the shafts had struck true, burning into her, and her cries rose in intensity, creating an unearthly uproar that must have reached every corner of the swamp. Then, a chorus of other cries rose up from all around them as the swamp came alive with the reverberating cries of an army of male marsh ticks.

"Kill her, kill her!" screamed Idwal.

First one, then several more, and then a score of marsh ticks appeared at the base of the hillock. They rushed up its slope, past the female, charging at the line of soldiers. In seconds, a storm of fire arrows flashed toward the insects. Most of Owen's arrows missed, but several struck true, pinning giant bugs to the side of the hill. The stench of burning tick washed over them. Within moments, the entire base of the hill was burning with scores of small shafts and dead and dying ticks, but more of the creatures kept coming.

An eruption of heat and flames lit up the night. Someone had thrown a firepot, which was instantly set aflame by the burning arrows. Ticks screamed in agony, forced back by the inferno, but through the flames, Owen saw scores more of the insects, massing and waiting for the flames to die down. His fingers were numb from loosing so many arrows. Then, another firepot exploded, then two more. The entire base of the hillock was burning—but still swarming with marsh ticks. The female raged down below, her cries bringing still more.

To his left, a man screamed in pain, and Owen realized with horror at least one insect had reached their line. More ticks bounded up the hill, and Owen threw one of his own firepots then the other. Burning insects darted about in all directions. He grabbed his last arrow, lit it, and sent it into a tick that had been almost on him, pinning the creature to the ground. Two more took its place. He grasped his spear and, lunging forward, impaled one of the ticks in the killing spot behind its head, but the second one was on him, rushing forward. Then, someone else rushed past him and stopped it with a spear thrust—it was Hrawlgir—but he was supposed to be on the other side of the hillock! Other guardsmen also moved down from the summit, reinforcing the line. He had been wrong earlier. The battle would be fought on his side of the hill that night.

The stench of burning insect was horrific, almost more than he could stand, forcing him to breathe through his mouth. More firepots erupted along the line, forcing the insects back again, but it couldn't stop them for long. The female still shrieked, still forced the males against them.

Then, Keep-Captain Awde and Lord Palin moved among them, Awde screaming at them, trying to force order out of the chaos. Lord Palin's face reflected his terror, but the young man stood his ground with spear and shield next to the keep-captain.

To Owen's right, two ticks launched themselves onto a guardsman. The man screamed and thrashed but went down. Owen was about to throw himself back into the fray when someone grabbed his arm. It was Dilan, his eyes wild, blood running down the side of his nose and dripping off his chin.

"Come with me. I need your help," he said.

Owen looked back at the others. "We can't leave our—"

"Now, or we're all dead!"

He knew his place was there, even if they were about to be overrun, but something in Dilan's face made him nod. Dilan turned and ran back up the hill, to the summit, with Owen following. *We've just deserted our posts during a fight. Men hang for that.* At the summit, the bonfires still blazed. The men who had been left with the horses were busy trying to calm the half-mad animals, leaving the wagons abandoned. Dilan headed straight for the wagon holding the oil and torches.

"What are you doing?" Owen yelled after him. "There's no time to bring more oil."

Dilan moved to the rear of the wagon, putting his shoulder

against it. "If we don't kill that bitch now, we're all going to die."

Owen could see her from there, still straining to get free, with fires burning all about her. He put his shoulder to the wagon beside Dilan. Together, they pushed it toward the edge of the hill. Owen looked around the back of the wagon, down the hillock. The distance was too far. Their chances of actually hitting her were impossible. The wagon would hit a rock and veer off course. Dilan took a burning brand from the bonfire and set the canvas covering on fire. Then, he tossed the log into the bed of the wagon.

"Push," he yelled.

"This isn't going to—"

"Push now!"

Together, they shoved against the wagon. It tipped over the side of the hill, started rolling, and then picked up speed.

"Look out below!" Dilan yelled.

Men, looking back wide-eyed, leapt out of the way as the burning wagon swept past them. It bumped, rolled, and flew down the hillside. Once again, the female marsh tick tried to fly away but failed. Then, as Owen had feared, the wagon veered away from her. It was going to sweep right past her. His heart sank. They were all going to die in that swamp. However, the wagon must have hit another rock because it suddenly veered back again, and impossibly, it smashed right into her. A giant fireball lit up the night. Burning pieces of insect and wagon flew through the air, falling to sizzle into the waters of the swamp.

The insects finally went silent.

Men cheered and attacked the remaining ticks. The insects broke and ran, perhaps understanding they no longer needed to protect the female.

Dilan grinned at Owen like a kid who had just done something bad and gotten away with it.

Not able to help himself, he grabbed the other man and hugged him hard, tears of laughter running down his cheeks.

We might just live through this night after all.

Chapter 17

Modwyn

Dawn was still hours away when Modwyn and Idwal sneaked back down the hillock to the smoldering carcass of the female marsh tick. The fire had been intense, and even the waterlogged tree trunk was now cinders. The horrific stench of burned insect would likely fester in Modwyn's clothes for days. At least the damned mosquitoes were finally gone, driven away by the smoke.

He had done what he could for the wounded soldiers. Five had died in the battle, torn apart by the insects. Several more would die before sunrise. While he had been tending to the wounded—like a dutiful physician—Idwal had retrieved his bear trap, throwing it away into the muddy waters, but only Modwyn could retrieve what they needed from the female.

Idwal stopped in front of the carcass of the female tick, staring at her. He had tied a kerchief over his face, perhaps thinking that might help with the smell. Idwal, it seemed, was as simple as any other peasant was. "Look at her," Idwal said quietly, almost reverently.

"She's beautiful, isn't she?" answered Modwyn.

The fire had burned away half her body. The remainder had been crushed by the impact of the wagon. Her legs were gone, which was a pity—the pincers alone would have been priceless—but that didn't matter. They only had time to search for the venom sac near the end of her stinger. He cast a worried glance up the hillock, but the soldiers were all too busy in the aftermath of the battle.

Those who believed male marsh ticks to be dangerous truly had no idea. Unlike the males, the females had stingers in their tails with which they could stab, like a wasp, or spray from a distance. Modwyn quickly found the poison sac—the size of his hands—and cut it free before securing it in a waterproof container. The poison, he knew, would cause near immediate torpor in an animal the size of a horse.

What chance would a man have?

Chapter 18

Owen

Owen cinched Gale's saddle straps tight and glanced over at the other scouts—Fin, Dilan, and Hrawlgir—as they readied their own mounts. The sun had risen, and the marsh ticks had remained at a distance, allowing the Wolfrey soldiers to tend to their wounded and bury their dead. Owen paused, staring at his friends.

Dilan shook his head.

"I should say something," Owen said.

"We've been over this," said Dilan. "There's nothing there. No one will believe you."

"I'm sure I saw a chain on that tree," Owen said.

Fin walked his mount over. "There's no chain," the tall, thin man said. "He's the family physician, for Father's sake."

Hrawlgir's face registered his confusion. "What are you talking about?"

Dilan glanced at Hrawlgir. "Nothing. Let it go, Owen. You can't prove anything, and emotions are high enough as it is right now."

Owen ground his teeth. "I don't trust—"

"You men!" called out Keep-Captain Awde as he approached. "I want to talk to you before you go."

Sayer followed along behind him, hurrying to keep up.

The four scouts, holding their mounts' bridles, turned to face the keep-captain, who stopped before them, his thumbs resting behind his sword belt. Dried blood was still crusted next to Awde's ear. According to the other men, he had killed a score of the insects himself the night before.

The keep-captain's gaze drifted over each of them, resting on Dilan. "You two left your posts last night," he finally said.

Behind him, Sayer smiled, his eyes shining.

"We had no choice," said Dilan. "The line wasn't holding."

"Not your call," snapped Sayer.

Keep-Captain Awde raised his hand toward Sayer. "He's right. It wasn't your call. It was mine, and I should have made it."

"Captain—" said Owen.

"It's all right, Toscovar," said Awde. "I'm not angry. I'm grateful. You did the right thing."

Sayer looked as though he had just swallowed something sour. His gaze snapped to Awde's. "But, Captain—"

"I'm a big enough man to admit my mistakes. I should have seen the line wasn't holding. Well done, Reese. Well done, Toscovar. You saved all of our lives, I think. I've spoken to his lordship, and he agrees with me. When this is over and we're home again, I think he'll present the two of you with arm-rings—his first as Duke. Be proud of yourselves this day."

Dilan inclined his head. Fin and Hrawlgir patted both men on their backs. Sayer stared at the ground.

"Be careful out there," Keep-Captain Awde said. "We've still got a long way to go, but from everything the hunters say, the greatest danger has now passed. It should be an easy trek to the witch's fortress. Idwal says the Vale is grassy hill lands. Just remember, we're far from home and have no friends here."

All four men nodded, softly muttering assurances they would be careful.

As Keep-Captain Awde turned to leave, Owen spoke up. "Captain?"

The warrior paused and waited.

"In… in place of the arm-ring, do you think you could broach the subject of releasing me from my—"

Keep-Captain Awde put his hand on Owen's shoulder. "We won't insult his lordship by turning down his gift, but I'll try, lad. I'll try."

He turned and left them, and Sayer hurried to catch up, only pausing to scowl at Dilan. Their spirits high, the four men mounted their horses and led them down the hill. Father Craftsman willing, they were going to be free of that damned swamp soon.

#

Just past midday, Owen and the others rode free of the old forest and out onto the Haunted Vale's grassy, wind-swept hills. The wild had long before reclaimed the old road to the witch's fortress, leaving only small mounds of fallen stone, the final remains of where small walls had once stood. They followed the trail of the stones to a small river blocking further passage northeast. A wooden bridge had spanned the river, but it had collapsed long before, leaving only the supports on either bank. They split into two pairs, with Owen and Hrawlgir riding north, seeking a fording spot for the wagons, while Dilan and Fin rode to the south.

Owen halted Gale and stood in his stirrups to see farther. Before them rose leagues and leagues of grassy hills, like an ocean. Once, that must have been farmland, the ground tended by the servants of the Greywynne family. Now it was wild, overgrown, abandoned. That was a lot of good land to abandon.

Owen pointed at a large hilltop standing higher than the surrounding terrain. "That's the high ground," he told Hrawlgir. "We should be able to see for leagues from up there."

The other man nodded and steered his horse toward the hill. As they rode, the tall grass brushed beneath their mounts' bellies. They would need to check the horses for ticks later, Owen knew, otherwise the animals might become sick. In fact, they should check each other for ticks as well. He shuddered when he pictured the marsh ticks once again.

They rode up the hill, traversing it on an angle so it wasn't as steep. At the top, the grass was shorter and windswept. Shading his eyes from the sun, Owen gazed out over the Vale. The river twisted on their right, disappearing into the distance. It wasn't wide—barely a river at all—but with its soft, muddy banks, the wagons would become stuck.

"All this land," said Hrawlgir as he dismounted and walked about the hilltop, "all abandoned. What a waste."

Owen pulled a waterskin from his saddlebags and upended it, drinking deeply. He wiped his mouth with the back of his hand. "The islanders think this land is haunted by the ghost of Serina. It's taboo for them. They'll never work it again, nor will they let anyone else work it."

Few trees dotted the hill lands. What little vegetation was growing there were mostly stunted bushes. The river began at the tall ridgeline to their south and ran north to the coastline. They were too far away to see the Promiscuous Sea, but sometimes when the wind picked up, Owen could smell it.

"There's something here." Hrawlgir squatted in the grass, brushing the stalks aside.

Still atop Gale, Owen saw shards of rusted metal and rotted straps of leather. A prickling itched at the back of his neck. "What is it?"

Hrawlgir made a noncommittal grunt and pulled something free of the grasping weeds. It had been half-buried in dirt, and Hrawlgir shook it, revealing an old helmet, rotted and falling apart. A single chin flap remained, dangling from it.

Hrawlgir stared at Owen in confusion. "It looks like one of ours."

Owen stood up in his stirrups once more, examining the hilltop more closely. "There's more, about us."

Hrawlgir dropped the helmet and brushed his fingers against his pants. He stalked about. "Father bless me, there are bones on the ground."

Owen dismounted and moved about, spreading the stalks of grass aside with his hands. "Bones everywhere," he said softly.

All about them lay blackened bones and rusted metal, the remains of warriors and their weapons—here, an axe head, the wooden handle long gone; there, the rusted sleeve of a ring-mail coat.

"Stron's army, or at least a part of it, must have fought a battle here," Owen said.

"Owen"—Hrawlgir bent down on one knee to examine something—"here's something… different." The tremor of fear in Hrawlgir's voice was unmistakable.

Owen stared over the other man's shoulder at the half-buried remains Hrawlgir was examining. Some moments passed before he finally realized what he was looking at, covered by decades of dirt—a rusted suit of plate-mail armor. Unlike the rest of the hilltop, no grass or weeds grew there. The ground around the armor for at least a foot in every direction was bare, discolored—as if it had been salted. The plate mail was corroded and flaking but still showed the intricate designs that had once been etched into it. Such a suit of armor would have been worth a fortune—not the armor of a soldier but that of a knight or a prince. A great helm lay half-buried and still mostly intact at the top of the chest plate.

Hrawlgir let his fingers trail over the plate mail. "Who in Stron's army could have—"

"No one." A shiver ran down Owen's spine. *This armor hadn't belonged to a man at all.*

Owen bent down and yanked the great helm free of the dirt. Unlike their half-helms with leather chin flaps, that knight's helmet had completely covered his face and head, leaving only a slit for the eyes, reinforced by brass with intricate flanges. As Owen held it up, dust and dirt—and who knew what else—poured out. In revulsion, Owen dropped it and wiped his palms against his pants as he stepped back. "Blood fiend."

Hrawlgir swore. "The bones are all around it—here and here." He moved farther back, pointing. "Skulls… fragments of skulls."

"Must have been one of Serina's captains. They said she always chose the best warriors to serve her, turned them into monsters against their will. How many men did it kill before they brought it down, I wonder?"

"How did they bring it down at all?" Hrawlgir asked. "They didn't stake it. The armor's intact."

"Priests." Owen looked about himself at the bones of the dead. "Some of these men must have been priests."

"Or wizards. A wizard could have burned one of them with magical fire."

"Maybe, but I know of only one wizard who fought with Stron—Belion, the battle mage."

Hrawlgir moved back toward the horses, which stamped nervously, perhaps sensing the foulness around them. "We need to go."

Owen nodded, putting his back to the remains of the demon. "Let's leave the dead be."

Both men mounted their horses and rode back down the hill.

A blood fiend? And I touched it.

#

Later, Owen and Hrawlgir met up with Dilan and Fin again. While Owen and Hrawlgir had been unsuccessful in their search, the other two had found a suitable fording spot. They all rode back to the main party and led them to the narrow, gently sloping bank. While several of the wagons still became stuck in the mud on the far bank, they managed to push and pull them all across before the afternoon grew too late.

Owen and Hrawlgir had reported the remains of the Wolfrey soldiers—and the blood fiend—to Keep-Captain Awde and the others, and Father Bowen promised to return to bury the remains and say a prayer, but that would have to wait until after they had found Sight-Bringer. The northern dead had lain on that hilltop for forty-eight years, so a week or two more would make no difference.

Once again, they found the remains of the old road, and Owen, riding Gale ahead of the others, led them northeast across the hills of the Haunted Vale toward the high cliffs along the northern coast, where they would find Serina's ancient fortress. When they reached the base of the cliffs, Owen heard the crashing of waves on the other side. They had forced their way completely across the island.

The dirt path led up the cliffs, twisting back and forth in a series of switchbacks. Seagulls circled above them, crying out. As the sun dropped below the horizon, they saw high, dark walls rising above them—Greywynne Fortress, Serina's ancestral home. Half a century before, Stron and his northern army had breached those walls and sacked the fortress. Owen had assumed they would find nothing more than ruins, but the fortress remained mostly intact despite the decades, merely abandoned, not destroyed. As they approached, the walls seemed to grow, looming over them.

The Greywynnes had been an ancient noble family, with vast holdings and once-great wealth. That fortress—far larger than Castle Dain—was proof of that. Its long curtain wall was three times the height of a man, with round stone towers spaced regularly along its length. A large gap ten paces across remained in one portion of the wall, where the stones had collapsed inward. Owen figured that must have been where Stron and his army had forced their way in. Somehow, they had brought siege equipment up there in what must have been a massive undertaking.

Keep-Captain Awde and Lord Palin rode past Owen, taking the lead through the dark, silent towers of the gatehouse. The walls, cracked and crumbling with age, were overgrown with weeds. The gatehouse was designed in such a way as to funnel visitors between the outer and inner gatehouse. Arrow slits built into the walls on either side created a killing ground. Owen warily watched those slits as they rode past, imagining enemies watching them.

No one spoke as the expedition rode into the fortress. The only sounds were the crashing of the waves on the far side, the creaking of harnesses, and the clomping of the horses' hooves. Past the gatehouse, the inner wall rose before them, higher even than the outer curtain wall. Owen stared up at it, amazed that Stron and his forces had somehow taken that monstrous fortress.

They rode into the fortress's ward, its courtyard, a vast open space. Once, it must have been filled with structures, stables, and warehouses, but it sat nearly empty. Judging by the charred, weed-covered skeletal remains everywhere, Stron's army must have put the wooden buildings to the torch. Only one wood-and-stone structure remained, against one of the far walls, a large stable with dozens of stalls. The main keep, built entirely from stone, awaited them, a single round tower jutting from its summit.

Keep-Captain Awde turned in his saddle to face the column of men, horses, and wagons. "We set up camp here in the courtyard," he called out loudly enough for all to hear. "Tomorrow, we'll explore the keep, see if it's safe to move inside."

The men set about, preparing camp. Owen secured Gale with the other horses in the stable near the inner gatehouse. The animals were skittish, clearly uncomfortable with the place—as were the men. Just for a moment, Owen felt a prickling in the back of his neck, as if he were being watched. He stared up at the keep, scrutinizing the dark windows, but saw nothing.

"Help me with the tents?" Dilan asked, startling him.

Owen nodded and moved to help him.

Chapter 19

Owen

Hours later—with the camp established in the courtyard, sentries in place, and everyone fed—Owen, Dilan, Fin, and Hrawlgir sat by one of the many small campfires. Many of the Wolfrey soldiers were already asleep, exhausted after their ordeal in the Feldwyn Swamp, but Owen and the others were still too wound up.

"Do you think," asked Fin, his eyes darting to the walls of the keep, "that if we were to climb to the top of that tower, we'd be able to see Echo Isle and the ruins of the monastery?"

Owen shuddered. "Why would you want to?"

"You know," said Fin, "just for the history. That's where her rebellion started. That's where she became a… well, you know."

Dilan, running a sharpening stone over the blade of his sword, snorted and shook his head.

Fin frowned at him. "You're not from Wolfrey. You wouldn't understand. My grandfather fought and died with Stron. Those might have been his bones Owen and Hrawlgir found."

Dilan paused halfway through a stroke with his stone and met

Fin's gaze. "You're wrong about that. Even in Shellat's Fief, we grew up with the tales of Serina and her undead army. I just don't know what good it would do to see the ruins of that monastery now, after all these years. Leave the dead be."

"I don't want to see that monastery," said Hrawlgir with a shudder. "The stories about what the witch did to those men…"

"That's why Father Craftsman cursed her," said Owen, "why he made her a blood fiend."

Dilan ran his stone along the length of his blade again. Sparks flew off, burning brightly for an instant before fading away. "Think so, do you?"

"You find this amusing?" Owen asked. "Torturing and sacrificing an entire monastery of holy men—and all because Serina was angry at the king?"

"Angry at the king?" Dilan shook his head. "The king murdered her father, her brothers, almost destroyed the Greywynne family."

"They were traitors," said Hrawlgir.

"Oh, aye, I have no doubt," said Dilan. "Especially *after* the king arrested them and seized all their holdings on the mainland." He pointed at them with his sharpening stone. "Every single king that's ever moved against a political opponent has claimed that they were traitors. History favors the winners. The losers all become villains."

"You're saying that Serina Greywynne wasn't a monster?" Owen asked. "All those villages she destroyed, all those people she killed? What crime did they commit?"

"I'm saying Serina was many things at many times—a master sorceress, the last of her line, a proud woman. Look about yourself. Look at this place! She was like a queen here. If her rebellion had been successful, there'd be different tales told now about who was and wasn't a traitor."

"More likely, she'd have drained the kingdom of every last drop of blood. She was a soulless monster."

"Aye." Dilan stared at his blade. "She was at that, and maybe much worse."

"So why defend her?" asked Hrawlgir.

Dilan sighed, his face red in the glow of the crackling fire between them, his eyes sad. "I'm not defending her. I'm just trying to show that not everyone felt—or feels—the same way. Nothing is ever as simple as you might think."

"Why?" asked Owen.

"I knew a man in the Rams," Dilan said, "a Greywynne Islander named Shabsil." His teeth flashed as he smiled at the memory. "Huge, ugly—smelly—man, with the same bright-red hair as the rest of them and a long, shaggy beard, but he was also a good man and a good friend… once you got to know him. Mind you, it took a long time to earn his trust. He knew Shellat's Fief was in the north, so he had lumped me in with you lot, considered me little more than just another Wolfrey man."

"They all hate us?" Fin asked. "Still? After so many years?"

"They still hate you," said Dilan. "And likely will for another fifty years. You committed the greatest of all sins: you killed their dreams."

"Dreams of conquest," said Fin.

"Because of Serina?" Owen asked.

"Aye," said Dilan, "because of Serina. These people, they've never accepted us. Shabsil once told me that the Fenyir word for *mainlander* is the same word for *stranger*… or *enemy*. These people have always lived separately… differently than we have in the kingdom."

"They're still *part* of the kingdom," snapped Owen.

"Tell them that," said Dilan. "Not only do they not care for us, they don't much hold with our beliefs—our Father Craftsman. They still worship the old gods, their ancient gods."

"Heathens," said Hrawlgir.

"I wouldn't say that too loudly in these islands," said Dilan. "Axe and sword, sea and storm, the old gods—Wodor, Hrum, Orkinus—that's who these people worship. A hundred years from now, they'll still worship them. The Greywynnes were about as… progressive a family as you'll ever find among the Fenyir Islands. When Serina's father, Tarlock Greywynne, gave his blessing for the church to build a monastery on Echo Island and begin to preach the ways of Father Craftsman, it was a huge deal for these people—world shaking—but it never took, especially after Serina… did what she did to those priests."

Owen shivered, once again feeling ghostly eyes upon him. Echo Island wasn't that far off the northern coast of Greywynne Island.

"These people—all the Fenyir clansmen, not just the Greywynne islanders—live separate from us, existing from the sea, fishing, sailing… raiding. Don't kid yourselves—they don't give a red rat's ring for the Kingdom of Conarck—or any of us. But to them, the Greywynnes *were* kings, their own royal family."

"The Fenyir Islands were never more than just another duchy," said Owen. "Not a kingdom. The Greywynnes were just another royal family. Thinking they were more, that's how their treason started."

"As far as these people were concerned," said Dilan, "Serina was a queen."

"She was no queen," Owen said. "Tarlock Greywynne was a duke. That made Serina, at best, a lady."

"Shabsil never spoke of Serina," said Dilan. "And understand this—every man in the Rams was my brother, including Shabsil. There was nothing we wouldn't do for one another, but he wouldn't discuss *her*. When some of the others tried to get him to talk of her, he'd become angry, violent—and this was not a man you wanted violent. But one night, when Shabsil was very, very drunk, he spoke of her, spoke of the shame he and his people endured at our hands. In the kingdom, they say that Tarlock Greywynne, the last duke of the Fenyir Islands, plotted against the king. The king, suspecting his treason, summoned the duke and all three of his sons to the capital. There, they were arrested, imprisoned, and executed."

"They admitted to their crimes first," said Hrawlgir. "Everyone knows that."

Dilan frowned at Hrawlgir, raising his thick eyebrows. "And so would you if you were tortured, but you're wrong—they didn't *all* confess. Shabsil said the old duke never confessed. They say everyone breaks under torture… eventually, but Serina's father, Tarlock, didn't. In the end, he was simply executed along with his sons, and the Greywynne estates and ships seized—all except this island, this fortress, where Serina's rebellion started. Because she was a woman, the king never considered her a threat." Dilan shook his head and snorted.

"Serina was always more than just a lady, Owen," Dilan continued. "They say magic ran deeply within the Greywynne bloodline, particularly in the women, and Serina more so than others. Long before she became a monster, Serina Greywynne was already a powerful sorcerer, a necromancer. Some—including Shabsil—believed that she was even more powerful than Stron's famous battle mage, Belion."

Fin leaned forward and met their eyes. "Do you think… Is it possible… I mean if Sight-Bringer has survived… what of Serina?"

Owen shivered. "Not according to Lord Palin. His father confirmed she was dead."

"But still," insisted Fin.

"She must be dead," said Dilan. "After all these decades, only her ghost could haunt this place, and that I don't doubt. Even if she were a wizard, she couldn't cheat death."

Owen shook his head. "She was a witch, not a wizard. Any powers she had were dark. No, Dilan. You're wrong. Serina Greywynne was a petty little island witch, a heathen, who sold her soul to Old Grim and murdered the monks on Echo Island—priests who were under her family's protection. And for this, Father Craftsman cursed her and turned her into a blood fiend."

"Aye, that's the story, isn't it?" said Dilan.

"You don't believe that?" asked Owen.

Dilan shrugged. "I have no idea, Owen. This all happened long before I was even born. But I know Shabsil didn't believe the Greywynnes were traitors." Dilan began sharpening his sword again. "Shabsil would tell you that our king falsely accused the Greywynnes just to seize their wealth. If you were to bring up Father Craftsman's blood-fiend curse, he'd laugh in your face—before punching it. These people don't believe in our Father Craftsman or Old Grim. He'd tell you that Serina wasn't cursed for killing the monks but *rewarded* for embracing the old, true gods."

Once again, the wind picked up, howling through the walls of the fortress.

Chapter 20

Owen

Owen dreams.

And in his dream, he walks through the low, curved tunnels of the Greywynne family catacombs. He doesn't know how he got here, doesn't know where he's going, but knows that he must keep going, that to stop now is to die. Holding his burning torch before him, he moves forward into the darkness. Desiccated corpses—dried-out husks of former Greywynne family servants, now honored in death—lie in recesses along the walls. Over the years, some of the bones have fallen and now lie scattered across the surface of the passage. When he accidentally steps on one, the cracking noise reverberates down the dark passageway, causing him to wince. He shouldn't be here, he knows. No one should be here, but he needs to find something, something important, something he needs in order to leave—

Another crack echoes down the tunnel, this time from behind him. Someone else is with him in the catacombs. He holds out his torch behind him, stares into the darkness, but sees nothing.

"Who's there?" he calls out.

The darkness giggles, an evil mocking laugh.

His hand goes for the hilt of his sword—but he isn't wearing one! He's unarmed. That isn't right. He's a man-at-arms—where are his weapons? His skin turns clammy, and his pulse races.

"I'm not afraid of you," he yells, hearing the lie in his voice.

More giggles, now followed by whispers, indistinct, too soft to make out, except for one word—his name.

Turning, he bolts. When he comes to an intersection, he chooses a direction at random. Boot steps now pound behind him, getting closer. Wild-eyed, he pauses long enough to throw a quick glance over his shoulder, seeing nothing but darkness. He runs on, breathless and terrified, for what seems an eternity. He stops again, now gasping for air, unable to go any farther. He glares behind him.

"Not afraid of you," he pants, wheezing, barely coherent.

More whispers, more laughter. Emrys Ballard? Is that Emrys Ballard? That isn't possible. Something has happened to Emrys, something that…

He remembers a rope squeaking, a body twisting. Crows.

With new fear driving him on, he turns and staggers away, taking turns at random, probably running in circles. Have these tunnels no end?

And then, he finds himself at the top of a flight of stairs, red stone stairs leading down. Each step is intricately carved with markings that seem to flow and alter as Owen looks at them, as if they were somehow alive. Carved into the wall over the stairs is the motif of a winged griffin, the once-proud Greywynne family insignia, now reviled throughout the kingdom. An unnatural coldness rises from the depths of the stairwell.

"No," he whispers. "I can't go down there."

Something *is down there, something that hates the living.*

More laughter from behind.

He spins about and, for the first time, sees his pursuers, three shadows, three men, standing just beyond the light of his torch, but he knows who they are, just the same—the Ballard brothers.

"Go on, Owen. Go down," Emrys whispers. "She's waiting for you."

Owen shook his head. "No. Can't."

"Can't go back," mocks another of the Ballard brothers, Trystan perhaps. "Go down."

His torch flutters weakly and grows dim.

"Go down," the Ballards whisper together, now almost chanting.

Just as his torch dies out, they rush him. He stumbles backward, his arms flailing at empty air. He's falling, falling down the red stairs. He screams—

Owen bolted upright, his blanket falling from him. His hair, wet with sweat, was stuck to his forehead. Running his hands over his face, he groaned. The air was cool, with the salty tang of the sea. He was still outside, still in the courtyard of Greywynne fortress, near the embers of a campfire. His friends were sleeping nearby. For long moments, he sat there, breathing deeply. Although still dark, the sky was just turning red in the east. The others snored, farted, and shifted about in their sleep.

A nightmare. It had been only a nightmare. Was it any wonder?

Nearby, one of the men, Fin perhaps, mumbled in his sleep, thrashing about. Owen wasn't the only one having nightmares that night, it seemed. The islanders were right—that place had to be haunted.

Then, Fin jerked in his sleep. "Can't go down the red stairs," he mumbled before twisting away.

Owen felt a wave of cold nausea sweep through him as he stared at his friend.

#

As the sun rose over the walls of the fortress, the camp stirred, and the men awoke, bleary eyed and lost in their own thoughts. Owen watched them, wondering how many others had dreamed of the red stairs.

They broke their fast, and led by the sergeants, they set about exploring the keep. In large groups, they combed through its passageways, searching each level, each chamber. Nothing of any value remained. Stron's army had ransacked it, taking everything, including the furniture. Its walls, though, stood firm and strong and would protect them from the elements. Under Keep-Captain Awde's orders, they moved their camp inside, taking over the upper levels, where the Greywynne servants had once lived.

When they were alone, Owen pulled Fin aside and asked him about his dream, but Fin said he couldn't remember any dream, just a feeling of unease and a bad night's sleep. Most of the men were in a foul mood as well, as if none of them had slept well. When he closed his eyes, Owen could still see the red stone stairs leading down to the Great Crypt, where generations of Greywynne family members had buried their dead. The old stories said that Serina had lived down there, that she had held court in the Great Crypt, surrounded by the vaults of the dead. It was there that Duke Stron had confronted her, striking her down with Sight-Bringer.

They found the sealed-up entrance to the catacombs almost immediately. It was hard to miss, a walled-up stone archway bearing the Greywynne family griffin at the end of a long passageway in the cellars of the keep. The stones blocking the archway had been hastily placed—with too much mortar, the stones inexpertly and too quickly set—the excess mortar having run and dried in long rivers, like candle wax. Priests had painted religious wards over the stones, seals against evil. The men who had walled up the underground catacombs had clearly been frightened. Even a half-century later, Owen felt a sense of foreboding when he stared at the entrance.

Young Lord Palin stood before the wall for several long moments before he turned to Keep-Captain Awde. "Tear it down."

#

The tight corridor had only enough room for two men at a time to work with hammers—Hrawlgir and a guardsman named Jon. Most of the other soldiers stood back, watching. Both men were stripped to the waist, taking turns striking the stones with large rock hammers. Sweat glistened on their skin as they tore down the barricade. Just behind them stood Lord Palin, Keep-Captain Awde, Modwyn Du'Aig, and Father Bowen. Owen jostled forward to see better, past Fin, just as Hrawlgir's hammer smashed a fist-sized hole in the wall. Instantly, a cloud of dust whistled out from the opening, coating Hrawlgir and giving him the appearance of a statue.

Silence settled with the dust.

Keep-Captain Awde was the first man to move, stepping up to examine the opening Hrawlgir had made. He looked over his shoulder at the crowd of men behind him. "Bring me a torch."

Father Bowen moved closer. "Captain, please… a prayer first."

Keep-Captain Awde paused and then nodded. The young priest, holding his Craftsman's hammer before him, recited his holy verses, beseeching the Father's protection. The air continued to whistle through the opening for a while longer before abruptly stopping. Father Bowen, his prayer complete, nodded to Keep-Captain Awde, who held the torch to the hole, trying to see through.

Although it was cool down there, the keep-captain's face glistened with sweat. "There's open space on the other side," he said. "Looks like stairs."

Every man in the north had grown up hearing the legends of the

Greywynne family catacombs, which were said to be older than the fortress itself. Owen remembered the old graybeards who had accompanied Stron, saying that the Greywynne family had built their fortress there on those cliffs *because* of the ancient mazelike catacombs beneath the ground.

Nonsense, Owen told himself. *If the Greywynnes didn't build the catacombs, then who did?*

"Captain," Lord Palin said, concern in his voice, "what's wrong with that man?"

Owen followed his gaze to where Hrawlgir still stood, transfixed, drool running down his chin, his eyes vacant. His lips softly opened and closed, as if he were whispering.

Keep-Captain Awde shook Hrawlgir's shoulder. "Hrawlgir, what's wrong? Speak up, man!"

Hrawlgir stared past him at nothing.

Keep-Captain Awde snapped his fingers, but the young man didn't react at all.

Modwyn hurried forward. "Captain, if you please."

The keep-captain stepped out of the way while the doctor peered into Hrawlgir's face and then placed his ear against his sweaty, dirt-covered chest. The others pushed in closer, straining to see what was going on, but Awde ordered them all back.

"What is it, Doctor?" asked Lord Palin.

Modwyn shook his head. "I don't know yet, my lord. He's… clearly confused about something but unhurt." The doctor took a step back, looked from Hrawlgir to Jon to the hole in the wall. "How are you feeling?" he asked Jon.

"I'm… I'm fine, Doctor. Will he be okay? Will *I* be okay?"

"Almost certainly," said Modwyn. He turned to Keep-Captain Awde. "This man needs rest and sleep. I think there must be deep vapors down here, freed when the wall was broken."

"Deep vapors?" repeated Lord Palin, moving back a pace. "Are we…?"

"We should be fine," Modwyn said, "but the men working on the opening should wear masks over their faces. That would help, I think."

"I've never heard of deep vapors before," said Keep-Captain Awde.

Modwyn raised a thin eyebrow. "I suspect not. We studied them in the Physician's University. The air belowground—once sealed up—becomes stagnant, dangerous."

Keep-Captain Awde nodded and turned to Sayer. "Have someone bring Hrawlgir upstairs and stay with him. The rest of you, if you're going to stay and watch, find cloth to cover your faces." Then, he used his dagger to cut away a strip from the bottom of his shirt and tied it to his face. He reached out and pried the hammer from Hrawlgir's grip before facing the fist-sized opening. Hefting the hammer in two hands, he glanced at Jon. "Together, then?"

Jon's face went slack, his eyes widening. "I… Captain—"

"I'll take a turn," said Dilan, moving forward and covering his own face with a cloth as he took the hammer from Jon.

Keep-Captain Awde and Dilan nodded at one another and beat upon the opening. Rocks fell and dust rose to the rhythmic pounding of the hammers.

Soon, the catacombs lay open before them.

Chapter 21

Modwyn

Some hours later, Modwyn stood back while Keep-Captain Awde spoke with Lord Palin near the opening to the catacombs. Modwyn needed to be with them when they entered the catacombs—*had* to be with them when they entered the Great Crypt—but that wasn't going to be easy. He knew there existed no practical reason to bring him along. While no one had come out and openly blamed him for the marsh-tick attack, Modwyn suspected that large blond cretin the others called "Horse-boy" must have said something about him and Idwal even though they had covered their tracks, for Modwyn was certain Awde was suspicious of him. No doubt, that fool would pass that suspicion along to the boy. Fortunately, the odd affliction that had overcome Hrawlgir had given Modwyn an idea, and they all seemed to have bought that nonsense about "deep vapors," but he needed to act quickly. Inhaling deeply, he approached the two men.

Lord Palin and Awde ceased their conversation at his approach. Once again, Modwyn was certain he saw suspicion in Awde's eyes. He ignored the soldier as the boy was the real power there.

"My lord," said Modwyn, bowing.

"Doctor," said the young man, his freckled face reflecting his uncertainty. "How is…?" He paused as his eyes flashed to Awde.

"Hrawlgir, my lord," said the keep-captain.

"How is Hrawlgir?" asked Lord Palin.

"He rests comfortably," Modwyn said. "Father Bowen is watching him."

"Why aren't *you* watching him?" asked Awde. "That's why you're here, isn't it?"

Modwyn paused, his back stiffening, but he ignored the challenge. "Hrawlgir will recover nicely. He only needs rest. But I am more concerned about those of us who will go deeper into the catacombs."

"Why?" asked Awde.

"My lord, the deep vapors will likely be worse once we're underground. You'll need me nearby."

The young man's face reflected his confusion as he looked from Modwyn to Awde.

Modwyn softened his voice. "My lord, it will be very, very dangerous down there. Without me, I don't think you'd be able to recognize the signs of vapors, act in time."

"Tell us the signs," said Awde. "We'll manage."

"Doctor," said Lord Palin. "We do need to go into those catacombs. That's the entire point of coming all this way. Now that the catacombs have been opened, how long before these… vapors go away on their own?"

"My lord, they could remain a threat for years, dozens of years."

"Dozens of years?" asked Awde, the scorn clear in his tone.

"These catacombs have been sealed for decades, filled with Serina's foul taint. Believe me when I tell you they will be dangerous for men for at least another lifetime. You could easily be leading your troops to their deaths—or, Father help us, *your* death. I can prevent that."

Lord Palin's hands pulled at the fabric of his pants, his gaze drifting from Modwyn to Awde, and he bit his lower lip. "What... what can you do, Doctor?"

I have him. Modwyn stepped closer, hefting his physician's bag before him, letting the small glass vials inside clink. "My lord, I suspected the deep vapors could be a concern before we sailed from the mainland. When we arrived in Port Ollechta, I visited an alchemist and purchased a medicine, a counter to the deep vapors."

Awde snorted. "Why wait until now to mention this?"

Modwyn lowered his gaze, trying to look contrite. "Because I couldn't be sure it would be a problem, not until I knew for certain. Besides, the cure itself is dangerous."

"I find that questionable," said Awde.

"Enough," said Lord Palin as he stepped between them, holding his hand up. "We can't blame the good doctor for Serina's evil." He inclined his head to Modwyn. "What do you need?"

"I need to go with you when you enter the catacombs. And we should bring along one or two of the hunters."

"What?" asked Awde. "Why would we want to go into a dangerous situation with people that are only a generation removed from open rebellion?"

"Because they *are* removed from rebellion. You can't blame them for the actions of their grandparents forty-eight years ago." His eyes snapped to Lord Palin. "That wouldn't be very lordly."

"I think I can blame them, Doctor," said Awde. "I don't think they're all that far removed from those men Stron fought."

"You're wrong, Captain," snapped Modwyn. "Besides, Master Idwal and his family, like all Greywynne islanders, have a long history of working the island's silver mine. They've built up a natural resistance to deep vapors."

"Those mines have been dry for decades, how is that poss—"

"Because, Captain, the resistance is hereditary! They have it, and we don't. It's really that simple."

"Gentlemen, please," said Lord Palin, his voice cracking. "Doctor, yes, you and one or two of the hunters may come. After all, Captain, they are *my* subjects now. If I expect loyalty, I need to show it to them."

Awde glared at Modwyn but nodded. "Yes, my lord."

Pleasure rushed through Modwyn. *Yes! All is now possible.* He tried not to grin as he thanked the young lord and moved away. Moments later, he found Idwal lurking in the shadows farther back, waiting for Modwyn.

"It's all arranged," said Modwyn. "You and I for now. We'll bring in your brothers as necessary."

Idwal nodded, squinting down the tunnel to where the opening remained. "I dreamed of her last night," he said softly, almost too softly to hear. "She called for me."

Modwyn nodded, feeling for the first time in his life that he belonged somewhere. "She called to me as well. She speaks to us through our dreams."

Idwal shivered, rubbing his palms against his upper arms. "How do you know all this, then? Who knows such things?"

"Ever since I was a boy, I have studied everything I could find about blood fiends, or vampires as some call them in the far east. Most of it was rubbish, superstitions, but some of it… I'm sure was true."

"Why?" asked Idwal, staring wide-eyed at Modwyn.

They stood there in silence for some time before Modwyn finally answered. "Because, like you, she's all I've ever had."

Chapter 22

Owen

Owen led the way through the catacombs. Accompanying him were several other men-at-arms, including Dilan, as well as Lord Palin, Keep-Captain Awde, Father Bowen, and Modwyn—ten men in total, a party small enough to move quickly through the low, curving stone corridors, but still large enough to fight if they had to.

Fifty years before, Stron and his army had fought ghouls—living corpses of men, reanimated by Serina—through every step of the catacombs. No one knew how long such abominations could survive, but Owen was happy Father Bowen was with them. The old stories said that priests could force their will on ghouls—some particularly pious men could even face down blood fiends. Like the other men-at-arms, Owen wore his ring-mail coat but carried no shield. Instead, he held aloft a lit torch in one hand and a fighting axe in the other. Nothing killed ghouls like an axe—at least, that's what the old greybeards back home had claimed. However, no one had seen a ghoul since Serina's rebellion.

The chilled air stank of mildew and rot. Along the passageway, at regular intervals, brass braziers still hung from the walls, still waiting for servants to fill them with oil and relight them. Giant cobwebs covered the curved low ceiling, hanging from the corners, often obscuring their way. As Owen forced his way through them, he shuddered, imaging large hairy spiders running down the collar of his mail coat. *Are the spiders poisonous on this damned island? They can't be worse than the marsh ticks.* Ahead, the tunnel intersected another at a right angle, offering three different paths from which to choose. Owen waited, with Dilan beside him. Each man held his torch high, but Owen saw only darkness in every direction.

"I don't know which way," Lord Palin said.

Keep-Captain Awde moved past Owen, looking down the left-side corridor. "The veterans of Stron's army did say the catacombs were mazelike."

"Those were simple men," said Modwyn. "Any catacomb would seem a maze to men like that. This isn't the capital. These tunnels can't be *that* extensive."

Lord Palin glanced at the doctor. "I thought these catacombs predated the Greywynnes?"

Modwyn shrugged. "Who truly knows such things, my lord? More likely, people invented those stories to make the Greywynnes seem more ominous."

Owen stared at the ancient crumbling stones along the wall and low, curved ceiling. *How old are these supports?*

"We should mark the floor at the intersections," said Keep-Captain Awde. "So we don't end up going in circles."

"Indeed," said Modwyn.

"Which way, then?" asked Keep-Captain Awde, turning to Lord Palin.

The young man hesitated only a moment. "Left."

"Left it is, my lord," said Keep-Captain Awde as he squeezed the young man's shoulder and walked past him, moving beside Owen. "Let's go, Toscovar. We have a Great Crypt to find."

#

Despite Modwyn's skepticism, the catacombs were indeed large and mazelike. They walked for what seemed hours but couldn't possibly have been that long. Occasionally, they passed chambers, old storerooms filled with rotting boxes and barrels, all blanketed by a thick layer of spiderwebs and glistening dust. As they walked, Modwyn sketched a map on a large piece of parchment. After the swamp, Owen no longer trusted the doctor, but he had to admit the man was clever. Then, he realized he smelled something strange and paused, sniffing the air. Keep-Captain Awde stared at him.

"You smell that?" Owen asked.

"Smell what?" Awde asked.

"Salt," said Owen. "The sea, I think."

Having gone his entire life without ever having smelled the sea air, Owen would never mistake that heady scent again. He was sure he could smell the ocean air. He closed his eyes and concentrated and then nodded with certainty. "I can hear the waves, too. There must be an opening somewhere."

"How is that possible?" Lord Palin asked from behind them.

"I smell it, too," said Dilan. "He's right."

"The fortress was built upon the cliffs," said Modwyn. "The roots of the catacombs dig into those cliffs. We may not be as deep underground as we thought."

"There's another chamber up ahead," Owen said. "I think that's the source."

They moved farther down the tunnel. Soon, all of them smelled the sea air and heard the crashing of waves. A large chamber opened on their left with two wooden doors, long since fallen down, rotting on the floor. Moisture hung in the air.

Owen extended his torch into the chamber. The others crowded around behind him. It wasn't a chamber, after all, but a natural cavern, its ceiling high above them. Daylight poured through a large opening on the opposite side of the cavern—it was the cliff face, after all. They could hear the echo of seagull cries. The center of the cavern was sunken and filled with seawater, like a pool. A stone landing rose up on the other side of the pool, with an ancient wooden walkway leading to it across the water. Atop the stone landing was a large wooden crane, the kind used to load ships. Wooden boxes and barrels were stacked everywhere—most falling apart. The air was rich with the sea, salt, and stench of centuries of bird shit.

"I'll be damned," whispered Keep-Captain Awde. "It's a pier, a secret dock."

"How's that possible?" asked Lord Palin.

The keep-captain stood silent for several moments then reached out and gripped Owen's forearm. "Just you and I, Toscovar." He turned and addressed the others. "My lord, this place is falling apart. Best if you wait here."

The young man bit his lower lip but nodded.

Keep-Captain Awde faced Owen. "Hold the torch as high as you can, but don't get too close behind me. Stay back until I'm all the way across. I don't know if it'll hold both of our weight."

Owen stared at the rotting wooden walkway and at the water around it. *How deep is that pool?*

"Take your armor off," Keep-Captain Awde said as he removed his own.

Dilan took his torch and axe and helped him undo the straps at the back of his ring-mail coat and pull it over his shoulders. Once free of the armor, Owen flexed his arms, feeling nimble and light.

"Ready, Toscovar?" Keep-Captain Awde asked, standing in his

padded undershirt and reattaching his sword belt around his waist.

"Almost, Captain," Owen said as he did the same.

Dilan handed him back his torch. "I'll hang onto the axe for you," he said. "Every little bit less should help, right?"

Keep-Captain Awde looked from Owen to Dilan, and then at the rickety walkway.

"I'm not *that* big," Owen said.

Keep-Captain Awde snorted. "Wait until I'm across, then come over—quickly." He turned and stepped onto the walkway, which creaked under his weight but held. He took another step and then another. "It's still sturdy," he said, looking over his shoulder. "Well built."

Moments later, the keep-captain was all the way across and onto the stone platform. A set of stairs led up along its side to the top, where the crane sat. The keep-captain waited at the stairs for Owen. "Let's go, Toscovar."

Owen gingerly stepped out onto the wooden walkway. It groaned and creaked but held. Halfway across, though, he heard a board crack, and he froze, his heart skipping a beat. When nothing further happened, he kept going. Moments later, he was safely across and following the captain up the stairs. At the top of the platform, he paused and examined the dock opening. Bright sunlight poured in, exposing the stunted bushes growing out of the cliff walls. The remains of an old wooden pier still hung from the opening. The keep-captain had been right—it was a dock, a secret dock built right into the side of the cliffs. They moved to the edge of the opening and peered out over the side. Five feet or so below, waves crashed against the cliff face.

Owen leaned carefully over the edge of the cliff and stared into the water below. "How did they…?"

"It's high tide right now," Keep-Captain Awde said. "They must have used the crane to lower people and supplies to ships during low tide." Turning, he leaned back, peering up the cliff face. "I can just see the fortress walls above us. Modwyn was right. We're not that far belowground."

"You can see Echo Island from here," Owen said, pointing.

Just across the water, a small isle rose out of the sea. The white stone ruins of the monastery gleamed in the sunlight.

"Never thought I'd be this close to such a place," whispered Keep-Captain Awde.

"Nor I," answered Owen. "Father Craftsman, bless us."

Keep-Captain nodded and gripped Owen's shoulder. "Let's get back to the others."

Owen paused. "Sir, if… if she had her own secret dock… then why…?"

The waves struck against the rocks below, throwing cool mist into the air.

"Why did she let herself get cornered by Stron?" Keep-Captain Awde sighed and shook his head. "I don't know. Maybe there were no ships in which to escape, or… maybe she just wasn't afraid of Stron."

A chill ran down Owen's spine.

"Do you know what I wonder about, lad?"

"No, sir."

"I wonder what our physician would say about the presence of… foul vapors when there's an opening like this bringing in fresh air?"

"I… I don't know, sir, but I don't trust him."

"Neither do I. Let's keep an eye on Modwyn. What do you think?"

"Yes, sir. I think that's a very good idea, sir."

They made their way back across the walkway, to where the others were waiting for them. After explaining what they had seen and putting their armor back on, they moved farther down the corridors, continuing their search of the catacombs. Not long afterward, they found the entrance to the Great Crypt of the Greywynne family, bloodred stone stairs leading down, a winged stone griffin watching over the entrance. A cold wave swept through Owen's core.

The stairs looked exactly the same as in his dream.

Chapter 23

Owen

The red stairs disappeared into darkness, a straight path down to the bowels of the earth. Staring at them in bewilderment, Owen felt himself sway.

"Owen," whispered Dilan, gripping his forearm. "You all right?"

The others clustered behind him. He felt himself become the center of attention.

"What is it, Toscovar?" asked Keep-Captain Awde.

Someone else whispered something about deep vapors.

Owen shook his head. "Nothing. It's nothing."

Keep-Captain Awde watched his face carefully. "All right, then. Maybe one of the others should go first. You've done enough for one day."

"I'm fine, Captain."

The keep-captain shook his head and turned to Dilan. "Reese, you go first. Watch your step."

Hefting his fighting axe in one hand and his torch in the other, Dilan slowly went down the steps. Keep-Captain Awde followed and then Lord Palin, Father Bowen, and Modwyn. Owen went last, with the last four other guardsmen. He counted the steps as they descended—anything to take his mind off the impossibility of having pictured the stairs perfectly in his nightmare. After thirty steps, they came to a landing, and then the stairwell turned, descending even farther into darkness. However, after another twenty-two steps, a cave-in blocked the rest of the way. The others clustered in front, examining the rubble. Owen glanced at the ceiling above them. *What would it take to start another cave-in?*

"Can we clear it?" asked Lord Palin, his voice reflecting his uncertainty.

"I don't know, my lord," said Keep-Captain Awde. "I have no experience with mining."

"We can clear it," said Modwyn. "I'm certain of it."

Awde snorted.

"It's true," said Modwyn, turning to face Lord Palin. "This is just as your father described it. We must almost be at the bottom, the Great Crypt of the Greywynne family."

"All this was the work of Belion the battle mage?" asked Lord Palin, staring at the collapsed ceiling.

"When Belion broke his own staff," said Modwyn, "the magical eruption brought down the ceiling."

"I don't understand this. If Serina was already dead, why did Belion break his staff?" asked Keep-Captain Awde.

Modwyn shook his head. "You've been in more battles than I, Captain—the confusion of war? Who knows?"

"Who, indeed," said Keep-Captain Awde. "Tell us again what Duke Oskaley told you, in detail this time. I'd hear—"

"The details are unimportant," said Lord Palin sharply, his tone clear that the discussion was over. "All that matters now is Sight-Bringer." He adjusted his sword belt, which had a tendency to move about on his thin hips. "We'll need to clear this rubble. Set up a rotation. Have the men work in teams. Support beams, whatever it takes. We need to get inside the Great Crypt. I hate this damned place, and I don't want to be here a moment longer than I have to."

Owen understood that sentiment perfectly.

#

The next week was a blur of backbreaking labor for Owen. The Wolfrey soldiers worked in shifts, two men at a time. They carried the stones back up the red stairs, depositing them farther down the corridor, out of the way. Many of the fallen stones were too large for any single man to carry and had to be hoisted up the stairs on a wooden platform built on rails, with ropes attached to a pulley. Sometimes as they worked, the partially collapsed ceiling would groan, sifting dust and grains of rocks, making Owen think the ceiling was about to come down again.

Some of the men broke under the strain, their fear sending them fleeing to the upper catacombs. Others became ill from dust coating their lungs, sending them to their blankets, coughing and hacking, their mucus black.

As the men became ill, the shifts became shorter and more frequent. Owen would fall exhausted into his blanket only to be woken up—seemingly right away—to be told he needed to go back to work again. He barely slept, and when he did, nightmares plagued his dreams. The others also complained of their dreams.

Throughout it all, Hrawlgir remained the same. The young man didn't speak and barely slept but merely lay like a dead man, eyes wide open, staring at nothing—but then, seven days after the work had commenced, late at night, while Owen and Fin were on shift together, the two men uncovered the landing at the base of the stairs that led to the entrance of the Great Crypt.

And Hrawlgir woke.

Chapter 24

Owen

Owen stood beside Fin as Lord Palin and Keep-Captain Awde examined the landing, the scaffolding, and the narrow opening through the rocks that led—they assumed—to the Great Crypt. Modwyn and Idwal stood nearby, waiting while the keep-captain and Lord Palin discussed the best way of proceeding. The tiles of the landing formed a mosaic of shapes, creating an overall geometric pattern, with words inscribed that none of them could read. Every time Owen stared at them too long, they set his nerves on edge, giving him a headache.

By using a framework of support beams, they had managed to create a small tunnel beneath the rubble—three times the length of a man—with just enough room to crawl through. Fin and Owen had been on night shift together when they broke through, pushing the last large stone aside and opening up a path to a vast chamber on the other side. According to legend, the Great Crypt had been built within a massive cavern housing the Greywynne family's dead. That late at night, most of the soldiers were still sleeping up in the keep far above them. They had immediately gone and found the keep-captain, who brought Lord Palin, who insisted on bringing Modwyn, who dragged along Idwal.

With the Great Crypt open before them, Modwyn had argued that a small party could easily crawl through, find Sight-Bringer, and get back out again—perhaps taking only minutes. And while Owen was terrified at the thought of crawling through that tunnel into the crypt where Serina had died, the only way to leave that cursed place again was with the sword. They had gone all this way, fought through the Feldwyn Swamp, and then labored for days at unblocking the opening. The end to the expedition was tantalizingly close.

"My lord," said Keep-Captain Awde, repeating his argument once more, "there's no need for you to go. I can do this with one of the men." The keep-captain had been trying to convince the young man for some minutes, but Lord Palin wasn't listening.

"It's my responsibility," said Lord Palin.

"The tunnel is dangerous. It can come down at any moment. If that happens, your sister will be the last surviving member of the Dain family, and your cousin will become duke. Do you want that?"

The young man looked away but shook his head. "I'm going in."

Keep-Captain Awde sighed. "At least let me go first, with another, just to make sure it's safe."

"I'll go. I don't mind," said Owen. He had no desire to go, but if the young lord felt he owed Owen, he might be more likely to consider Owen's request to free him from his oath of service.

"I should go as well, my Lord," said Modwyn, stepping closer. "There are undoubtedly deep vapors within the crypt. You'll need me."

"No, I don't think we will!" snapped Awde.

"We've talked enough," said Lord Palin. "Let's go find the sword and leave this damned haunted place and all its nightmares. I haven't had a decent sleep in days. You can go first, Captain. I'll follow with the doctor behind me. This one"—he pointed at Owen—"should come last, just in case he gets stuck."

Owen stared suspiciously at the tunnel. *Can I get stuck?*

"Maybe I should go," said Fin.

Keep-Captain Awde glanced at Fin, but Owen spoke up first. "No, I'm going."

Fin frowned, pursing his lips. "Owen—"

"Enough." Lord Palin unbuckled his sword belt. "If we're fast, we can find the sword and be back out again before we finally decide who is and isn't coming. It's those I've already named—and let's get on with it. If we're lucky, we can be back on our way to Stron's Watch and Port Eaton before the sun rises."

Keep-Captain Awde nodded. "All right, Toscovar, you come. Bring the fighting axe along with you—just in case ghouls *do* live forever."

Owen handed Fin his sword. His armor was up in the keep, with the rest of his belongings.

Once ready, Keep-Captain Awde looked over them all. "What about these deep vapors, Doctor?" he asked.

The physician patted a satchel hanging off his shoulder. "I have something that will help, but it's best to wait until we get to the other side."

"Is it safe?" Lord Palin asked, watching the opening.

"It's doubtful there will be deep vapors this close to the entrance, my lord. Once we get within the Great Crypt, though, we can apply my protections then."

"Why wait?" asked Keep-Captain Awde.

Modwyn looked away. "Because the protections will… make us sick as well, nauseous, perhaps a bit unsteady. It's best to wait until we have no other choice."

"What stupidity is this?" Keep-Captain Awde asked.

"It's not stupidity. It's necessary. Would you prefer to be slightly ill or dead?" Modwyn glared at the captain, his lower lip trembling slightly.

"It's all right," said Lord Palin. "We'll wait until we're inside as the doctor suggests. This man"—he pointed at Fin—"can sound the alarm if anything happens, go back for more help."

"Master Idwal can help as well, I'm sure," said Modwyn.

"Yes, of course," said Lord Palin. "And we're happy for your service, man."

Idwal inclined his head. "'Tis an honor, my lord. The times are different now. Maybe this expedition will help us all forget the past and start over again."

Lord Palin smiled. "Yes, I'd like that. The past needs to stay in the past. A new start."

"Indeed, my lord," said Idwal with a slight bow of his head.

Keep-Captain Awde, wearing only his padded undertunic, held his hands out to Fin. Fin stared at him in confusion for a moment.

"Lantern, man, and the axe," the captain said.

Grinning at his own foolishness, Fin handed both to the keep-captain, who then dropped down on his belly at the tunnel opening. He put his wrist through the loop on the bottom of the axe handle, placed the lit lantern ahead of him on the dirt, and crawled into the opening. Within moments, his wriggling legs were out of sight, the lantern's light receding. Seconds later, the captain called out to them, saying he was through. Lord Palin followed next and then Modwyn. Then, it was Owen's turn.

Owen, following the keep-captain's example, looped his axe handle around his right wrist, dropped down, and crawled into the tunnel. His shoulders and back scraped the rocks above him. He hated being in the tunnel. Fin had been the one working within it before, pushing the stones back to Owen to pile up. *Maybe I should have let Fin go, after all.* He saw the light from the lantern ahead of him at the other end of the tunnel, and he pushed on, shoving with his knees and pulling with his elbows. His breathing was amplified in the tight space, and he knew that he needed to calm himself, that he was getting himself worked up. He couldn't help how he felt. All that rock was hanging over him, threatening to bury him. He had to get through, had to get out. *Never should have come. Never should have volunteered.* Then, just as his panic welled up within him, his head emerged into open space. A moment later, someone grabbed him and pulled him to his feet. The others stood about, staring around themselves in wonder.

Keep-Captain Awde held the lantern high, the haft of his axe against his thigh, and Lord Palin stood beside him. Modwyn had been the one to help Owen up, and the doctor turned his gaze to the chamber surrounding them—a scene unlike anything Owen had ever seen.

The giant cavern opened before them, extending even beyond the considerable reach of the lamp's light, but what the lamp did expose was vast, magnificent. Ancient brown skulls stared down at them, completely covering the walls. Someone must have nailed them all in place, Owen realized. The surface of the floor was all tiles, a mosaic of black and white, with the same strange lettering he had seen at the landing. At regular intervals stood giant, sturdy pillars supporting the arched stone ceiling high above them. Each pillar was easily six or more feet in diameter, and each base was carved into the likeness of a snarling human visage so that it appeared as though giants were watching them. In front of each pillar sat a huge cast-iron brazier at least four feet across. As far as the lantern's light reached stood even rows of crumbling stone coffins and larger stone vaults—the remains of countless generations of the Greywynne family. A thick layer of sparkling dust lay atop everything, shining in the light of the lantern. The winged griffin of House Greywynne was prominent everywhere, etched into all the coffins or sitting as statues atop vaults.

"The Great Crypt," whispered Modwyn, almost reverently. "I never dreamed…"

"What?" asked Owen.

The other man shook his head. "Nothing."

Lord Palin reached out and gripped Modwyn's forearm. "Doctor, the protection you spoke of?"

"Yes, of course, my lord." Modwyn knelt and rummaged within his satchel and laid out four strips of cloth, each long enough to serve as a mask. Next, he removed a small glass vial, unstopped it, and proceeded to pour several drops of a thick, dark fluid onto the rags.

Instantly, a vile stench washed over Owen, making his eyes water.

"What is that?" he asked.

Modwyn grimaced. "It's harsh, I know, but a little sickness now will ensure the effects of the deep vapors don't take us by surprise." He held out a piece of cloth to Lord Palin.

"Doctor," said Lord Palin, looking ready to faint. "Is this really—"

"It is, my lord. Please believe me. It will make you sick and dizzy, but you must resist removing the mask. If you do, it won't work a second time."

Keep-Captain Awde stepped closer to Modwyn, gripping the wrist of the other man. "You first, Doctor."

Modwyn paused, and a look of uncertainty flitted through the doctor's eyes, like that of a cornered animal.

What's going on here?

Modwyn glared at the keep-captain but then tied the cloth behind his own neck and wore it, masklike, over his face. He breathed deeply, staggered for a moment, but then righted himself and met the keep-captain's eyes again. "Satisfied?"

Awde sighed and held his hand out for a strip of cloth. "Let's get this over with."

As Owen tied his cloth over his face, a wave of nausea rushed through him, making his legs go wobbly. He bent over, trying not to vomit, and slowly concentrated on breathing, first one breath and then another. His vision grew dim, and he found it increasingly hard to concentrate. The others looked just as unsteady. Lord Palin was bent over, gagging, but Modwyn was beside him, patting his back. Keep-Captain Awde forced himself erect and staggered forward, his axe-head trailing on the tiles behind him. Lord Palin followed, swaying drunkenly, but when Owen tried to follow, he fell to his knees. He shook his head, his vision blurry.

Modwyn knelt next to him, his hand on Owen's shoulder. "Are you all right?" Modwyn's voice sounded disinterested, and his gaze was directed away, toward Keep-Captain Awde and Lord Palin, who held each other up as they staggered forward. The keep-captain had dropped his axe several paces back.

"I... sick," Owen managed, closed his eyes, and shook his head once more. "Catch... breath." His eyes closed again, and he was aware he was lying on his side.

"You stay here, soldier," said Modwyn. "Rest a bit, but keep the mask on."

Something was... wrong with Modwyn, but Owen couldn't put his finger on it. Before he could ponder it anymore, another wave of revulsion swept through him. Modwyn moved away, quickly catching up to the other men. Owen closed his eyes to stop the chamber from spinning, and when he opened them again, he saw that Modwyn was supporting Lord Palin and had taken the lantern from the keep-captain, who stumbled along behind them. Owen rolled onto his belly, his cheek lying against the cold stone tiles. His blurry eyes tried to focus on something just before him—Modwyn's mask. That's what had been bothering him about Modwyn. He wasn't wearing his own mask.

Why not?

The answer surged through him, momentarily burning away his lethargy and clearing his thinking—*Modwyn has betrayed us!* With trembling fingers, Owen yanked the cloth from his face and pushed it away. His eyelids fluttered as he fought to stay awake. *Can't sleep… Must… move.*

He blinked rapidly, forcing himself to his knees. The gigantic crypt spun wildly around him. He breathed deeply, feeling as if he had been drinking fire. He swayed in place, but his gaze slowly focused again. His limbs, impossibly heavy, trembled uncontrollably, refusing to move properly, but somehow he managed to stagger to his feet. Stumbling forward, he fell against one of the stone vaults, using it to catch himself and remain upright.

Where are the others?

He pushed away from the vault, almost falling again as he lurched forward. He made his way thus, farther into the Great Crypt, stumbling from vault to coffin, always heading in the direction of the lamplight. The vaults and coffins seemed to blur, to move on their own, as if he were drunk.

Then, Owen felt something… different. He felt a vibration in the air, a throbbing that coursed through his entire body—it seemed to be pulling at him. Stumbling forward, he staggered toward a large stone vault. The stone griffin perched atop its roof leered menacingly at Owen. The mysterious, unearthly throbbing in his skull grew stronger as he approached the vault.

He slowly circled the vault, leaning against it for support. As he came around its corner, he stared in disbelief at the sight before him—the skeletal remains of a large man in full plate armor, still standing upright, pinned right through his chest plate into the stone vault wall by the strangest longsword he had ever seen. The sword's hilt was carved out of white stone into the shape of a bizarre, unworldly naked woman. Her outstretched arms composed the sword's quillons—its cross guard—and her animallike hoofed feet formed the pommel. The blade itself was longer by at least a foot than any other sword Owen had ever seen. It was double edged, with a long fuller containing perfectly formed but indecipherable runes, extending most of the way down its perfect blue blade. It was the most beautiful thing he had ever seen. Mesmerized, Owen slowly reached out a hand. The moment his fingers touched the blade, a current of energy flowed into him. He yanked his fingers back and stared at his fingertips and again at the blade. *Sight-Bringer.*

The Illthori, that strange race who had died out centuries before men had crawled out of caves, had left behind three relics that had become the kingdom's greatest treasures—the crown, the rod… and the sword.

I'm actually standing before Sight-Bringer, the reason we've come all this way. His gaze drifted about the area around him now, seeing for the first time the dozens of other skeletons. Some of them had been torn apart, with legs, arms, and heads lying separate. All wore mail armor, rusted and falling apart. Among the discarded swords, axes, and pole arms lay shattered wooden shields bearing the Lion of Wolfrey. It looked eerily like the hilltop where he and Hrawlgir had discovered the remains of the blood fiend. *This was where the battle with Serina took place,* he realized with sudden clarity. Looking behind himself, Owen saw that he hadn't come that far from the collapsed entrance. Owen's gaze went back to the corpse impaled by the sword. *Stron! It can only be Duke Stron.*

His heart hammered within his chest, and his blood chilled. Only paces away was another vault that had been reduced to rubble, the ground around it black with scorch marks, not unlike the ground where the female marsh tick had been killed. Blackened bones lay scattered among the scorch marks. *Was this where Belion had broken his staff, bringing down the entrance?*

At that moment, Owen heard movement, footsteps. Still barely able to stand, let alone fight, he dropped down and hid behind the corner of the vault. Someone had just crawled out of the tunnel, carrying a fluttering torch before him, joined a moment later by another man–Idwal and one of his brothers. The men stalked past, moving farther into the Great Crypt in the direction that Modwyn, Lord Palin, and Keep-Captain Awde had been heading. Idwal had been with Fin, guarding the entrance.

Owen stared at the corpse of Stron, at the strange longsword pinning him to the wall of the vault.

"Sorry, my lord," he whispered, grasping the hilt of the sword in both hands. The moment he touched it, power coursed through him again, amplifying his senses. Stunned, he released the sword and staggered back. The moment he did, the sickness and lethargy rushed back in, threatening to knock him to his knees. *Magic. It's real magic.*

He once again gripped Sight-Bringer's bizarre handle, feeling the occult power of the Illthori relic rush through him. That time, he held on, shoving the longsword upward in an attempt to dislodge it. It held fast. He yanked it down again, trying to rock it free. The blade moved, just a fraction, but enough to drive Owen to redouble his efforts. Grunting under the strain, he shoved the blade up and down. Then, without warning, the sword slid free of the wall all at once. As it came loose, the desiccated corpse of Duke Stron unceremoniously slid off, the plates and bones falling apart.

Panting, Owen held Sight-Bringer upside down against his chest, its point near his feet. He still felt wobbly and weak from whatever Modwyn had poured on the masks, but the sword's magic was helping him. He didn't think he would have been able to go any farther without its help, but Lord Palin and Keep-Captain Awde were in danger, and he had to do something. His skin clammy, his heart pounding, Owen stumbled after the retreating figures of Idwal and his brother.

The two hunters were moving farther into the Great Crypt and came to a large stone dais the size of a house. Atop the dais sat a massive throne of polished wood, decorated with antler horns and animal hides. Modwyn stood waiting atop the dais. At his feet lay Lord Palin. Keep-Captain Awde lay unmoving behind Modwyn, asleep or dead, Owen couldn't tell. A monstrous pile of corpses, dozens of them, as high as a man's waist, lay piled up before the throne.

As he stared at the pile of dead, a wave of fear and revulsion washed over Owen. Terror such as he had never felt before gripped his heart. The urge to turn and run built up within him the longer he stared at the corpse pile. He closed his eyes, his heartbeat pounding in his ears like a drum. *I have no business here. No living man does.* Some dark and horrible thing lay hidden away within that pile of bodies, a dark presence that hated all life.

Just as his terror was about to send him fleeing, the magic of Sight-Bringer throbbed, sending a wave of energy through him, driving away the worst of his fear. He couldn't run. His duty was there.

Forcing his eyes open again, he saw that the lantern the captain had been carrying was sitting on the landing, illuminating the corpse mound and the three men standing around it. While Modwyn watched, Idwal and his brother pulled bodies from the pile, throwing them unceremoniously onto the ground around them. Some of the corpses, little more than withered husks, fell apart as the men handled them. Owen's dread grew again, becoming palpable, and he began to hyperventilate.

"Don't," he whispered. "There's something in there, something—"

All three men stood staring down at something they had just uncovered—another corpse, but that one wasn't ancient. It was a young woman, naked but for a rusted old ring-mail coat, filthy with grime and dried blood. Her hair was blond and tightly woven into braids. Intricate blue tattoos covered the entire upper half of her face, like a mask. Her hands lay clasped atop one another on her stomach, as if she were only sleeping.

It's Serina Greywynne, Owen realized, *the Blood Queen.*

He suddenly grasped the full implications of Stron's corpse, run through by his own sword—the legends were all wrong. *Stron didn't kill Serina. She killed him.*

She killed everyone.

Idwal and his brother picked up young Lord Palin and held the boy poised over Serina's corpse. Once again, Owen's dread grew. That time, the magic of the sword couldn't push it away, and his mind raced.

Modwyn drew a dagger and placed it against Lord Palin's throat. Owen knew that he had to do something right then, had to help somehow before it was too late—but he couldn't. His terror froze his limbs.

"No," he whispered, spittle running down his chin. "Don't!"

With one quick movement, Modwyn cut Palin's throat, severing an artery. Bright arterial blood spurted over Serina's pale face, drenching it. A wave of dizziness swept over Owen, and he felt himself swaying.

I've just failed my liege lord—stood by watching while another man murdered him. I'm cursed.

As horrific as his failure to act was, what happened next was infinitely worse as the corpse of Serina Greywynne suddenly moved, reached up with blood-splattered hands, and pulled the young boy's head down toward her before burying her mouth against his neck.

Even from where he hid, Owen could hear her drinking.

His courage shattered, Owen ran, stumbling back toward the entrance.

Serina Greywynne, the Blood Queen of Greywynne Island, was alive.

Chapter 25

Modwyn

Modwyn stood before Serina, his pulse matching the excitement in his fevered mind. *She's alive! It's worked!*

It had seemed impossible, but there she was before him, nonetheless. When the three men had pulled off the last of the withered corpses, revealing her—still young and beautiful, as if she had merely gone to sleep—he knew his plans had worked. Despite having been trapped in that cavern for forty-eight years, she hadn't aged a day—and she never would. She'd remain young and beautiful forever—as would he once she rewarded him for freeing her and gave him her gift.

Clearly, she had been trapped when Belion, having no other choice, broke his own staff, causing the cave-in that collapsed the entrance. With no source of fresh blood, she had fallen into a coma-like sleep. The boy's blood had brought her back, waking her from forty-eight years of nightmare-inducing dreams. All his life, he had studied blood fiends in a futile attempt to be like her, but her godly condition couldn't be duplicated by mortals. He realized that only she, the master, could pass on her gift and create more immortal beings.

Her long blond hair was pulled back tightly, tied in braids, in the Fenyir style, interwoven with gems and talismans. A series of elaborate blue tattoos covered the entire upper half of her face. Her eyes—the color of blood—were so beautiful, so otherworldly. As she stared at him in challenge, his heart skipped a beat. The tales of her beauty had been incomplete, unsatisfactory. She wasn't merely a beautiful woman—she was a goddess. She leaned back upon her elbows atop the pile of dead and then wiped one forearm against her mouth, smearing the blood across her perfect features.

"Who are you?" she asked, with the clipped accent of his true people.

Modwyn fell to his knees, as did Idwal and his brother, Hywal. "Your servant, majesty," Modwyn answered. "Modwyn Du'Greywynne. I am your great-nephew."

She stared at him blankly with those beautiful dark eyes for several long moments before finally answering. "I don't have a great-nephew, but there was a boy, my brother's bastard son. He lived on Felorin Island. Perwin, Perwin Du'Greywynne his name was."

"My father," Modwyn answered.

Her eyes tightened. "But you have the accent of a mainlander."

"It... it wasn't safe after the war for anyone with Greywynne blood," Modwyn said. "They called you a traitor, killed anyone even remotely connected to your bloodline."

"It's truth, my queen," said Idwal, speaking for the first time.

Nodding, she offered her hand to Modwyn, who took it—forcing himself not to snatch it back when he felt the chill of her flesh. He helped her to her feet. Idwal rushed forward to help as well. Hywal remained on his knees, his head down, shivering in terror.

"So how is it then that you are alive, great-nephew?" she asked.

"My parents ran, hid on the mainland, and changed their name. I was born far from these islands, far from my true people. I only ever knew of you from tales my parents told me, but we've always remained loyal, always. I've had to hide my entire life from these Dain dogs." Modwyn kicked the corpse of Lord Palin for emphasis.

"Dains?" asked Serina, licking the blood from her perfect lips. Just for a moment, Modwyn saw her fangs.

"Yes, your majesty," said Idwal. "This one is the new lord of the northern invaders, them what claim to rule us."

She cocked her head and considered Idwal for some moments. Then, she approached him and ran her bloody fingers through his hair and down his cheeks, leaving a trail of wet blood. She leaned in closer and sniffed him. "You are one of mine, aren't you, you and this little one down here?" She glanced at Hywal, who was smiling like a puppy.

Idwal's eyes took on a fervent glaze. "I am—we are, your majesty. We're loyal. We've always been loyal: my grandfather, my father, all of us."

"Grandfather? Great-nephew? How long have I slept?"

"Forty-eight years," said Modwyn, staring at his hands. "It's been forty-eight years since Duke Oskaley sealed the catacombs after he claimed you were dead."

"Forty-eight years?" Her face reflected her confusion, and her red eyes darted about the crypt. "I know it was a long time… but *that* long?"

"I'm so sorry, Majesty," whispered Idwal, tears running down his cheek. "The northerners said you were dead, killed by Stron with that sword. Had we suspected the truth, every man, woman, and child on this island would never have stopped until you were free."

"It's true," said Modwyn. "The old duke, Oskaley, claimed Stron killed you with Sight-Bringer. It was only a week ago, on his deathbed, that he admitted the truth, that you were only trapped down here."

"Oskaley?" Her eyes narrowed.

"Stron's younger brother," answered Modwyn. "He was… here during the battle."

Serina turned about, looking over the Great Crypt. Her gaze drifted near the entrance. "I… I remember that fool Stron. He was no threat, even with that Illthori talisman. Belion—him I remember well, damn him—he was the one who trapped me in here by bringing down the entrance. There were others, priests, soldiers. I killed them all, but another? Wait!" she spun back to face him, her eyes widening in remembrance. "*A boy*, a frightened little boy who hid near the entrance and then ran? *That* was a Dain?"

Modwyn snorted. "The mighty Duke Oskaley. The hero who helped kill you. The only survivor of the battle."

Serina raised an eyebrow. "Where is the mighty Oskaley now?"

"Dead, majesty. It took me years, but I found employment with the Dains as a physician. I poisoned him weeks ago. I had planned to kill all of them eventually. After he became ill and admitted his crime, I finished him for you."

She glided up next to him—so fast, like a dream—then ran one palm down the side of his face. "Such a loyal boy, such a…" Her voice trailed off, and her gaze went slack. She spun from him, staring away into the darkness. "I don't feel it," she said, so softly it was almost a whisper.

"Feel what, your majesty?" Modwyn asked.

She bolted, so fast she became a blur as she disappeared into the darkness. Then, moments later, she screamed in rage, shattering the silence of the Great Crypt. In a moment, she was back, her face a mask of rage, glaring at Modwyn. His knees went weak as fear swept through him. With no warning, she pressed up against him, crushing him against her chest, wrapping her thin arms around him. He felt like his spine would snap. "Where is it?" she hissed into his ear. "Why did you move it?"

"What… I… I… don't—"

"The sword, Sight-Bringer. Where is the sword?"

"Majesty… please," he begged.

"*Someone* has taken it!"

"Majesty… there's… there's no one."

Then, he remembered the young blond soldier. Spots of light popped in his vision, and Serina turned his head to expose his neck. Her fangs glistened.

"Wait… please… I think… I know. There was one other, a soldier. He must have taken it."

"Another enemy? And you've allowed him to live?"

Her fangs brushed against the skin of his neck, but then she dropped him, and he fell crashing to the stone floor. He lay there, staring at her bare feet, trying to breathe. After another moment, she would have broken him, he knew. His eyes darted to Idwal and Hywal, standing just behind her, their mouths hanging open like toads'.

"Go," Modwyn croaked. "Find the soldier and kill him before he can warn the others. Bring us back the sword."

They stared at him in open contempt.

"Do it," said Serina. "Bring me back Sight-Bringer, and hurry—it is dangerous."

As the two men ran for the opening to the crypt, Modwyn rose to his knees before her.

"Now, grandnephew," the terrible beauty before him said. "You will tell me of these *others* within my home."

Chapter 26

Owen

With the overwhelming terror driving Owen on, he barely remembered crawling back through the tunnel to the landing and the red stairs. When he saw Fin's body lying in a pool of blood—his throat cut—his anger burned through his fear, finally forcing him to stop. In death, Fin stared at Owen, as if accusing him of letting him down.

As he had let down Lord Palin and Keep-Captain Awde.

He couldn't help it—he felt as if someone else had had control of his body, forcing him to run. Even then, even after seeing her with his own eyes, he had trouble accepting the truth—Serina Greywynne, the greatest evil that had ever plagued the kingdom, once again walked the land.

A lit lantern sat in the blood beside Fin, and Owen picked it up, realizing he still held Sight-Bringer in his other hand.

He looked down upon his friend. "I'm sorry, Fin."

Then he turned and bolted up the red stairs, into the catacombs above. He was out of breath by the time he reached the top and staggered down the passageway. Even with Sight-Bringer's aid, he was still groggy from whatever poison Modwyn had given them. Stumbling, he fell, dropping the lantern. As it tipped over, its wick dimmed. Frantic, he snatched at it, placing it right side up and softly blowing onto its burning wick. His hopes sank as the wick went dark.

Without light, he would surely wander around for hours.

Then he realized he could see after all—not perfectly—but well enough to make his way. Once again, Sight-Bringer's magic was helping him. He stumbled down the tunnel, lined with corpse-filled recesses. He had to reach the others, to bring help. Maybe together they could defeat Serina and save the captain, maybe they—

At the sound of boot steps behind him, he realized they were coming for him.

His mouth dry, his pulse racing, he staggered forward. He was a capable enough swordsman, but in his present state, a child could have beaten him, and if he were attacked by Serina, he'd stand no chance at all. Once again, terror gripped his heart, threatening to unman him. If he stood and fought, he'd die there—he knew that for a certainty. He had to hide but didn't know where. Torchlight flickered behind him. Frantic, Owen looked down upon the corpse-filled recesses along the catacombs passage—a bad choice, he knew, but his only one.

He pulled himself into the recess and lifted the feather-light corpse that had been inside it over himself, like a foul, moldy blanket. If they even glanced inside the recess, they'd see him. He edged farther back, as far as he could manage. The footsteps were almost upon him. He held his breath and prayed to the Father for help.

A moment later, two pairs of legs swept past—the hunters. They didn't stop, not taking the time to search the crevices. *And why should they? There are hundreds of these openings. What's one more? Besides, what kind of a coward hides among the dead?* His face heated with shame. The hunters moved farther down the tunnel, heading toward the entrance to the keep—the only way out.

He knew if he stayed there, they would eventually find him, so he crawled out. As he did, the corpse fell apart, its bones falling onto the stones. Then, he heard a sound—the soft crashing of waves against rocks, the secret dock, another way out.

He made his way back down the dark tunnel toward the sound, still amazed that he could see somehow, even if poorly. Soon, the air became wet and pungent with salt as he came upon the chamber with the dock. Moonlight shone through the dock's opening, illuminating the rotting wooden walkway across the pool.

He crossed over again, ignoring the creaking, and climbed the stairs to the cave's opening. Leaning against the opening, he stared out into the night. The cool, wet breeze on his face energized him. Clouds partially obscured a full moon that provided only enough light to make out the dark, churning waters below. The tide was low, the waters at least twenty feet away. He bit his lip as he stared into the waves. If he jumped, the waves would batter him against the cliff face.

Tilting his head back, he stared up the cliff. He could just make out the shape of the fortress walls above. He was a superb climber—had been all his life—but he didn't know if he could manage a cliff face at night and reach those walls. The rocks would be wet and slick, but the last time he had been here in the daylight, he had seen bushes growing out of the cliff. Owen didn't know if they would be solid enough to hold his weight.

Do I really have a choice?

He knew he couldn't stay there. The hunters would find him. At least another hour was going to pass before the next two men came on duty. Besides, the fresh air was beginning to revitalize him, to wash away the last of Modwyn's poison. He had to do something to warn the others.

He pulled off his padded undertunic, exposing his upper body to the chill, and wrapped his tunic around Sight-Bringer. Next, he removed his belt, looped it in a knot around the longsword's strange cross guard, and refastened the belt over his chest so that the sword hung down his back. The blade of the longsword, although wrapped in his tunic, rested against his spine, which wasn't the safest of choices, but he couldn't think what else to do. He couldn't leave it there, not after traveling all that way for it. Nor could he climb with it in his hands.

Facing the sea, he leaned out again over the edge of the opening, still holding onto the side of the cliff. Tentatively, he placed one boot on the rotting pieces of the pier. It groaned under his weight but held. To his right was an outcropping of stone that looked as though it could hold his weight. From there, he figured, he might be able to—

Something smashed into Sight-Bringer, almost knocking Owen from the ledge. The object, a hand axe, ricocheted into the sea. His arms flailing for balance, he grabbed at the rocks. As he did, a figure rushed at him, moonlight glinting off a knife's blade. Instinctively, he let go of his handhold and grasped at the wrist of the man's hand, somehow connecting, but as the man collided into him, they both fell back into the open air.

A feeling of weightlessness lasted only a moment, and in that moment, Owen sucked in a mouthful of air. Then, they hit the water. The sudden impact of the freezing-cold water was like being smashed in the face with a shield. As they sank, the other man grasped at Owen's neck with both hands, trying to pull him in closer, to use him to climb above the water. Owen raised his knee and forced it between them. Then, he kicked out, shoving his attacker away. He saw the shadow of the other man sink deeper, flailing, bubbles rising. Free, Owen followed the bubbles, heading for the surface, where he could just make out the moonlight. When his head broke free of the water, he gasped for air, still swallowing a mouthful of salty water.

Choking, he went beneath the waves again.

Frantic, he pushed for the surface once more, managing to break free again. The turbulent waters grabbed him, tossed him about like flotsam, and smashed him into nearby rocks. Pain lanced through his chest and knee, but he grasped at the rocks, feeling his fingers slip over the seagull shit that coated them. Somehow, he managed to hang on, just barely keeping his head above the waves. Coughing, he gasped for air as the waves tried to pry him loose and drag him back beneath the water. The cold sapped his strength, and his fingers numbed. He knew he couldn't stay there as the waves would tear him loose and dash him against the rocks, but then, the clouds over the moon must have parted, because he suddenly saw a dark opening in the cliff face, not twenty feet away. *A cave!*

He let go of the rock, pushing off it with his legs, and swam with all his might.

Chapter 27

Brice

When Brice drifted back to consciousness, he was certain he was still asleep, still having a nightmare because—although his head pounded and his throat burned—a woman was chanting. The words were foreign, undecipherable, yet *wrong* somehow... foul. An overwhelming sense of dread came over him. The tales other men had told of him, of his exploits in battle, were vast exaggerations, he knew. He had been frightened in every single battle he had been in, but the sensation had never been anything like what he was feeling at this moment. He was literally trembling in fear, gasping for air, as chills shook him. He didn't know what was going on, but somehow he recognized he was in great danger. He needed to get up, to act, but found it difficult to move.

What is happening?

He recalled that he had been with Lord Palin in the Great Crypt. They had just broken through when he... *What? I must have passed out.*

Why?

The answer came to him in a flash of insight. *Modwyn! He's done something—his medicine was a trap after all, but how? I watched him breathe through his own mask.* The chanting increased in volume and became more demanding in tone.

Do something, man. Do it now!

He forced his eyes open, willing himself fully awake. The first thing he saw was the foul-smelling piece of cloth Modwyn had given him to wear. It lay nearby, just before his eyes. *I remember now. I pulled it from myself before… before all went dark.* Then, his gaze fell on the face of the young man he had been responsible for, Palin Dain. Palin's eyes were glassy in death, his blond hair matted down with his own congealing blood.

Oh, Palin, Danika, I'm so sorry. All my fault.

As the chanting grew in intensity once more, Brice's gaze drifted beyond Palin to the woman with the pleated blond hair who was standing before him, her back to Brice, her arms outstretched. She wore only a coat of rusty ring-mail armor, her shapely legs naked and white, her feet bare. Before her lay a pile of dead, dozens of ancient corpses. Watching her with wide, frightened eyes was the weasel Modwyn. Next to the physician, shaking in terror themselves, stood two of the Greywynne hunters.

All traitors!

A hot rage burned away Awde's self-loathing, pushing back his terror. His heartbeat pounded in his ears—he had failed Palin but could still avenge him. His fighting axe lay not three feet away, where he must have dropped it before passing out. Modwyn had made a mistake—he should have killed Brice when he had the chance. Brice prepared to act. He inhaled deeply, gritting his teeth.

Now!

He moved, scrabbling forward, and gripped the haft of the fighting axe as he staggered to his feet. His body was refusing to move properly—he was too slow, too clumsy, as if moving underwater, but he drew the axe back with both hands and prepared to cut the woman's head from her shoulders. Modwyn—his eyes filling with terror—pointed at Brice, spittle running down his chin. Brice froze in midstrike when the withered corpses moved. Their dead heads turned and stared, eyelessly, at Brice. The blond woman in the ring-mail armor spun to face him, her eyes impossibly red, her forehead covered in tattoos.

He struck, hacking down at her with the axe, but she swept upon him, impossibly fast, and caught the axe in one hand, wrenching it from him as if he were just a child. She tossed the axe aside, where it clattered against the stones. Gripping him by the collar of his undertunic, she drew him in close against her blood-drenched chest.

Fangs! She has fangs. What—

"What have we here—a hero?" She spoke with the clipped accent of a Fenyir islander.

In that moment, he knew who she was—Serina Greywynne.

He struggled, but she merely tightened her grip, choking him. Then, she turned to Modwyn. "First, the one who stole my sword, now this one?"

"Awde, my queen," said Modwyn. "Brice Awde… the leader of the Wolfrey soldiers." He snorted derisively as he came closer, a sneer on his face. "Men call him a great warrior, a hero of the north. Not so great now, though. Have you wet yourself, coward?"

"Damn you, traitor. How?" Brice squeaked.

A huge grin lit up Modwyn's skeletal face. "Do you think me so stupid as to handle such a dangerous poison without first administering an antidote to myself? The marsh tick poison made me ill, but not insensible."

Brice struggled helplessly in Serina's iron grip. "You'll die for what you've done, bastard." Serina nuzzled her face into his neck, softly licking it with her tongue. Revulsion shuddered through him. Her lips brushed his ear as she whispered into it. "A great warrior, are you?"

"Fu… fuck you… witch!" he managed. Spots of light danced in the edges of his vision.

"Perhaps later. Your loyalty to your northern masters is admirable but misplaced. I can use a man like you. I'll need new battle captains now, new childes."

"Bu… Burn, witch!"

"In time, perhaps." She bit into his neck.

Pain coursed through him, setting him afire in agony, and he jerked helplessly in her grip. Then, she began to drink his blood, sucking it from him. Waves of pleasure coursed through his body, mingling with the pain. He shuddered in obscene joy and felt his erection grow. Shamed, he moaned in pain… in pleasure. Darkness edged in on him, and he felt himself slipping away—escaping her. His thoughts were of Danika, how he had failed her, too.

I'll find you in the afterlife, my love.

But then, Serina stopped drinking. "Now, childe, *you* drink."

With one hand, she held him up by the back of his neck while she bit into her own wrist. Dark blood welled against her pale skin, and she thrust her wrist against his mouth.

He couldn't help it, couldn't stop her.

He drank.

Then he began to change.

Chapter 28

Dilan

Dilan bolted upright, his blanket falling away as he gasped for air. His chest hurt, and a thick layer of sweat coated him. He had been dreaming of Prophet's Bridge again, that damned bridge. Everything was dark around him, but when he heard the snores of other men, he realized he wasn't back with his brother on that cursed bridge but in the witch's old fortress. Most of the men had complained of near-constant nightmares, and Dilan was no exception. Tonight, though, was the first time his nightmare was of the bridge instead of the red stairs. No matter how far he ran, he couldn't escape that bridge.

Rubbing the sleep from his eyes, he got up and pulled on his pants and undershirt then his boots. He figured he might as well relieve himself since he was up. He glanced at his sword and belt lying beside his blanket. In the Rams, the penalty for being caught without your weapon had been weeks of mucking out stables and shoveling horseshit. He picked up his sword and belted it on. He wasn't a Ram anymore, but some habits remained.

Moonlight spilled through the open window, providing just

enough light by which to make his way. Sleep would evade him that night, so he might as well stay up. He cautiously stepped over the lumps of sleeping men, many of whom tossed and turned in their sleep. At the open doorway, Dilan paused and glanced back at the room and its occupants.

We need to leave this place. We shouldn't be here.

He slid out into the corridor. Although the halls were dark, Dilan had little difficulty finding his way along the stone passageway, up the circular stairs, and out onto the keep's outer wall. The Wolfrey soldiers had built a wooden privy up there so they could drop their scat over the side of the wall. A light breeze blew against his face, carrying with it the smell of the sea and the promise of the coming fall.

Just then, boot steps pounded up the stairs behind him. Father Bowen, his face flushed, ran right into Dilan.

Dilan caught the young priest by his shoulders before he could fall back down the stairs. "Easy, Father."

The priest's eyes were wide with fear. "Have you seen him?"

"Seen who?"

"Hrawlgir. He's awake."

"Finally. Well, that's good news for a change."

"No, it's not. He's gone… disappeared."

"What are you talking about?"

"I was sitting with him, reading by candlelight when he just… sat up."

"Well, he had to wake up eventually."

"You don't understand. He looked at me and said, 'She's awake.' He wasn't right, so frightened. I went to get him something to drink, was only a moment, but when I returned, he was gone. I searched but couldn't find him anywhere. I thought maybe he came up here."

"Who's *she*?" The hairs on the back of Dilan's neck rose, a prickling in his scalp.

Father Bowen shook his head. "I think he must have fevers, or… I have no idea. Where's Modwyn? He's supposed to know these things."

"I don't know, Father, but we need to find Hrawlgir now—especially if he's not right in the head."

Dilan looked about, scanning the parapets. Father Bowen paced beside him.

"He's been asleep for days now," said Dilan. "Maybe he had to piss. I know I would."

"He's been doing that in his bedroll," said Father Bowen. "I've been the one cleaning up after him."

Isn't that also Modwyn's job?

Dilan stopped abruptly. There, near the wooden privy, a man stood outlined against the moonlight—standing atop the parapet.

"Hrawlgir," said Dilan softly, not wishing to scare the man, for if he were sleepwalking, he might slip and fall, a distance of at least a hundred feet to the rocks below.

The two men stepped closer and saw the man standing atop the privy was indeed Hrawlgir. The other man gave no indication he was aware of them, merely swaying in place atop the wall.

"What's he doing up there?" Father Bowen whispered.

Dilan shook his head. "Hrawlgir, come down."

Then, as if finally aware of them, Hrawlgir turned and stared at Dilan. "We shouldn't have come," he said. "We don't belong here."

Dilan shuddered. That was exactly what he had been thinking. Slowly edging closer, Dilan wondered how fast he could rush forward if Hrawlgir made any sudden moves. He figured if he could reach the other man without startling him, he might be able to grab him and pull him down from the wall.

"It's all right, Hrawlgir. There's nothing to be afraid of."

Hrawlgir cocked his head, a smile on his face. "There's *everything* to be afraid of." Then, without another word, he turned and stepped off the edge of the wall, disappearing into the night.

Dilan stared, frozen by the suddenness of it. A wet splatter sounded against the rocks far below. He turned and stared wide-eyed at Father Bowen, but the priest wasn't looking at Dilan. Instead, he was gazing up at the night sky.

"The moon is blood," the young priest said.

Chapter 29

Owen

Owen collapsed on his belly just inside the cave opening and lay soaking in a shallow pool of water. At least he wouldn't drown, he thought—until the tide rose and flooded the cliffside cave. With every breath, sharp jabs of pain cut through his lungs. Never had he been so exhausted. Every single part of his body hurt, but forcing himself to his hands and knees, he crawled away from the cave opening until he could stand upright. The rocks inside the cave were wet and—judging by the smell—covered in bird shit, making the footing even more treacherous. He cautiously made his way farther back into the cave. The pommel of Sight-Bringer—somehow still strapped to his back—scraped against the rocks above him, so he untied the belt, removed the sword, and once again pulled his sopping-wet undertunic over his body.

What now?

He held Sight-Bringer against his chest. Once again, his vision and other senses became sharper, his thoughts more coherent. If he didn't get out of that cave, he'd freeze to death, he knew—long before the tide rose and drowned him. He couldn't go back out into the sea. Even if he left the sword in the cave, which he couldn't do, he was too exhausted to swim against the waves again. Finding that cave had been very lucky, but maybe the entire base of the cliffs was honeycombed with them. If that was the case, perhaps they were all connected. If they were connected, he might find another way out. Slowly, on shaky feet, he edged his way along, farther back into the cave.

"Please… Father Craftsman," he said, his teeth chattering, "show me a way out."

The cave's ceiling narrowed, and he had to scramble along on hands and knees, but he kept moving back until he could no longer see the cave opening and the moonlight. Then, he ran out of room, with solid rock before him. *So much for that plan. What do I do now? I'm trapped down here.* Dejected, he curled up on his side, the sword's pommel held against his chest. His teeth chattered so hard that his jaw hurt. He was so tired, so exhausted… Maybe if he just closed his eyes for a moment, just until he—

He woke with a start, not realizing he had fallen asleep. A strong vibration had woken him, one he had felt throughout his entire body.

The sword—it was the sword.

Still resting against his chest, the bizarre handle was thrumming with occult energy, as if alive. He wrapped his numb fingers around the hilt and gasped when strength and energy flowed back through him, forcing him fully awake. He then saw an opening above him that he had missed earlier, a crevice perhaps two feet wide that led upward. At the very top of the crack was a streak of stars—the crevice led up and out of the cave.

Wrapping his belt around the hilt of the sword again, Owen tied it to his waist and then braced his back against one of the crevice walls and his feet against the other. Slowly, he began to worm his way up. The climb was torturous and felt as if it took him hours, though that couldn't possibly have been true. Nonetheless, when his head finally broke free of the crevice and into fresh air, he inhaled deeply, grateful to be finally free. Using every bit of energy he had, he managed to pull himself free of the opening and roll over onto the wet rocks.

The sound of waves crashing nearby forced him to move again, to stumble wearily to his feet. The rocks became high cliffs behind him but dropped down onto a beach. Down was easier than up, so he staggered down onto the sand. With the sea on his left, he stumbled down the beach. Looking up, he stared in confusion at a red moon, which made no sense at all. Then, the red moon spun wildly, and he collapsed, the longsword slipping from his fingers as he fell onto the wet sand.

Chapter 30

Dilan

Dilan stared at the moon in disbelief. *How is this possible?* He rubbed his eyes with his palms, but the moon remained a deep bloodred. Lightheaded, he turned and gaped at Father Bowen. The young priest whispered a prayer, his face reflecting the same bewilderment Dilan felt.

"Father Craftsman, help us," Dilan said. "What… what does this mean?"

The young priest reached out with trembling fingers and grasped Dilan's shoulder, as if to hold himself up. "I don't know, but this has nothing to do with the Craftsman. This is dark magic."

A scream rose from the stairs leading down into the keep. Dilan's fingers brushed his sword hilt, glad for the habit the Rams had instilled in him. "We need to get below. Rouse the others."

Father Bowen nodded. "I'll follow."

Dilan drew his sword and slowly made his way down the stairs in the darkness, Father Bowen just behind him, breathing down his neck.

"A little space, please," Dilan said, "just in case I need to fight."

"Yes, yes of course." The priest moved back a bit.

They heard another scream, but that one was abruptly cut off. A moment later, someone began beating a metal shield boss with his blade—the call-to-arms.

"We're under attack," said Dilan.

"Are the islanders rebelling again?"

At the bottom of the stairs, they came out onto a long corridor. Most of the men had been asleep but were scrambling to pull on armor and grab weapons. Beams of crimson moonlight stabbed through open window slips in the corridor's outer wall, giving everything the illusion of being drenched in blood. Dilan shivered as he moved down the corridor, sword in hand.

Dilan paused only long enough to dash back into the chamber he had shared with the others. Owen and Fin weren't there. They had been on shift clearing the stairs. The other men, though, were awake and preparing for battle. Dilan grabbed his shield, slipping his left arm through the enarme strap and gripping the handle of the metal boss. He considered taking the time to pull on his ring-mail coat and helmet, but just then more men screamed in terror and pain down below in the great hall, and Dilan knew he was out of time.

When he moved back out into the corridor, he saw he had lost Father Bowen in the press of men moving toward the stairs. Dilan joined the herd, following the other guardsmen downward. He heard the fighting before he reached the bottom, but what he then saw made no sense.

The great hall, a massive chamber with arching stone columns bearing the groin ceiling, was pure chaos. Wolfrey men-at-arms, some wearing little more than undergarments, were battling walking corpses. Living dead men, some little more than bone and dry, parchment-like flesh, came at them with grasping skeletal hands. The walking corpses seemed weak, barely able to remain upright. Every time a guardsman lashed out at one of the attackers, he severed an arm or a leg or split an entire body in half—the withered internal organs spilled out like rotted grain onto the stones of the great hall. None of the corpses had eyes, yet somehow they unerringly went after the living men, an unstoppable wall of the dead. When they did manage to reach past the soldiers' weapons, to grasp and hold onto the men, they soon overwhelmed them, pulling them down in a knot of dead, grasping flesh, biting and tearing.

"Ghouls!" Dilan cried out. "We're fighting ghouls, walking corpses."

A steady stream of ghouls shambled out of the corridor leading down to the catacombs' entrance. The hundreds of recesses filled with the mummified remains of the Greywynne-family servants flashed once more in Dilan's memory. *How many corpses are there in the catacombs? Hundreds? Thousands? Are they all ghouls now?*

He rushed forward, smashing his shield into the dried-out face of a ghoul, knocking its head clean off and sending the rest of the body flying. It had such little weight, as if it were paper. Two others came at him, reaching out for him with skeletal hands missing fingers. He stepped into them, shield high, moving from the back guard and swinging his sword forward and low in a powerful cut that severed the front leg of the closer ghoul at the knee. The second ghoul had been grasping for Dilan's shield, trying to pull him off balance, so Dilan simply smashed the metal boss into it, knocking the monster back and creating space to thrust his sword point into its face. The blade went clear through the ghoul's skull in an explosion of dust, coming out the back of its head, but then the ghoul pushed forward, forcing its head up the length of Dilan's sword blade, still reaching for him. The other ghoul—the one whose leg Dilan had severed—reached up and wrapped its bony arms around his thigh as it tried to pull him down. Terror gave Dilan strength, and he yanked his sword back savagely, taking the ghoul's head free of the body. He yanked his rear leg free of the other ghoul and shoved the headless ghoul into the other, quickly backpedaling to get out of their reach.

This is impossible. How do you kill something that's already dead?

He realized the answer a moment later: *the same way Stron and his army had—with axes, fire, and organization.* Fighting as individuals was going to get them all killed.

"Shield wall!" he yelled, slashing out at a ghoul that was trying to pull down another Wolfrey soldier, cutting the damned thing nearly in half and saving the man. "Form a shield wall, or we're all dead. And somebody bring axes!"

Wild-eyed, he looked around himself. The hall was complete pandemonium. Then, he caught a good look at the face of the warrior he had just saved: it was Hooper Tibs, Marlin Ornkey's friend, one of the two men most vocal in asserting that Dilan was a deserter. Hooper was staring stupidly at Dilan, his piglike eyes shining.

This isn't going to work. They're all like him. No one will listen to me.

Then Hooper moved to Dilan's left and stood shoulder to shoulder with him. "Shield wall," Hooper screamed. "Form a shield wall, you whoresons!"

Dilan lapped his shield over Hooper's, protecting Hooper's right side. Two more men ran to join Dilan on his right. All four men locked their shields together, overlapping them, as a small knot of ghouls rushed them.

"Ready," Dilan yelled, and the men leaned into their shields, bracing themselves.

The ghouls hit but with no real force, no strength, and were thrown back several feet. All their strength was in numbers and unyielding effort, Dilan realized. As the ghouls came at them again, the men struck down at them over their shields, knocking them to the floor. "Back," Dilan yelled, and the men stepped back a pace, opening enough room for them to cut downward at the still-moving corpses, to hack them to pieces.

More men joined them, and a true shield wall formed. Each time the ghouls attacked, the men threw them back. Soon, the ground before them was littered with arms, legs, and hacked-up torsos—but the only blood came from the soldiers. Behind him, he heard Father Bowen praying, calling on the Craftsman to give strength to their arms. A grim determination came over Dilan, forcing back his fear.

We can do this, he realized. *We can beat these abominations.* "They're nothing more than bones and dust," he yelled. "Hold the line. Stand firm."

More men joined them, extending the line all the way across the hall. Behind them, more men formed, and he felt a hand on his back, shoring him up. Someone handed war axes forward to the men in the front rank. As the ghouls came against them again, the men with the axes began cutting them down like cords of wood.

"Forward!" Dilan yelled.

As one, the men stomped forward with their left feet, throwing the ghouls back. The shield wall moved forward, the front rank stepping over the still-moving ghouls on the floor, trusting the men behind them to cut them apart. Dilan grinned, overcome by battle rage. *This is working. We're going to—*

A small, thin woman—a warrior-queen in a ring-mail coat with long blond hair tied in braids—swept into the hall behind the ghouls. At first, Dilan thought she must have been wearing a mask, but then he saw the upper half of her face was painted with intricate blue designs. She didn't walk as much as she flowed—like a spirit, leaving a shimmering distortion behind her, as if Dilan were watching her from across the flames of a bonfire. Even from where Dilan stood, dozens of paces away, he could see she was beautiful—and horrible—with impossibly all-red eyes. The entire front of her ring-mail coat glistened with fresh blood. She paused, staring at Dilan, and then she smiled at him, opening her lips and exposing her fangs.

Then fear washed over him, and although the horror made no sense, he knew just the same—that was Serina Greywynne, the necromancer, the witch, the Blood Queen of Greywynne Island. With a cry of inhuman rage that shook him to his core, she swept forward, like a tidal wave, singlehandedly rushing in on the shield wall. It should have been ridiculous—a lone woman, barehanded, attacking a shield wall.

It was horrifying.

She shattered them utterly. In an instant, she was among them, a blur of fangs and talon-like hands. The shield wall disintegrated before her. She lashed out, and a severed head flew through the air. She gripped one man by the leg and swung him at the others like a club, knocking them over as if they were merely toys. Behind her, the ghouls swept into the broken line, pulling the men down to tear at them. Everywhere Serina moved, she brought horror and death. She rammed her entire hand through a guardsman's body, mail armor and all, her fist coming out his back.

Just then, something grasped at Dilan's ankle, and looking down, he saw a ghoul, headless, legless, but still clawing at him. In revulsion, he brought his sword blade down, severing the ghoul's wrist, and kicked the hand free. Everywhere, men screamed and died.

Everyone is dying.

But then, Father Bowen stood his ground before the demon, confronting her with the power of his faith. She paused before him, her arms drenched in blood. He held his Craftsman's hammer out, dangling it before him from a leather cord around his neck while he chanted, praying loudly, his visage stoic, although Dilan was certain the man was terrified.

When Dilan had been a young boy, his mother had told him tales of Serina and how some of the most pious of the priests had been able to stand against her undead captains and even immobilize them with sheer force of will and prayer while other men came forward and drove wooden stakes through their black hearts.

Bless you, Father Craftsman, for sending us a man like Father Bowen. He's given us a chance this night.

Dilan's gaze darted about—there, not five feet away, was the broken shaft of a spear! He darted forward, dropping his sword and shield to pick up the spear. He ran straight at Serina's motionless back, intent on driving the spear through her heart.

Another ghoul grasped at his legs, tripping him. He fell forward, dropping the spear as Serina stepped forward and gripped Father Bowen's outstretched hammer. With complete contempt, she yanked it free and threw it aside. Father Bowen's eyes grew wide in terror as she reached out, gripped both sides of his head, and squeezed. His head shattered, drenching her in blood and gore.

Dilan kicked at the hands grasping at his legs and climbed to his knees. Serina turned and saw him and smiled at him again, Father Bowen's blood and brains dripping off her face.

Dilan's courage shattered. He ran, as did all the others, intent only on escape. Dilan bolted past several pockets of still-struggling men. He smashed into someone and saw the terrified bearded face of Marlin Ornkey before the press of men running and dying pushed them apart. He couldn't stay there. Nothing but death was there.

Then, somehow, he was past the ghouls and out of the hall. He sprinted for the keep's entrance and the inner ward. Reeling off a wall, he staggered past the keep's entrance and out into the cold red night. His heart pounded, his breathing strained. From somewhere deep within his soul, he knew he shouldn't be running, that he should stand and die like a man, but he couldn't help it.

The horses were screaming, as mad with fear as he was. As he reached the stables, a guardsman tried to stand before him, babbling at him. Dilan barreled past the man, barely noticing as he knocked him down. The horses were stamping and snorting, desperate to break free. Spittle ran down Dilan's chin, and he gasped for air, his limbs shaking.

The guardsman who had tried to stop him was back on his feet. He grabbed at Dilan's shoulder again, but Dilan shoved him away again. The man drew a sword. Then, a new man rushed into the stable—one of the hunters—and rammed a spear into the back of the guardsman, killing him. The hunter yanked his spear free then screamed in rage as he rushed at Dilan. Only Dilan's training with the Rams saved his life, as—at the last moment and acting on muscle memory, he spun inside the man's clumsy attack, striking the spear shaft with his palm, kept turning, and elbowed the hunter hard in the jaw, cracking it. Then, he was in close against the man, well inside the reach of his weapon. Dilan elbowed him again, and the man howled incoherently as he fell back, dropping his spear. Dilan caught it, spun it about, and rammed the metal spear point up into the underside of the man's chin, through the roof of his mouth, and into his skull. Dilan stumbled back, dropping the spear, his skin flushed with a cold sweat.

He needed to get away from there—away from *her*—immediately. The first two horses he approached wouldn't let him get near them, but the third did.

Gale... it's Gale.

The tall black colt was trembling, eyes wide with fear, but he remained still long enough for Dilan to throw a saddle over him. Hanging on a peg on a nearby wooden wall was a prepacked patrol bag, ready for the next time Keep-Captain Awde needed to send out men to scout the surroundings. Dilan grabbed it, tossed it over the animal without even looking inside it, and mounted. He rode the colt out of the stables at a gallop and out into the red night.

Gale needed no encouragement. The horse bolted, and Dilan hung on, letting the animal pick his own path in the night. They galloped through the inner gatehouse and then the outer and then down the winding trail leading from the fortress. Still shivering, still gasping for air, Dilan focused only on staying in the saddle. He didn't look back until they were near the bottom of the winding trail.

Dilan could still hear the screaming.

Chapter 31

Modwyn

Modwyn stepped gingerly over the corpses of the Wolfrey soldiers, wishing to keep blood off his boots. The hall was worse than a slaughterhouse, with bodies and pieces of bodies lying strewn everywhere. Human blood gelled beside the desiccated body parts of the undead—many of which were still twitching. Modwyn's skin was clammy, and his pulse was racing. He didn't care about the fate of the soldiers—they had been little more than animals to begin with, but he hadn't expected so much… carnage.

Are all battles like this?

Those ghouls that hadn't been hacked to pieces stood silently along a wall, awaiting further orders from their mistress. His eyes kept drifting to them, certain that only Serina's will kept them from killing him and Idwal and his brothers. Serina—her beautiful face storming with emotion—strode purposely among the bodies of the Wolfrey dead, still searching for the sword she blamed Modwyn for losing. As frightened as Modwyn was of the ghouls, he was far more terrified of her.

The sword has to be here. It has to.

His gaze darted to Idwal, standing dutifully nearby and watching Serina like a loving dog. Serina's rise had altered the dynamics between the two men, Modwyn realized. Where before, Idwal had been almost subservient—following all of Modwyn's orders—he wouldn't even acknowledge him anymore. Modwyn felt a knot of anger at the man's betrayal, growing in his belly. That damned peasant had never truly been loyal to him, yet releasing the queen had all been Modwyn's doing. Without him, Serina would still be trapped in torpor. *However, despite all I've done, who does she reward with eternal life? That damned idiot warrior, Awde!* The injustice was staggering.

Modwyn sighed, forcing himself to approach Serina. Her beautiful red eyes held a wild, manic look as he approached. Her entire upper body was drenched in blood, as if she had dunked her head and shoulders into a bath of gore. Modwyn lowered his gaze before her and stared at the ground dutifully. She was still barefoot, and even her small, delicate feet were drenched in blood. Fifty years of lying trapped beneath the ground, buried within a corpse pile, had rotted all of her clothing. She would need new garments—clothing fit for a queen. He smiled, thinking of that bitch Danika back at Stron's Watch. She seemed almost a match for Serina in size. Perhaps Serina would give Danika to Modwyn as a reward.

She laughed then, a soft titter that hinted at madness. "It's not here. I can't feel it anymore. All those decades and now… nothing."

Modwyn glanced up. "Majesty, I… I'm sorry, but you're free now. What matters some old sword?"

She closed her eyes for a long moment, but when she opened them again, they were livid with rage. Unbelievably fast, she gripped him by the collar of his physician's robes and lifted him—one-handed—into the air. "An old sword? Fool! That sword is Sight-

Bringer, an Illthori relic. It. Kills. My. Kind. Do you have any idea how many of my childes have been slain by that thrice-damned sword?"

Modwyn couldn't think clearly. His eyes focused on her fangs, so close, only inches from his face. "I… My queen, I… I don't—"

"I should have destroyed it myself decades ago, but I couldn't bring myself to—it's still an Illthori talisman and contains priceless, long-forgotten magic from another age."

"Your majesty," said Idwal, sliding up beside them, "my brothers and I have looked for the sword but found only Wolfrey blades. Not a one of them carried a sword with a woman on the hilt. We'll keep looking, but I fear… at least one of them escaped."

Serina dropped Modwyn. He lay on his side near her bare feet, gasping for air.

"Escaped?" Serina addressed Idwal. "*Of course* one escaped, and of course he has Sight-Bringer. The gods mock me, test me. Stron the monster used that foul weapon against my childes—would have used it against me as well. I *will* have it back. It's too dangerous to be out of my hands."

"They won't get far, my queen. I will kill them. For you, I will kill anyone." The look on Idwal's ruddy face was one of utter devotion, his eyes shining in the torchlight. Behind him, three of his brothers edged closer.

"Why do you say *they*?" asked Serina.

"One was the guardsman in the Great Crypt." Idwal sneered at Modwyn. "That one's poison didn't work on him, nor did he make sure he were dead. That guardsman were the one what took the sword and ran. My brother Hywal and I went after him, but Hywal didn't come out of the catacombs, and now I fear my brother must be dead. I think the guardsman leaped from the hidden dock into the waters of the sea. If so, it's still there. He must have drowned."

Serina shook her head and ran her fingers over Idwal's cheek, leaving trails of smeared blood. The hunter shuddered with pleasure.

"No," she said. "The sword has moved away. I can no longer feel its foul presence—and I would if it were close by—even underwater."

Idwal bit his lower lip and nodded. "Then he's gotten free somehow, got out of the water, managed to avoid getting smashed like an egg by the rocks. Another of my brothers were murdered in the stables. Likely another soldier got away as well."

Modwyn climbed to his knees, his throat still sore. "Please, great-aunt. It's not my fault, but I can—"

"It *is* his fault, my queen," said Idwal. "It was his fool plan to use the marsh-tick poison on the others, but he didn't make sure they were all dead. He let that soldier steal the sword. Had I known, I would have—"

"Lies! Outrageous lies!" Spittle flew from Modwyn's lips as he rounded on the hunter. "*I* freed her—not you! This was my plan. I am her loyal servant. You're just a foul, dirty peasant."

Serina said nothing, but a small ghost of a smile danced across her bloody lips.

"My queen, I am loyal," said Idwal, glaring at Modwyn. "Me and my kin have always been loyal. This one—for all his claims of kinship—is an outsider. Even if he were of our blood, he's hidden as a craven among the mainlanders all his life. He isn't one of us and never will be."

"Damn you, you cretin." Modwyn advanced on Idwal, a murderous rage gripping him. He stopped when he saw Idwal had slid his hunting knife free of his sheath and was holding it loosely against his leg. Modwyn's gaze snapped to Serina. "Please. I live to serve you. I would be *as* you. It's all I've ever wanted."

Smiling, Serina swept forward and gripped Modwyn, pulling him in against her bloodstained armored breast. Her lips nuzzled his cheek, his neck, murmuring soft incoherent whispers into his skin. She was so cold. Urine soaked his hose, and he whimpered.

"Please… please… I love you," he whimpered. "I only wish to serve you."

Her tongue darted out, licking the side of his neck. "You have failed me. You are not worthy of the gift."

His legs went weak. Had she not been holding him up, he'd have fallen. The hall spun about him as his heartbeat pounded in his ears.

"Please. Please don't." Despite his terror, he felt his erection grow as she nipped at his throat. "Please… please… I would serve you."

"You *will* serve me," she whispered. "But in a manner more appropriate to one such as you—as a blood thrall."

Holding him tightly against her with one arm, she gripped the front of her ring-mail coat and ripped it apart, sending metal rings popping and flying, exposing her naked breasts. She gripped one of them, the veins visible against her pale white skin, and pulled Modwyn's head toward it. She squeezed her nipple and tugged on it, and watery pink fluid, blood mixed with what looked like mucus, oozed from its tip.

She stared down at him with tenderness, as a mother might gaze upon her baby. "Drink."

"Please, no." He whimpered.

"Come, take mother's milk."

"No… no, please."

She turned her attention to Idwal. "You will take your brothers and kill these men. You will bring Sight-Bringer back, do you understand?"

"Yes, my queen," said Idwal.

"Please, please," begged Modwyn. "I freed you. I'm loyal. I'm of your bloodline, your own blood."

She gripped the back of Modwyn's head with one hand and

forced his mouth over her nipple. Modwyn gagged on the putrid fluid, which smelled like the infected flesh of plague victims but tasted far worse. He tried to pull back, but she held him tightly against her breast as she made soft cooing noises. Unable to avoid doing so, he drank—then he gagged.

"What… what of the other soldiers, the ones in the keep?" Idwal asked.

"What keep?" Serina asked.

"Stron's Watch they call it, my queen, near the bay. There's one more Dain there—but just a girl."

"Another Dain?" She tightened her grip on the back of Modwyn's head as he writhed, his lips crushed against her nipple. "How many of those foul Dains can there be?" She sighed. "Just bring me the sword. I'll deal with this keep—and this last Dain-child."

Modwyn winced as blinding pain wracked his body. His spine arched—so forcefully that he feared it would snap—and still she held him tightly, his screams muffled by her breast.

Then the pain grew far, far worse.

Chapter 32

Dilan

Dilan let Gale take him south of the fortress, along the shoreline. As they followed the beach and moved farther away from the fortress, Dilan's horror began to recede, and his thoughts cleared. His shame threatened to crush him. He had fled, leaving his comrades to Serina and her ghouls. *What kind of a man am I?* He had fled after Prophet's Bridge as well, but that had been different, he told himself—he had had no choice then. *Is it any different this night?*

The old warriors had described an overwhelming aura of terror that had always surrounded Serina—the Dread. Only Stron, with Sight-Bringer's help, had been able to stand against her, encouraging others to do the same. He didn't know if he had experienced that same Dread, but Dilan had never—not ever—felt such soul-crushing fear as he had earlier that night. At the time, it had felt like someone else had run away and he had been a helpless prisoner in his own body.

Whether it was foul magic or not, he had still run away, leaving the others to their fate, and he was alone on a hostile island. *What now? Stron's Watch.* He needed to get back, to warn the others, the men they had left behind to garrison the fort. Serina would be coming for them next.

He let Gale move along the shoreline. He knew he would've made better time along the old road, but he never would've found it in the dark. Besides, if he rode cross-country at night, he risked injuring Gale, which would leave him on foot. At that point, the shoreline was the best path.

Looking back over his shoulder, he stared at the dark fortress on the cliffs, growing smaller. The waves crashed against the beach, flowing in and then receding, casting cold mist into the dark night. The smell of salt washed away the stench of dead flesh but could do nothing to clear his inner turmoil. Serina Greywynne, the legendary necromancer and blood fiend, was alive and free.

What fools we were, thinking we could come back to this haunted place. We woke her.

As he rode, he rummaged through the patrol bag. As expected, it was packed for a single day of scouting, no more. Inside the bag, he found a waterskin, some dried fish, flint and stone, several torches for night patrols, and a short length of rope. However, the bag contained no weapons, and that was his greatest concern. He had no way to defend himself.

Fall was coming. Already, the days and nights were getting colder, but all he had to wear were his pants, undertunic, and boots. When the sun rose, he was certain he could once again find the old road and follow it into the Feldwyn Swamp again, but he knew he would have to face the ticks alone.

I'll never make it.

He figured he could follow the shoreline south and then west all the way around the island to reach Stron's Watch and Port Eaton, but doing so would take a week if it were even possible at all. A wall-like ridge of jagged hills cut across the island's interior to the southeast. If he could find a pass over them, he'd cut his travel distance down considerably and still come out near Port Eaton. The expedition couldn't have come that way before, not with the wagons, but maybe a single man on horseback could. If he could get over the hills, he'd be back at the fort within a day or two. Then he could—

He yanked back on Gale's reins. Just ahead, a dark shadow lay across the sand. In the ghastly red glow of the moon, he hadn't seen it until he was almost upon it—it was a body, lying near the water's edge, the waves edging closer.

A spasm of fear coursed through him, and he steered Gale away from it, farther up the beach. Whoever it was, it wasn't his problem. *Best I stay away, stay alive to warn the others.* He made it another twenty paces before he sighed and turned Gale about.

"A quick look, that's all," he told the horse. "We'll be careful."

As he rode closer, he saw the man lying facedown in the sand was dressed as he was—in pants, boots, and a padded undertunic designed to be worn beneath ring mail. Then, the figure moved, rolled over, and groaned. Dilan tensed, fearing an ambush, but long moments passed with nothing happening. Something glinted in the sand next to the man—a longsword. Dilan waited, but the man didn't move again.

Climbing down from Gale, Dilan moved closer, still holding Gale's reins, ready to mount and flee at a moment's notice. Whoever the man was, Dilan guessed it was probably one of the Wolfrey men-at-arms. *But how did he get here?* Dilan glanced back. The fortress and the cliffs upon which it sat weren't that far away. The man could have stumbled out of the fortress just as Dilan had. If the man had been wounded, perhaps that was as far as he could make it. *Help him, you gutless coward,* Dilan admonished himself. Kneeling down in the wet sand, Dilan grasped the man's soaked shoulder and turned him over onto his back.

Owen. It's Owen. How is this possible?

Owen had been on duty clearing the entrance to the Great Crypt. Placing his ear next to Owen's mouth, Dilan heard him breathing and felt the moisture of the other man's breath on his ear. He didn't see any wounds, but he couldn't be sure under the moon's eerie red glow. His confusion grew when he stared at the longsword lying beside Owen. In the moon's light, the blade seemed to glow crimson. It was unlike any sword he had ever seen. The handle was a carved white figure of a woman with her arms outstretched. As he gripped the white handle to examine the weapon, a wave of energy coursed up his arm, causing him to drop the sword and fall back onto his ass in astonishment. Pushing himself up on his elbows, he stared in disbelief at the weapon and then at his still-tingling fingers. The sword's touch hadn't hurt him so much as surprised him. In fact, it had felt refreshing. *What could possibly—*

A flash of insight cut through him, sending shivers down his spine. *This is Sight-Bringer.*

Owen moaned, and his eyes opened. He reached out for Dilan, grasping his forearm, but his grip was weak. "Serina…" he managed. "She's free."

Dilan sighed. "I know."

Owen closed his eyes again, his head falling back once more.

"I know," Dilan repeated.

Chapter 33

Danika

Danika tosses in her sleep. Her breathing quickens as cold sweat drenches her skin. Earlier, she was dreaming of Brice, of the way he looked at her the last time they were alone. Then, the dream changed. He's with her now but sitting on the edge of her bed, his naked back to her, his head in his hands as his broad shoulders shake. Is he crying? *Moonlight pours through her bedchamber window, spilling across the room, coloring everything silver. Sitting up, she reaches for her lover and wraps her arms around his neck.*

His skin is ice.

She jerks away as he turns to her, his eyes filled with soul-shattering sorrow.

"My love," he says as he reaches for her hands, holding them tightly in his frigid grip.

"Brice, what's wrong?"

"I love you. I will always love you." Tears run down his cheeks and freeze solid.

She tries to pull back, to get away—his fingers are so cold. Gasping in pain, she sees her own breath before her eyes—but no moisture comes from her lover's mouth.

"I love you," he repeats, softly, an ocean of sadness.

Fear grips her heart. Something is wrong here. She pulls harder, but he won't let her go. "Brice, you're hurting me," she whimpers.

"You should have gone with me," he says. Now, blood pools over his teeth, painting them red. His eyes have also turned completely red. She screams—

And bolted upright in bed, instantly fully awake. She was alone—Brice wasn't with her, wasn't dead. She pressed her palm against her sweaty breast, holding it tightly against her pounding heart. Pain shuddered through her but receded almost immediately as relief washed it away.

"Just a dream," she whispered to herself, closing her eyes. *It was only a dream. Brice is with Palin—far from me but safe. Thank the Craftsman.*

When she opened her eyes again and saw the moon outside her open window, she gasped.

The moon, full and bright, was the color of blood.

#

After breaking her night's fast, Danika found herself before the closed door leading to the office chambers of Wendel Dert. She rapped on the door, and following a pronounced wait, heard him call out for her to enter. When she opened the door, Dert was bent over his desk, writing.

When he glanced up, a flicker of annoyance passed through his small eyes. "My lady, can I be of service?"

"I was looking for Father Cotlas," she said.

"In my chambers, my lady?"

"I'm... I'm sorry. He's not in the fort."

"Well, he's old. I'm sure he couldn't have toddled off too far." He returned his attention to his ledger.

She stood there for a few more moments, fighting down her anger, and then stepped back, closing his door. Every single time she had visited that island with her father, Dert had been like that, full of his own importance. Her father had claimed he was a competent reeve and had served well for decades on that windswept rock, managing the island's affairs, but she knew he had become like a lord, the only real authority on the entire island, clearly not used to deferring to anyone.

Still, I am a Dain.

She sighed, moving back down the circular tower stairs. Dert was right, though. Father Cotlas couldn't have gone that far.

#

As Danika entered the fort's stables, still looking for Father Cotlas, she heard Wren, her handmaiden, pleading with somebody, clearly upset. Wren was eighteen and not used to travel or the hard conditions in a fort filled with men. She had been miserable since coming to the island, and more than once, Danika found herself wishing she had left the younger woman back at Castle Dain despite her need for a servant. Appearances mattered, though, and it was unseemly for a lady to travel without a handmaiden. Still, she didn't like the tone she was hearing in Wren's voice. She put her back to the wall of the stable and listened.

"Come on, my little pretty one. I have a young girl like you, and I miss her," a gruff voice said. "Just a quick kiss, and we'll let you go."

"Please leave me alone," said Wren. "You'll get in trouble."

"Think so, do you?" another man asked with a chuckle. "I think not, pretty one. We're not doing anything. You came in here to bother us while we were working. *You'll* get in trouble."

"That's not true," Wren pleaded. "I just wanted to see the horses. I'm sorry. I'll leave."

"I've got something better than a horse for you to see, my little one."

Anger, not fear, coursed through Danika, and she stormed inside the stables, her face dark with indignation. As expected, two of the garrison soldiers had backed Wren into a corner. Tears were running down the young woman's cheeks. *Have these men no shame?* The soldiers in the fort possessed entirely too little respect, and it was beginning to infuriate Danika. *First, Wendel Dert's cavalier attitude toward me, now this outrage?* At Danika's entry, the men spun about, guilt on their faces.

Both men backed away quickly from Wren, lowering their heads in respect. "My lady," they said.

One of them, a particularly ugly brute with a shiny face, said, "My lady, the stables are no place for—"

"If I hear one more word out of either of you, I will have you both whipped and sent to the gaol for a month. You sicken me."

Both men's faces went white, and they stared at their feet.

"Get out now!" Danika said, forcing them to go around her.

Wren rushed forward, buried her face in Danika's shoulder, and began to sob.

Danika patted her back. "It's fine, Wren. It's fine. Some men know no better."

I really should have left her back in Castle Dain.

#

Later, Danika stood alone atop the fort's single tower. She leaned against the battlements, staring out to sea, where a flotilla of small fishing boats bobbed on the water, their brightly colored single sails catching the sun's rays. She smiled as she watched the boats. She had learned to sail there, years before, when she visited with her father. Forts were no place for a teenaged girl, and she had been bored to tears, so a townsman had been found who was willing to teach her how to sail.

Despite the Greywynne islanders' surly reputation, the fisherman had been surprisingly patient with her—and her obligatory guard—explaining that he had already taught his own daughters to sail, "So why not one more lump-headed girl?"

Once out upon the waves, Danika had found a sense of freedom that she had never experienced in the north with all its customs and expectations of appropriate female behavior. There—and throughout the entire Fenyir Islands—women were the equals of men. The civilized Kingdom of Conarck considered the Fenyir clans to be little more than barbarians, but on the islands, a woman could achieve anything a man could—many even fought as warriors alongside the men or skippered their own raiding longships, pirating the merchant vessels traveling along the island chain.

Soft footsteps on the stairs announced the arrival of Father Cotlas, his face white from the exertion of climbing all the way up the tower. She rushed over, took his arm, and led him to a wooden bench, helping him down onto it.

"I should have found *you*, Father," she said.

He waved his spotted hand at her. "I'm old, not dead. I can still climb stairs." He coughed, and she patted his back. After some moments, his coughing eased, and he nodded. "You wanted to talk to me, my lady."

She opened her mouth, paused, and then bit her lower lip, suddenly realizing how pointless talking to Father Cotlas about her dreams would be. *I shouldn't have bothered him.*

"Come, come, my lady, you can talk to me. I'm a priest of the

Craftsman. You can tell me anything." He patted her hand, sliding over on the bench and making room for her.

She sat beside him, gathering her thoughts, feeling foolish in the bright light of the day. "Father, I don't want to waste your time, but… I had a bad dream last night."

He nodded. "You're not the only one, not after that business with the moon. That's why I was out of the fort. The locals are terrified—feel it must mean something."

"What do you think? Have you ever seen such a thing?"

"I didn't see it last night. I was sleeping. But a long time ago, I saw something like it… once," he said softly, looking away toward the forest.

"When was that?"

"How old are you, Danika? Twenty-two?"

She felt a fluttering in her stomach as she recognized the tremor of fear in his voice.

"I'm twenty-five, Father."

He smiled weakly. "Yes, yes, of course you are. I remember when you were born. But you're still just a child, too young to have known the bad days, the days of Serina's rebellion."

"I know her war nearly destroyed us all."

He snorted. "That might be a bit of an exaggeration, but maybe you're right. Who knows where her hunger would have stopped? At any rate, coming back here, looking for the sword, going to her fortress… I fear these actions have stirred up the past."

"What are you talking about?"

"I was with Duke Stron at Roald's Farm when we fought her ghoul soldiers, her undead captains."

"I didn't know that. Were you—"

"On this island, at her fortress? Yes, but I was just a young man. I didn't go down into the catacombs with the others. They were all better, more pious priests than I ever could be." He paused. "But I'm old, and my mind wanders. I was talking about Roald's Farm, where we first managed to stand against her—to win.

"We were all terrified. We had heard the stories... about her being a necromancer, that she could raise the dead. It was all true. That night, her army of ghouls attacked." He shivered, trembling at the memory. His hands shook so badly that he placed one atop the other to hold it. "It was an army of corpses driven by hatred and malice. As they came at us, we felt the Dread of Serina—that soul-numbing fear that always surrounds her. We'd have all turned and fled that night had it not been for your uncle with Sight-Bringer. He was everywhere that night, or so it seemed. Wherever the fighting was the worst, your uncle was there to drive the monsters back. You should have seen him. Ghouls and blood fiends fell before his righteous power."

Father Cotlas's eyes gleamed with the memory. He smiled at her, his whiskers white with age. "We beat her that night—for the first time! We stood our ground and fought her army. That was the beginning of the end for her rebellion. Her blood-fiend captains couldn't stand before that sword, and its holy touch burned the ghouls, sent them back to whatever hell Serina had dragged them from. Her army—defeated for the first time—fell back, and we pursued, chasing them all the way across the Promiscuous Sea.

"You should have seen that army, my lady. The ships filled that bay below us. Even some of her own people among the Fenyir clans joined us. Port Eaton burned that night. Then, we pushed her back all the way to her dark fortress, destroying her there. Well... you know that tale, how only your father survived the confrontation, may Father Craftsman keep his soul."

"But what does this have to do with last night, the moon?"

Father Cotlas was silent for long moments. When he finally spoke, his words were barely a whisper. "Nothing, my lady, nothing at all. I'm old, and my mind wanders to the past."

"Father, what aren't you telling me?"

He sighed and bit his lower lip.

"Please, Father."

He nodded. "The night… that night at Roald's Farm, just before her ghouls came upon us, the moon also turned red."

"That's… what does that mean?"

"Nothing." He patted her hand, smiling weakly. "It means nothing. Last night was probably just a trick of the eye."

"But—"

"Don't worry, child. Your brother and… Your brother will be back shortly. Then, we'll leave this cursed rock behind us. You'll see. All will be well."

Danika forced a smile upon her lips, a weak, fake thing. She stared past Father Cotlas, out at the dark interior of the wood line.

Be safe, brother. Be safe, my love. Come back to me, both of you.

I'll leave with you then, Brice. The world be damned, I'll run away with you then.

Chapter 34

Owen

Owen woke to the familiar gait of being on horseback, but he was tied by the wrists to a saddle horn. He jerked in surprise, almost falling off despite the bonds, but a strong hand held him in place.

"Easy, Owen," said Dilan, walking beside him and holding him upright with one hand while carrying Sight-Bringer across his shoulder with the other.

The sun beat down upon Owen, baking his aching head and making it feel as though a donkey had kicked him. He winced in pain, shading his eyes with his hand.

"Dying," he muttered then shivered despite the heat.

"No, you're not." Dilan handed him a sloshing waterskin. "But it was a lucky thing I found you."

Owen took the waterskin and tried to drink but couldn't manage more than a few sips before he started coughing. Dilan took the waterskin back and thumped Owen on his shoulders. When he finally stopped coughing, Owen took in his surroundings. He was sitting on Gale. A length of rope secured him to the saddle, wrapped around his waist, his wrists, and the saddle horn. Owen fumbled with the knot, untying it.

"You kept falling off," Dilan said. "Not sure why people call you Horse-boy."

"It's an insult," Owen muttered, "not a reflection on my riding skill."

"Nor your ability to recognize a joke."

Knee-high grass brushed against his legs. Rolling hill land surrounded them. In the distance ahead, he saw a forested ridgeline, rising like a wall before them. Flies buzzed his pounding head, and his eyelids seemed impossibly heavy. His thoughts were terribly disjointed… but he remembered the Great Crypt and… Serina! He jerked back, almost falling again.

"Where… where are we?" he asked.

Dilan turned, shading his eyes as he walked backward. "Southwest of the fortress. We've been walking since last night, when I found you on the beach near the cliffs… with this." Dilan hefted the sword. "What happened?"

A cold anger burned through Owen's sickness. "Modwyn. Modwyn happened. The effeminate bastard betrayed us, murdered Lord Palin. Fed him to… to *her*. She's alive. Serina Greywynne is still alive."

Dilan's face was tight, but he didn't seem surprised. "How?"

Owen related the events of the previous night, how Modwyn had poisoned them with his cure for deep vapors and then murdered the young lord. When he got to his own part—how he had fled—his face burned with shame. Dilan said nothing, merely nodding his head in understanding.

They walked in silence for a bit before Dilan spoke again. "She sent the ghouls into the keep—so many corpses, an army of the dead."

"The others?"

Dilan shook his head, staring at the ground.

"Father Craftsman, keep their souls," said Owen.

"There's more," said Dilan. "I was attacked by one of the hunters."

Owen gripped the saddle horn tightly. "They're traitors, too. Idwal killed Fin, cut his throat. They must be working with Modwyn. They must all be serving her."

"*Her,*" repeated Dilan. "Serina Greywynne. It's so impossible to accept, even now, even after seeing her with my own eyes last night."

They walked on in silence, and Owen's throbbing headache receded slowly. When he spoke again, his voice was no more than a whisper. "Dilan, I… I failed them, failed my oath. I ran from her last night, like a coward."

Dilan looked away quickly. "You're no coward. It was the Dread. It emanates from her, like a poison."

"What now?" Owen asked.

Dilan ran his hand through his hair and nodded toward the hills before them. "We cross those, but it won't be easy. We have some water—not much—a bit of food."

"Weapons?"

Dilan hefted the longsword. "This amazing weapon. Did you… feel it?"

"I felt it," said Owen. "I'd be dead if not for its magic."

"It's longer than I'm used to, more like a great sword, but it'll do."

Owen, like all other guardsmen, understood how to use a two-handed sword, as well as other weapons, but his training had focused on sword and shield, spear, and axe. A two-handed great sword was a knight's weapon, intended to either beat down a plate-mail-wearing opponent or batter past pikes. Furthermore, if Sight-Bringer had indeed been crafted by the mysterious, long-dead Illthori—the "precursor race"—then it had not been designed for the use of men at all.

"Why are we headed for the ridgeline?"

"We have to warn the others, but we'd never get through the swamp."

"Can we get over those hills?"

"I think so. They don't look that high."

Owen considered the hills. They certainly weren't anything like the mountains back home, but their summits were still high enough to be cloaked in mist and low-hanging clouds. The slopes looked rough, covered in thick brush and trees. Owen and Dilan were at least an hour's ride away still, but even from there, he could see steep gullies and crevices. A small river or stream must have cut through the range because he saw a valley with thick dark-green vegetation.

"There, I think." Dilan pointed to a crevice between two of the larger hills. "That looks like a pass. We should be able to get through it, maybe even before nightfall."

Owen considered it. "I'm not sure I can manage that today. Maybe we should camp, hunt, recover our strength."

A look of concern flashed through Dilan's eyes, and he glanced behind them. "We can't do that. I think we're being hunted."

"Her?" Owen's fear spiked. Once again, he recalled Serina's bloody hands rising from the corpse pile.

Dilan shook his head. "Men on horses. I saw them briefly earlier. I think it's Idwal and his brothers. Blood fiends can't move about in daylight, or so the legends say."

"You're sure?"

"I'm not sure of anything, Owen."

Owen looked behind them but saw nothing.

"They can't let us go, Owen, not after what they've done, not after freeing… her."

Owen felt his anger build. "They're hunting *us*? We're warriors, not marsh ticks. Let's kill them, take their horses and supplies."

"Don't be the fool the others think you are. There's twice as many of them, and they're mounted—all of them. They'll be moving faster than we are, and they'll have bows. We're tired. You're hurt. I've been walking all morning—and we have one sword." Dilan shook his head. "I've been hunted by men like these before. If we fight them in the open, we'll die."

"What, then?"

"Run, or at least walk as fast as we can and get over those hills. Port Eaton is on the other side and Stron's Watch."

"We can't go near Port Eaton. If Idwal has turned traitor, then the rest might have as well."

"Agreed, but we do need to cross those hills."

Owen scooted forward and patted Gale's flank. "Okay, then, get on. Gale can carry two, at least for a bit."

Gale, bless his sturdy heart, didn't so much as whicker in protest, and riding double, the two men headed for the ridgeline and safety.

Chapter 35

Idwal

Idwal pulled on his horse's reins. He raised his hand, motioning his brothers to stop as well. They rode across the low ground, avoiding the heights, not wanting to spook their prey. The two men they hunted were doing the same, so they likely realized they were being tracked, for all the good that would do them. Idwal and his brothers didn't know that part of the island, but they could follow two men and a horse easily enough. They were getting closer. Their prey was not that far ahead, near the base of the hills, where the forest grew thicker.

So they're trying to cross the hills and come out near Port Eaton, Idwal mused.

Idwal ground his teeth, determined not to let them get away. With only one horse, the soldiers could either ride together—and tire the animal out—or take turns riding and move at the speed of a walking man—either way, Idwal and his brothers were going to catch them soon. Once they were close enough, they'd bring them down with arrows and take the sword back to the queen. He felt giddy with excitement, like a little boy, when he thought about giving the sword to her.

The queen lives. It's amazing, impossible, a miracle.

Once, she had brought their people to the brink of conquest over the mainlanders—only Stron the Butcher and his foul blade had stopped her, a blade Idwal would present to the queen.

Perhaps, he mused, the gods hadn't wanted her free all those years—at least not until a strong enough leader had emerged among the people, one ready to lead the islanders and other Fenyir clans to conquest and glory—a leader like Idwal. He was a modest man, a humble, pious man, but he knew he would rise to the occasion. Perhaps in time, she would even make him like her, immortal. All he had to do was kill two northern dogs and bring her a sword. Running his fingers over the wooden beads braided into his beard, he smiled and then spat into the high grass.

He would have killed them for nothing.

Chapter 36

Owen

Owen walked beside Gale, with Dilan just behind him. The powerful colt had brought them both to the base of the hills but couldn't carry them up the rising incline. As Owen looked up the incline, the wind gusted behind them, carrying with it the unmistakable neighing of a horse. Both men turned and stared.

How close was that?

Thick brush and trees along the base of the hills surrounded them. They had made good time over the vale's hills, but from there, the journey was going to be rough—a hard uphill slog. Dilan stepped away, approaching a massive oak tree, its limbs long and gnarly, like grasping arms. Several of the thick branches reached almost to the ground. Standing behind one the width of his wrist, Dilan pulled it back, straining with it for several feet. When he released it, the branch whipped back into place with a resounding crack, throwing leaves through the air. Returning to grab Gale's reins, Dilan led the animal past the oak, shuffling his feet in the dirt.

Owen stared at the obvious tracks. "Dilan, no one's that stupid."

Ignoring Owen, Dilan removed the rope from Gale's saddle and ran back to the branch. He fumbled with the rope, unraveling its weaves, untwisting the smaller narrow lengths so that they soon resembled knotted hair. Then, using Sight-Bringer to hack off a branch the length of his forearm, Dilan held it between his thighs and used the longsword to shave off its end, creating a wicked point. He held it up and raised a thick eyebrow, utterly unconcerned that he had just used one of the kingdom's holiest treasures to chop wood.

Owen shook his head. "It won't work. They'll see it."

"It'll work. They know we're close. They'll want to kill us and be done with it."

Using the unraveled weaves of rope, Dilan lashed the pointed stick to the tree branch he had tested earlier, tying it at a right angle.

"They'll see it," Owen said.

Dilan braced himself against the branch. "Hurry." He pointed at the branch. "Use those muscles."

Together, they forced the branch back and tied it in place with a slip ring, with one of the unraveled weaves extending back across the trail as a trigger. Dilan paused and listened, staring back into the trees behind them. He wiped the sweat from his eyes before yanking several handfuls of grass and very carefully setting them over portions of the twine.

Owen could still see the twine, but he had to admit the grass did break up its outline. "They'll still see it," he repeated.

"No, they won't." Dilan ripped a strip from the hem of his gray undertunic and carefully placed it on a branch on the other side of the trap at shoulder height. Then, he stepped back and appraised his work, clearly pleased with himself.

Owen grabbed Gale's reins, and they climbed the steep terrain. At any moment, he expected to feel an arrow in his back. They should stand and fight, he knew, while they still could. Dilan was going to get them both killed.

The hunters are going to see the trap.

Chapter 37

Idwal

Idwal stopped his mount, climbed down, and examined the ground. The tracks were fresh. The two men had dismounted some time before, to walk their horse. The animal must have been nearly exhausted, and the men wouldn't be in much better shape. The hunt would soon be over. His eyes narrowed as he examined the trail. Likely, they were terrified, knowing they were running out of time. The ground was churned, as if they had gone over it several times.

Why?

His lips pursed as he stood back up, hands on his hips, surveying the terrain around him. One of his brothers, Hyrol, eighteen years old, ran up next to Idwal, leading his horse by the reins, excitement in his bright eyes.

"There." Hyrol pointed with his hunting bow and ran past Idwal.

Squinting, Idwal saw something indeed hung from a branch, not twenty feet away, in the direction the two soldiers were traveling. After a moment, he recognized the piece of fabric, as if one of the soldiers had caught his shirt and, in his flight, had ripped it loose.

Idwal didn't hunt men—he hunted marsh ticks and other game—but he was no idiot. Pieces of clothing don't just rip free.

"Wait!" he yelled. "Don't—"

Hyrol looked over his shoulder, confusion on his nearly beardless face. At that moment, something heavy rushed forward from the path ahead, whipping through the air and dislodging a storm of leaves. Hyrol squealed like a pig as a heavy branch struck him. His horse screamed and bolted away, but Hyrol hung bent over the branch, his intestines hanging out of his back from the spike that had impaled him.

Idwal stared at Hyrol, a coldness rising from his core. "No!" he finally managed, running toward his youngest brother as his other brothers cried out in concern behind him.

Hyrol, still living, tried to turn his head. Idwal leaned around his younger brother, hugging him. Irdlin and Agastor joined him, their faces white. Hyrol tried to speak but instead only spat up a gout of blood. Examining the wound, Idwal knew in a moment it was mortal. No man could survive such a horror.

"Don't… don't let me… don't." His brother grasped at him, his fingers surprisingly strong, but then, Hyrol had always been a strong lad.

He screamed as they pulled him free, blood spraying from the wound, the size of a man's fist, through his torso. They laid him out on the blood-soaked ground and waited with him. Idwal held Hyrol's hand in both of his while Hyrol whimpered and begged, asking for their long-dead mother. When the lad's breathing, wet and strained, finally stopped, it was almost a relief.

Idwal closed his brother's dead eyes. His frustration and loss burned away in a fiery rage. This is *my* fault. I should have expected something like this. The two men were dangerous, having killed three of his brothers. He saw his hatred mirrored in the faces of his two surviving brothers, Irdlin and Agastor. They were going to do far worse than just kill these men.

“We go slower now,” Idwal said. “More carefully.”

Agastor gazed down upon Hyrol’s corpse. They had always been close. “We can’t just leave—”

Idwal leaned in and grasped the back of Agastor’s neck, pulling him in close so their foreheads touched. “Brother, we will come back and honor him. Now, we kill his murderers. We avenge him.”

Agastor gritted his teeth and acquiesced.

Idwal glared at the trees ahead of them. The two men weren’t going to get far. He wasn’t going to just kill them, he was going to skin them alive and use their flesh to make a sheath for the longsword—a fitting gift for his queen and a tribute to his dead brothers.

Chapter 38

Owen

Owen leaned into the slope, breathing heavily, concentrating on placing one foot ahead of the other. Thick foliage surrounded him, but he knew the hunters were still coming. Surprisingly, Dilan's trap must have worked after all, because they had heard a man screaming in pain a while back. He hoped it would slow them down enough to allow him and Dilan time to get over the pass.

Maybe it'll just make them angrier.

The sun was directly overhead, baking them. Dilan had chosen their path well, and they were most of the way up the pass. The climb, though, was exhausting, far steeper than it looked from a distance. He needed to stop soon, or he wasn't going to last much longer, but he knew he couldn't. If he fell behind, they'd catch him. He no longer wanted to stand and fight. Dilan had been right. He was in no condition to make a stand, especially out there in the open, with only one weapon between the two of them. Gripping Gale's saddle, he let the strong animal pull him along, with Dilan leading the way, trying to find the easiest path.

"Dilan," Owen wheezed. "How… how much farther?"

Dilan moved back and stared into Owen's face. "Drink," he said, thrusting the nearly empty waterskin into Owen's hands.

Owen shook his head. "Almost empty."

"Drink," Dilan repeated. "We're nearly at the summit. Then, it'll all be downhill."

Owen drank the last of the water, almost immediately feeling some strength return, but he could have drained a river, he was so thirsty. He kept going, slowly but inexorably forward, with Gale pulling him along. The black colt was heroically strong. Owen knew they wouldn't have made it that far without him.

Then, like magic, they came out over the top of a sloping, bush-covered ridge and saw the sea, the bay, and the smoke rising from cook fires in Port Eaton. "Thank the Craftsman." Owen leaned against Gale. "How much farther do you think?" he asked.

Dilan paused as he looked out over the descending terrain. "Hard to say. But we should reach the base before nightfall."

"Can we rest for a bit? I'm exhausted."

Dilan glanced back the way they had come and then shook his head. "Have to keep going, make Stron's Watch. I haven't seen or heard anything, but—"

Gale screamed and reared up, knocking Owen down. Something flashed past his face, leaving a hot burn on his cheek, and his fingers came away from his face bloody. Gale staggered to the side several steps then collapsed onto his flank, wheezing in agony, an arrow shaft jutting from his throat. Owen, climbing to his feet, stared at the horse in confusion, but Dilan tackled him, throwing him to the ground behind the wounded horse. More arrows hit the animal. Gale screamed and tried to rear up but couldn't.

The hunters had caught up to them.

Dilan crawled forward, snatched the patrol bag from Gale's

saddle, and crawled back to Owen, dragging the bag with him. He cast a frantic gaze at Owen. "We have to run. We need to get some distance, or they'll just move around, find an angle to hit us."

Owen shook his head, trying to reach out for Gale.

"Owen!" Dilan yelled. "He'll be dead soon enough. Can you run?"

Owen stared at Gale, whose large black eyes were clearly in agony. "Give me the sword," he told Dilan.

"Owen!"

"The sword," he repeated, holding his hand out.

Shaking his head, Dilan handed him Sight-Bringer. The moment Owen touched its hilt, power and energy flowed into him, revitalizing him. He crawled forward, up to the dying horse, not worried for an instant that the animal, maddened by pain, might kick at him.

"I'm sorry, Gale. You were a noble horse." Owen placed the blade against the horse's throat and cut it open.

Hot blood sprayed in his face, and Gale thrashed and shrieked once and then lay silent, the light of life gone from his eyes. Dilan was there a moment later, prying the sword from Owen's bloody fingers. The moment he took it back, weariness rushed back into Owen.

"Can you run?" Dilan asked.

"Yes, but it has to be now."

"Let's go!"

Dilan stumbled to his feet and sprinted, bent over, carrying both the sword and the patrol bag. Owen followed but stumbled and fell to his knees. As he pushed himself back up onto his feet, another arrow thudded into the earth inches from his fingers. He ran, gasping and wheezing, after Dilan.

#

Owen wheezed, unable to catch his breath. His cheek throbbed as blood ran down his face. With the hunters right behind them, they couldn't stop long enough to try and staunch the bleeding. He could only concentrate on keeping up with Dilan.

The mountain pass they made their way down cut back and forth around rock outcroppings. High craggy rock faces lined with boulders and thick bush dominated the terrain. Near the foot of the pass, a narrow stream cut its way across a tree-filled gorge. The slope was treacherous, with loose rocks and shale. Several times, both men slipped and skidded before managing to stop. The trail would be worse for their pursuers on horseback, Owen knew. The problem, though, was that on horseback, they weren't going to tire—Owen and Dilan were.

Dilan, moving faster than Owen, had gotten farther ahead again. Owen couldn't maintain the pace much longer, he knew. Suddenly, he was lying on his stomach, his face skidding against the rocks. He lay there, unable to move. A moment later, Dilan knelt next to him, helping him up into a seated position. Dilan held him by the shoulders, looked behind them, and then examined Owen's face.

"It's a deep gash," Dilan said. "But it should heal. You'll need stitches, and won't be so handsome anymore."

Owen tried to laugh, but only an unhealthy squeak slipped past his lips. "Can't… can't… keep going," he finally stammered.

Dilan pulled him over behind a boulder so that Owen's back was to it. He then peered around the edge of the boulder. "We can't stay. They'll catch us, flank us. We'll die before I can get close enough to use this cleaver." He hefted Sight-Bringer with one hand.

"If I only had a longbow," Owen said, hearing the slur in his words. "I could—"

"I heard a horse." Dilan turned back to face him. "Can you move?"

"Maybe… maybe I should stay here. You go on. I'll have a bit of a rest—have some words with these bastards." He tried to smile but started coughing instead.

Dilan shaded his eyes with his hand as he examined the valley below. "There's water down there if we can get to it."

Water? He was so thirsty. So close, but he'd never get to it. Then he did laugh, smiling at the irony. "Go… go on."

Dilan frowned at him, his thick eyebrows bunching together. "We're going together, Horse-boy—you and me. This isn't so bad. I've been in worse."

Owen snorted, shaking his head. "Go!"

He shoved at Dilan's arm, trying to push him away, but he had no strength left, and Dilan ignored his efforts, still studying the terrain below them.

"There's a gorge down there," Dilan said, excitement in his voice. "I think I see structures. There's something down there."

"What?"

Dilan gripped Owen's arm and yanked him to his feet. "Move, soldier! You can rest when we get down there. It's not that far." He flashed a smile at Owen. "And it's all downhill."

Despite being certain he couldn't go any farther, Owen did. Somehow, he got back on his feet and staggered after Dilan. Time became a blur of pain and delirium. His only memory was placing one foot before the other and repeating the effort, as in a dream. When they reached the gorge, their arrival came as a surprise. Owen fell to his knees, gasping for air, his chest on fire, his heart ready to burst.

I did it. Oh, Father Craftsman, I did it!

He lay on his side, only vaguely aware that Dilan was stomping about, looking for something. When Owen finally caught his breath again, he saw the gorge was open and wide, clearly excavated by men—a quarry. They were in a quarry. The ground was rocky, the cliff walls orange and red. The dilapidated frames of wooden huts and buildings, long since rotted and collapsed, sat nearby—including what appeared to be an ancient pulley and frame.

Dilan, having moved farther into the quarry, called out to Owen, excitement in his voice. "The stream comes through here. Fresh water, Owen!"

His thirst empowering him, Owen staggered to his feet and stumbled over. As promised, a quickly moving stream flowed past what looked like an old slag heap.

"Is it safe?" He fell to his knees in front of it.

"Safe enough, I'd guess," Dilan said. "It's moving."

Owen filled his hands with cold water, drank deeply, gloriously, and splashed some of it on his cheek. It burned like fire, and he moaned.

"This is the silver mine." Dilan knelt next to Owen and pointed at a cave entrance, overhung by a large shelf of orange rock. "We saw the sign for it just before the swamp. Do you remember?"

He did, but the memory seemed a lifetime before.

Dilan gazed at the cave opening. "Owen, we need to go in there."

Owen stared at it. "How will we see?"

Dilan rooted through the patrol bag and pulled out two torches. He immediately set to the torch with flint and stone, casting sparks at it. The torch, wrapped with pitch and cloth, caught fire with an oily whoosh, casting flames and thick black smoke.

Dilan threw the empty patrol bag down and cast a worried glance behind them. "They'll be here any moment. We have to go now."

Owen stared at the dark opening, an unsettled feeling in his gut. "Is there no other—"

"No. We'll die if we stay out here. Then Serina will move against Stron's Watch. The others will be taken by surprise."

Owen nodded. "Go. I'll be right behind you."

The two men entered the mine.

Chapter 39

Idwal

Idwal and his two brothers sat upon their mounts just outside the mine entrance. The smell of burning pitch was still thick in the air. They must have just missed their prey. *Where did they find a torch?* Idwal wondered. Those two soldiers had the luck of Orkinus, the Sea God himself, but their luck had run out. That was the only entrance in or out of the mine. Idwal leaned over his saddle and spat. His horse skittered back a pace, clearly agitated. Maybe it smelled the blood from the one they had wounded.

"Should have come faster," Irdlin said with a sneer. "Coulda got 'em before they got inside."

"Shut it," snapped Idwal. "We've lost enough kin chasing these two. Horses trip and fall on steep terrain, break legs—maybe they break our necks when we fall with them." Idwal fidgeted in his saddle and then swung a leg over and dropped down onto the ground, still holding his short bow. "They're done. We'll kill 'em in there."

Idwal stared at the mine opening, remembering the last time he had gone in, a long-standing dare among the youth of the island. *I was what… twelve years old? I think I shat myself I was so frightened.*

Agastor joined him. Despite being two years older, Agastor always deferred to Idwal. Bald like an egg, with a long drooping mustache that ran down his chin, Agastor pulled the ends of his mustache, as he always did when worried.

Idwal frowned, feeling his irritation anger rise. "What?"

Agastor paused, staring into the dark mine entrance. "These are soldiers," he said. "They know how to fight."

"They're unarmed," Idwal said.

"Not true," said Irdlin, still sitting on his mount behind them. "They've got the magic sword."

Idwal shook his head. "Not a magic sword. That's just pig-shit lies these mainlanders made up to frighten us. It didn't kill *her*, did it?"

"They say it killed her captains," said Irdlin. "But even if it's just a sword, it's still a sword."

"We've got the range," said Agastor, holding his bow up.

Idwal shook his head. "Might have time to take a shot, might not. There's lot of places to hide in there, low ceilings. Remember?"

"I remember Naildlin lost her boy in there, what, eight years ago? His ghost might still—"

"There are no ghosts in there," snapped Idwal, "just two half-dead Wolfrey soldiers. They're in there now, hiding, shivering in their own piss. We're going to go in there after them and finish them. Then… then I'll bring her back the sword."

"We," said Agastor. "*We'll* bring it to her."

"We'll bring it to her," said Idwal. "That's what I meant."

"Why don't we just wait here?" asked Irdlin. "There's no other way out. Going in after 'em is stupid."

Idwal shook his head and ran his fingers over his receding red hair. "She won't want to wait. She's been waiting too long as it is. No way I'm making her wait anymore. There's a reckoning coming to these mainlanders, for all their murdering, stealing, and raping. It starts now."

Agastor bit his upper lip and grunted. Irdlin climbed down from his mount and ran his fingers over his hand axe and hunting knife, as if to check they were still there.

"You carry the torch," Idwal told Irdlin. Then, he met Agastor's gaze. "We come behind, with arrows nocked. If you get a shot, take it. Don't let them get close enough to use the sword."

Agastor, silent as always, watched with hooded eyes before nodding.

Once they lit their torch, the three brothers entered the mine.

Chapter 40

Owen

The catacombs beneath Greywynne Fortress had been narrow and confining, but the silver mine was far worse. Several times, Owen had to turn sideways to follow Dilan down particularly narrow passages. Dilan held the burning torch at arm's length ahead of them, the torch's flickering flames casting moving shadows, adding to Owen's unease.

They had only come a short way into the mine, but Owen was already worried they'd have trouble finding their way out again. None of its passages seemed to make any sense. Short, random tunnels led off in all directions. Perhaps the miners had followed the silver veins, or perhaps they were just digging at random, hoping for a hit. Several times, they even came upon openings in the tunnel floor, leading down. Some of those openings still had remnants of wooden ladders in them. Without the torch, they'd likely have fallen in and broken their necks. *This must be what it's like to be inside a giant anthill.* All along the passages, at regular intervals, were small niches, little shelves dug into the walls, each the size of his hand.

Owen ran his fingertips over the surface of one of the niches. It was slick with old wax.

"Candles," Dilan said from just in front of him, the torchlight flickering over his features.

"What?"

"They put candles in there and then stood in the same spot all day, holding tiny rock hammers, slowly chipping away and looking for silver, sometimes finding nothing at all."

"How do you know that?"

"Remember Shabsil, the man from this island, in the Rams?"

Owen inclined his head, staring at the hammer marks along the wall.

"Generations of his folk toiled in here, making the Greywynnes rich—before it finally ran dry. I think that's why Shabsil joined the Rams. He didn't want to spend his days fishing."

"So he fought alongside men he hated?" Owen asked.

"Men fight for all kinds of reasons, Owen. Some for adventure, some for money—some just 'cause they like the killing."

"Why'd you join the Rams?"

"Because my brother signed up and because I like to eat."

They passed the remains of wheelbarrows and storage bins, long rusted through and falling apart. Farther on, a large pile of rock debris almost completely blocked the tunnel where a portion of the ceiling had collapsed. They managed to climb over the rocks and continue on their way, but Owen worried the rest of the tunnel would collapse. As he dropped down from the rock pile, he saw Dilan was down on one knee, examining something. Owen came closer and saw the mummified corpse of a child, no more than seven or eight. The body appeared to have been a boy's.

"May Father Craftsman bless him," said Owen. "Must have gotten lost. What a terrible way to die, all alone in the dark."

Dilan, his gaze somber, reached out and traced his fingertips over the child's mummified eyes, the lids forever closed. "May whatever gods you worshiped keep you safe on your journey, little one."

They moved on, Owen growing increasingly uneasy, a prickling in his scalp. He desperately wanted to leave that place, to get back out into the fresh air and sunshine. He was getting sick of being underground—first the catacombs, then that place.

Several minutes later, the tunnel opened into a large cavern, the first natural cave they had seen in the mine. Then, a stench hit Owen like a punch in the face—acrid and revolting. Dilan extended the torch into the cavern. Long and wide, it was at least a hundred feet across. Its floor was a natural depression completely filled with dark, stagnant water. The top of the cavern was high above them, just barely visible in the weak torchlight. Massive stone pillars, looking like icicles, hung down from the ceiling, with water slowly dripping from their points into the pool and casting ripples across the dark water. Something fluttered above them—and a cold sweat coated Owen as he realized the shadows in the ceiling were moving—thousands of bats, hanging upside down, swayed softly back and forth.

And what is that sound, that chittering—"Father's breath!" Owen jumped away from the cavern's entrance.

The stone floor around the pool was alive with crawling insects, each the size of his thumb, looking like a cross between a cricket and a spider.

"It's all right." Dilan swept the torch back and forth near the ground, scattering the insects. "They're cave crickets, harmless… I think."

Owen glared at them. "You think?"

"Look," said Dilan, pointing with his torch across the pool "There's another opening, another tunnel, on the other side of the pool." He met Owen's gaze. "This is good. This'll do."

Chapter 41

Idwal

Holding aloft a torch, Irdlin led the way, and Idwal followed closely behind. In the narrow passage was only room for one man to walk at a time, so his older brother Agastor took up the rear, but both Agastor and Idwal held their short bows before them, an arrow notched but not drawn. In those close confines, they'd likely have time to loose only a single arrow, and then they'd be fighting hand-to-hand with the axes—but axes might do better than a longsword in those narrow tunnels.

Gods damn these shit-streaked mainlanders! Why didn't they die in the fortress like the rest of their mates?

"Look." Irdlin pointed at a small corpse leaning back against the wall.

Idwal sighed, his shoulders drooping. "Naildlin's boy—must be. Saur, was it?"

"Aye," said Agastor in a monotone voice. "Why didn't we find him before?"

"Never came this far," said Idwal. "This mine is a maze, goes on much farther than you'd think."

"Should we… should we do something?" Irdlin asked.

"Later." Idwal reached down and touched the dead boy's forehead. The skin felt like leather, and Idwal shuddered. "We'll come back and take him from this place, bury him properly."

"Shit way to go," said Irdlin.

Agastor snorted. "Ain't no good way."

"We'll come back for you, lad," said Idwal. "Give your ma some peace."

They moved on, watching for signs. Their prey left little marks on the rocks, the occasional scuff mark or boot print, but Idwal could still smell the oily pitch of their torch. At each intersection, he would go out alone and sniff each tunnel, never failing to find the one the two soldiers had taken. He smiled. The smoke smelled fresher, still hanging in the air. They had almost caught up to the two soldiers. He motioned for Irdlin, still holding the torch, to go first.

As his brother passed by, Idwal gripped his shoulder and whispered into his ear. "We're almost on them. When you see them, drop down on your belly. We'll loose our arrows over you."

Irdlin's eyes grew large, and his lip trembled. "Are you—"

"Just do it."

Irdlin nodded and moved on, more cautiously.

Soon now, thought Idwal. *Very soon.*

#

Irdlin reached the cavern entrance first. He paused and thrust his torch down near his feet, jumping back when he saw a living carpet of insects near the edge of the cavern pool. Idwal came up just behind him, trying to see over his shoulder.

"Gods-damned… ugly… stupid… gross… things," stammered Irdlin as he stamped at the ground, smearing several of the large cave crickets across the rocks.

"Calm down, you idiot," said Idwal. "They're just bugs. They won't hurt you."

Agastor snorted. "Ain't marsh ticks, boy."

"It's a sinkhole," said Idwal.

Irdlin turned to glare at his brothers then looked back over the pool-filled cavern. "Look! There they are," he cried out, pointing across the cavern.

Idwal's eyes narrowed as he saw a glow of torchlight fluttering from another opening on the other side of the cavern. The two men must have just crossed the pool and were only paces away, down the other tunnel.

"Come on," said Irdlin as he stamped out into the pool, the water rising to his knees.

"Wait, fool!" snapped Idwal, reaching out for him, but the other man was already out of reach. Idwal exchanged an exasperated look with Agastor and stormed off after Irdlin. Agastor followed.

They were halfway across the sinkhole when one of the soldiers—the one with the sword—jumped out from behind a boulder and started yelling like a fool, swinging the huge sword about in the air. Idwal drew his arrow back, but suddenly the ceiling attacked them, falling upon them in a storm of wings and wild shrieks.

Chapter 42

Owen

When Dilan attacked, yelling and frightening the bats, Owen paused only long enough for the creatures to swarm the hunters. Then, pins and needles stabbing through his legs, he stumbled to his feet from where he had been hiding behind a column of rock and rushed out at the men, coming at them opposite Dilan. In his right hand, he gripped a large stone the size of his fist.

Within the storm of bats, he had difficulty finding a target at first, but one of the hunters held a torch and was waving it wildly about, shrieking in fear. Owen, covering his face with his forearm, moved through the bats toward the man. Bats smashed into him, shrieked, and flapped away.

From the other side, Dilan came at the distracted men, swinging the longsword in both hands. He severed one man's outstretched arm at the elbow, slicing right through his short bow at the same time. Then he took the man's head off with the reverse cut.

The man with the torch staggered toward Owen, terror in his eyes. Owen slammed his shoulder into him, knocking him back into the water. The torch went out with a hiss, and the cavern went black, with the only light glowing from the opposite tunnel opening where they had left their torch propped up against the rock wall. Ignoring the bats, Owen dropped on top of the man and hammered down at his face with the rock. He connected solidly, hearing the crunch of the man's face under the impact. The man yelped once, almost in surprise, and Owen hit him again and again and again.

Strong arms grabbed him from behind, pulling him off his foe. Owen spun and flailed out with the rock, just missing the new attacker.

"Owen, stop! It's Dilan. Stop!"

In his rage, Owen took several deep breaths before being able to gain control of himself once more. His eyes adjusted to the dim light, and he could just make out Dilan's face.

"It's over. We've won."

"They're all dead?"

"No. One ran." Dilan moved away, picking Sight-Bringer out of the water where he must have dropped it when he pulled Owen off the dead hunter. Then, Dilan stalked off down the far tunnel. As he turned away, Owen saw an arrow jutting from Dilan's left shoulder. Moments later, Dilan was back with the torch, which sputtered weakly.

"You're hurt," Owen said.

"Later. You?"

"No… no, I… don't think so."

Owen gazed down at the man he'd been fighting, but his face was beneath the water. Owen wasn't sure he wanted to see what he'd done to him.

Horse-boy, good for nothing but breaking bones.

Dilan splashed through the pool, retracing their steps. "We need to get outside again before the torch goes out on us."

Owen stumbled after his friend. Behind them, the bats still shrieked, the sound of their flapping wings chasing after them.

#

When Owen and Dilan emerged from the silver mine, their torch was little more than a smoking stump, but they were out. Owen inhaled deeply, grateful for the fresh air and grateful to be alive. He shielded his eyes from the glaring late-afternoon sun. Three horses, small mountain ponies, were tied to a nearby tree. The animals stamped nervously at the sight of the two men, the smell of fresh blood still on them. Owen went to them quickly, calming them, speaking in a reassuring voice.

Dilan paused, his face white as he looked over his left shoulder at the arrow still jutting from it. Owen moved back to help Dilan sit down on a rock. Then, he examined the wound. The arrow protruded from the flesh at the back of his shoulder, which was bleeding around the shaft, but not too heavily. It had buried itself in the muscle—as good a location as any for an arrow wound, but all arrow wounds were bad, always creating internal injuries. If anyone pulled the projectile free, Dilan would start bleeding heavily. Owen went to the hunters' horses and dug around in their saddlebags until he found some jerky and water. Returning to Dilan, he gave him the waterskin first.

Dilan nodded in gratitude, his face flushed with sweat, and drank deeply. "How bad?"

"Just a small puncture," said Owen. "Almost nothing."

Dilan snorted, shaking his head. "Right."

"Can't do anything about it here. We need to get to the fort, get some real help."

Dilan took a bite of jerky and chewed it slowly, as if the effort was almost too much, and then swallowed.

"Can you ride?" Owen asked, gazing out over the forested land before them. They were close to Port Eaton. Owen could even see the gleam of the white walls of Stron's Watch, high up on the hill overlooking the town. "We're just southeast of the keep, maybe an hour's ride, maybe less."

"Do I have any choice?" Dilan asked, his head dropping to his chest.

Owen knelt down in front of his friend and looked into his face. "You've kept me going, Dilan. Now I need you to focus as well. We're almost there."

Dilan nodded weakly. Owen took Sight-Bringer from Dilan's weak grip and helped him climb atop one of the ponies. Mounting another pony, he took the reins of the last animal and led them northeast, skirting the edges of Port Eaton, toward Stron's Watch.

#

By the time Owen led Dilan up to the gatehouse of Stron's Watch, a small group of men were waiting for them, including Keep-Lieutenant Sayer. Three guardsmen stood beside Sayer, each carrying a spear. Sayer's eyes narrowed as he watched Owen climb down from his pony, leaving the wounded Dilan mounted. During the ride around Port Eaton to the fort, Dilan's condition had worsened, and he had swayed in the saddle, his head drooping.

Sayer's gaze went from Owen to Dilan to the longsword thrust through Owen's belt. "What's this then, Toscovar? What are you doing here? Where's the captain?"

"I don't know," Owen said, which was the truth. The last time he had seen Keep-Captain Awde was in the Great Crypt, just before Modwyn murdered Lord Palin. "But I think he must be dead."

Sayer looked as though he'd just been gut-punched. "Dead? What in the Father's name are you talking about?"

Through the open gatehouse, the reeve, Wendel Dert, was rushing over, a scowl on his ruddy face. Behind him, helping the elderly priest, Father Cotlas, was Lady Danika.

"Betrayal," Owen said. "Modwyn and the hunters have betrayed us."

"Truth," mumbled Dilan. "And Serina Greywynne is alive… free."

Sayer's unbelieving gaze darted to Dilan. "What nonsense is this?"

"What's going on?" asked Dert, his face flushed. "Who are these men?"

"Deserters, I'm thinking," said Sayer.

"I'm no damned deserter," said Owen, feeling his face heat.

The three nearby guardsmen exchanged glances with one another and moved closer.

"Lieutenant," said Lady Danika. "What's happened? Why have these men returned? Where is my brother?"

"Get back, my lady," snapped Dert. "These men are deserters. They're dangerous."

She frowned at Dert. "No, of course they're not." Then she saw Sight-Bringer, thrust through Owen's belt. Her eyes widened. "Is that…?"

"Sight-Bringer," answered Father Cotlas as he reached out a trembling hand, letting his fingers trail over the surface of the blade. "I'd never—not ever—forget that weapon. It's been decades since I saw it last, in Stron's hands as he went into the catacombs to kill Serina."

Dert's face reflected his astonishment. "That can't be—"

"May I?" Lady Danika held her hands out.

Owen drew the magnificent weapon and held it before his eyes as he stared at the perfect steel of its blade. Then, he dropped down on one knee and handed the sword, hilt first, to the Lady Danika. *We crossed the sea for this sword, braved the Feldwyn Swamp and its monstrous ticks, and lost so many fine men.* "My lady, Sight-Bringer. Blood Fiends' Bane, the Sword of Justice."

She hesitated, as if also overcome by the moment, then reached out and gripped the hilt in both hands. As she did, her eyes widened in astonishment, and she took a sudden deep breath. "It *is* Sight-Bringer." Then, she looked from the sword to Owen and then Dilan. "Your friend is hurt."

At that, Dilan slumped forward, against his pony's neck. Owen rushed to catch him, but one of the guardsmen rammed the butt of his spear into Owen's gut, knocking him to his knees.

"Here now, enough of that," said Lady Danika sharply.

"My lady, please," said Dert. "This is a dangerous matter."

When Owen could breathe again, he glared at the warrior who had struck him and was still standing over him, the spear point near Owen's face. Angry though he was, Owen forced himself to be calm. The situation was a misunderstanding, that was all. The other guards moved to lift Dilan down from the pony, but Dilan fell as they did, and they lay him upon the ground.

Father Cotlas rushed over to help. "I don't know what's happened, but this man needs help."

Lady Danika, still holding Sight-Bringer, turned on Owen. "Where is my brother?" Her voice edged toward panic.

"Your... your brother is dead, my lady," answered Owen. "Murdered by Modwyn. I saw it myself. He used... used your brother's blood to feed Serina Greywynne. She's alive."

Dert barked in laughter, glancing around at the others, incredulity on his shiny face. "Serina Greywynne? That's the best you can do, a ghost story?"

"It's the truth," said Owen. "She'll be here next."

Lady Danika dropped Sight-Bringer, which clanked against the stones of the gatehouse. “Dead?” she whispered, her anguish clear. “And what of Brice… of Keep-Captain Awde?”

Owen sighed. “I think he must be dead as well, my lady—as are all the others. I didn’t see, but my friend…” His eyes darted to Dilan. “My friend was there. Serina sent ghouls to kill them. Only we escaped.”

“My lady, don’t listen to these lies.” Dert moved closer, licking his lips. “Tell her,” he snapped at Sayer, who stood back, clearly confused and overwhelmed.

Sayer’s eyes shifted nervously, but then he nodded. “The reeve is right, my lady. There’s no way the captain is dead. More likely, these two stole the sword and made their way back here. That one”—he pointed at the unconscious Dilan—“was always going to be trouble. I warned the captain about him. What did you two do?”

Tears ran down Lady Danika’s face, and she threw her head back and howled in anguish. Father Cotlas immediately left Dilan and rushed to help her instead. She collapsed against his chest, sobbing and mumbling something about a red moon. Father Cotlas led her away, back into the keep.

Dert glared at Owen then Dilan before bending over and picking up the longsword. He paused, staring in abject wonder at the blade. “This really *is* Sight-Bringer,” he said in a whisper, almost to himself. Then, his gaze snapped back to Owen. “Lieutenant, maybe they’re deserters—maybe they’re not—but until we understand what *has* happened, I want them secured.”

“We didn’t do anything,” said Owen.

As he braced himself to rise, the guard before him moved his spear point closer.

“You have to listen to me,” said Owen. “Serina Greywynne is out there. She’ll come with the night.”

Dert snorted, his eyes filled with contempt. “Serina Greywynne.”

"Wait," said Owen.

"Just you try it, Horse-boy," snarled the guardsman. "Just you try it."

Dert, Sight-Bringer in his hands, walked away, back to the keep's tower.

Part Three:

The Siege of Stron's Watch

Chapter 43

Idwal

By the time Idwal stumbled down out of the hills and arrived at the alehouse in Port Eaton, the sun had long since gone below the horizon. He had failed the queen and failed his brothers. He needed help if he was to retrieve the sword—help from men drinking away their pitiful lives inside that alehouse. The two-story building was the focal point of the town. The men would gather there to drink and complain about fishing, bad crops, and the gods-damned mainlanders that were the root of all their problems.

He hesitated before the entrance, listening to the sounds of the men inside. The last time he had been in there, the others had been angry with him for agreeing to take the mainlanders inland, but that evening, he needed their help. As galling as asking for their help was, the only other option was to return to Serina and admit his failure. He pulled the door open and staggered inside toward the sounds of laughter and conversation—sounds which abruptly died at his entrance.

As always, several dozen men filled the alehouse. The large

common room was poorly lit by candles and the central fire pit. The innkeeper, a fat old fool with a cleft tongue and with a harlot for a wife, stared at Idwal, his eyes dim. Idwal knew how he must have looked, standing there covered in his brothers' blood, gripping his hand axe. He scanned the crowded common room, noting open hostility in many faces. Several men slid aside as Idwal reached the bar, giving him room.

"Something strong," he told the innkeeper.

The man stared at him stupidly for several moments, but when Idwal smashed the side of his hand axe against the bar top, the fool finally moved, pouring several fingers' worth of flame-rot into a clay cup and placing it in front of Idwal. The smell of the alcohol, a local home brew, was almost enough to bring tears to his eyes. Idwal drank it in one swallow then wheezed and coughed as the fiery liquor ran down his throat.

He squinted at the innkeeper. "More."

The innkeeper, still glaring stupidly, poured him some more. Idwal turned to face the rest of the men, silently watching him, including his once-friend, Galvin, the barrel maker, a big ruddy-faced man of middle years with a great shaggy brown beard.

Galvin stepped in front of Idwal. "What's happened, then? Where are your brothers?"

Idwal downed his second cup of flame-rot, which went down only slightly more easily. "Dead."

"All of 'em?" asked Galvin, astonishment in his gravelly voice.

Idwal nodded. Astonished whispers swept through the room.

Rage burned in Galvin's eyes. "This is what comes from taking their silver, from spitting on our laws. The gods have cursed you for leading them there, to her once-home."

Idwal hawked and spat onto the rush-covered floor. "Think so, do ye? No, master barrel maker, *I* haven't been cursed." Idwal let his eyes drift over all of them. "My faith has been *rewarded.* Something wondrous has happened, something we've waited our entire lives for." He let his teeth flash in the dark room, feeling his blood rush through him, reenergizing him. His eyes brimmed with tears as he thought about her. *They don't understand, but they will.*

"You've lost your mind out there, in the wilderness, as well as your brothers," Galvin said.

Idwal laughed. "You understand nothing, man—nothing. *She* lives. I went to bring her back, to free her—and I succeeded! Serina Greywynne once again rules this island!"

Disbelief had a sound, Idwal realized, and it was silence. Some men stared at him in openmouthed disbelief, but others glared with hatred and distrust.

Galvin was the first to speak. "Are you insane, man? What did those mainlanders do to you out there?" Galvin shook his head, not waiting for Idwal to answer. "I've always liked you, man, but you've gone too far this time. You led our enemies to holy ground. You've been damned by the gods for this."

Idwal shook his head. "I saw her. I spoke to her." He pointed at them with his hand axe, using it to punctuate his words. "You all failed her," he shouted, spittle flying from his mouth, "especially all you graybeards that were around when Stron came through! She was never killed, only ever trapped. Abandoned by all you!"

The alehouse erupted into yells and angry accusations, all directed at Idwal. At least four of the old men in the room had been alive when Stron's army had come through, and they led the jeers directed at Idwal, accusing him of lies, of heresy.

"She's alive, you fools!" he yelled, to be heard over their uproar. "She's alive, and she's coming, and she needs you to act like men again, like your fathers once did."

"The moon was red last night!" yelled Starlin Meergs. He was well into his seventh decade, stooped and tired, but he had been a young soldier during Serina's rebellion. As the ruckus quieted, he pushed his way through the others to stand before Idwal, wide-eyed. "I saw it. Saw it with my own eyes: red, just as it were when she raised her ghouls." Spittle ran down his chin into his gray beard as he watched Idwal. "Is it really true? They said… they all said she were dead. Dead."

"It's all true." Idwal reached out and clasped a hand on Starlin's frail shoulder. "She sent the dead from the catacombs—your honored ancestors—to rip the Wolfrey soldiers apart, killed all of 'em, too." He turned to point in the direction of the fort that had sat silent sentinel over them for decades. "Most of the mainland soldiers are already dead and rotting. All that's left alive now is them that hide up on the hill. We need to pull them out, hang them like they hanged your brothers, your fathers, your grandfathers. We need to show the queen that we can still act like men because she's coming, and she's going to finish her war. Glory is coming. Retribution is coming."

Pandemonium and furious jostling swept through the common room again, like a fire. They cried out that Idwal was a liar, shaking their fists at him.

Then, one man, Gars, a gap-toothed cretin of a local sheep farmer, grabbed Idwal by the collar and shook him, yelling, "Liar!" right into his face as he shoved him back against the bar.

Rage pounding in his ears, Idwal smashed his hand axe into Gars's temple, caving it in. The room went deathly silent as Gars fell to the floor, his legs twitching, blood pooling around his head. Then, as if released from a spell, they all rushed in, grabbing Idwal and disarming him. Someone punched him in the gut, taking his breath away, while another yanked out a handful of his hair. He fell to his knees, and someone kicked him in the chin.

Galvin rushed in, roaring and pushing back the others. "Enough!" the large barrel-maker yelled. "Enough of that, I said. That's not our way."

Two men lifted Idwal up, holding his arms behind his back.

"Galvin," Idwal gasped. "Thank you—"

Galvin shook his large bearded head, his eyes hard. "Don't thank me, murderer, we're gonna hang you."

A chorus of agreement resounded through the common room, followed by men rushing forward and spitting in Idwal's face. Rage swept through him, followed by panic. He roared like a lunatic as they dragged him outside into the cold night air. He lashed out, trying to kick at them and tear free, to spit and insult their mothers and their sisters, but he was powerless to resist so many men.

This is happening too fast!

They tied his hands behind his back, painfully. Then, someone else dropped a rope around his neck. He could only scream in rage—kicking and thrashing—as they lifted him up onto a pony, threw the rope over a nearby tree branch, and tied it off to the tree's trunk. His thoughts a whirlwind, he could only stare about himself in disbelief. The queen was alive and free, and those idiots were going to kill him. He would miss seeing her set the mainland on fire. The glory, the revenge he so desperately craved, would go to others—to lesser men.

"Does anyone have anything they want to say before he hangs?" Galvin asked the crowd.

Some yelled more insults, others spat at him, and still others recommended torturing him first. Idwal had grown up with those men, hunted with them, drank and laughed with them. He almost laughed at the irony.

"The moon is red," someone said, almost too softly to hear.

Whoever it was repeated it more loudly. Then others started swearing softly to themselves as they looked at the night sky. Then Idwal saw it, too—a gibbous moon the color of blood.

She's coming.

“I have something to say,” a man called out from behind the crowd, his accent identifying him as a mainlander.

Modwyn Du’Aig—no, Modwyn Du’Greywynne—former physician to the Dain family and once accomplice to Idwal, stepped forward, leading a clearly terrified horse. The animal’s eyes were wild, its flanks so badly scored by countless cuts from Modwyn’s spurs that blood glistened wetly as it dribbled down its flanks. No animal could survive that kind of mistreatment. It would be dead in hours.

“This is none of your business, mainlander,” said Galvin, staring suspiciously at the man and the tortured horse. “We deal with our own here. Go back to your fort.”

“I didn’t come from the fort. I came from Greywynne Fortress—*your* queen’s fortress.” Modwyn’s lips curled into a sneer as he walked past Galvin. The physician was a thin man, somewhat effeminate, but that night, he resonated with dread, and the islanders parted way before him. He stepped in front of Idwal, cocked his head, and squinted as if confused by Idwal’s present circumstance. Then, ignoring Idwal, he put his back to him and faced the angry men.

“Modwyn,” said Idwal, “help me. They don’t believe me. Tell them about the queen.”

Modwyn extended his arms out to the sides, his palms up. “What this man says is true. Serina Greywynne, your rightful queen, is free once more. Rejoice!”

The men stared at one another. Collectively, they turned to Galvin, who stepped forward. “You think us fools? Leave us before you join him.”

“She’s coming, man,” Modwyn said. “She’s coming, and she sent me here to help you find your lost courage. She wants you to take that fort for her.”

Galvin laughed, shaking his head. “Take the fort? It would take an army to capture that fort.”

"Exactly," Modwyn said.

Then, figures approached from the darkness. They had been traveling along the road behind Modwyn, the road that led through the forest to Feldwyn Swamp. A collective gasp ran through the crowd, and several of the men scurried backward. Modwyn's horse bolted away. Idwal took several moments to understand exactly what he was looking at, but when he finally did, a ripple of terror washed through him—scores of dead men, the corpses of the Wolfrey soldiers killed by Serina, approached, forming a ring around the terrified crowd. Their eyes were vacant, black. Many of the corpses were missing limbs, and all still had gaping wounds.

"Rejoice, men of Greywynne Island," said Modwyn. "Your rightful queen Serina Greywynne has returned. Now, all you need do is fight for her. Kill those mainlanders in the fort."

Relief flashed through Idwal as the men at last somberly accepted the truth that Serina had returned. Galvin was the first to drop to his knees before Modwyn, lowering his head to the ground and swearing allegiance. The rest followed almost immediately.

"Modwyn," said Idwal. "Thank the gods you came. Set me free."

Modwyn turned to stare at Idwal with mock puzzlement in his face. "Where is the sword you were sent after, Master Hunter, the one you blamed me for losing?"

"The sword must be in the fort by now. But we can still get it, still bring it to her. We can do this."

"Yes, we can," said Modwyn, resting his hand on Idwal's knee. Then, he raked his fingernails across the pony's flank, ripping through the animal's flesh as if it were paper.

The pony screamed and bolted. Idwal fell, swaying and choking, his vision exploding with lights. His head felt as if it were going to pop off. His last sight was Modwyn's gleeful face as he lifted his bloody fingernails to his lips and licked them.

Chapter 44

Owen

The tower's gaol was cold and damp and stank of mold. Owen stared at the locked wooden door, aware a guardsman was on the other side. Dilan lay on his side on a small cot nearby. Wooden boxes and barrels containing consumables filled the rest of the small stone cell. *The island garrison is so small there can't be that many incidents requiring a cell. On the other hand, Dert seems the kind to overreact, so we'll probably be hanged without a trial.*

Am I joking? he wondered.

The sun had been setting when they arrived at the fort. The old stories said that blood fiends couldn't come out during the daylight. If so, she'd come soon. *Damn Sayer, and damn Dert!* He kicked in the side of a wooden crate, exposing rotting potatoes.

At the noise, Dilan woke, turned, and stared at him in confusion. "What's going on?"

"We're prisoners. Dert thinks we stole the sword and ran away."

Dilan's head fell back, and he sighed. "Idiot. What about Sayer?"

Owen bit his upper lip and shook his head. "He's overwhelmed by all this. Besides, I don't think he's ever trusted you, but we need to get out of here, convince somebody that—"

The lock in the cell door clicked. A moment later, the door swung open, and Father Cotlas, holding a leather satchel in his thin arms, stood in the doorway, warily watching Owen and Dilan. One of the garrison soldiers, a man Owen didn't know, stood behind him, holding a drawn sword.

"If you promise not to cause trouble, I'll tend to your friend," Father Cotlas said.

Owen extended his arm toward Dilan and stepped out of the way. The guard closed and relocked the door behind the priest, leaving the three men alone.

Father Cotlas examined Dilan quickly, expertly. "That arrow needs to come out, or the wound will fester. If that happens, you'll take fever and die."

"Do what you need to, Father," Dilan said, beads of sweat on his upper lip.

Father Cotlas opened his satchel, revealing medical instruments and bandages, and set to work on Dilan's shoulder. "When I'm done, I'll sew up your cheek," the priest told Owen. "Should really be Modwyn doing this, though."

"He's a traitor," said Owen bitterly. His fingers traced the cut on his cheek. It was still oozing blood, but not as badly as before.

"Yes… well," said the priest, "I guess we'll know the truth of it soon enough. Although I must admit I never did like his looks." He paused and met Owen's eye. "If what you say is true, then what about Father Bowen?"

"I don't know," said Owen.

"I do. He's dead, Father. I'm sorry," said Dilan. "He was very brave. He actually confronted Serina himself, but…"

Father Cotlas, his face grave, sighed. "Let's look at that wound."

He began to tend to Dilan, softly probing the flesh around the arrow's shaft. Dilan, biting his lip, cried out in pain several times. Sweat beaded on his forehead.

After several moments, the elderly priest looked up, his fingers bloody. "It isn't as bad as it seems. The arrow buried itself in the flesh, but it didn't go far."

Dilan, his face pale and his breathing quick, nodded. "Man with the bow didn't… didn't have the time to make a full draw."

"All right, then," said the priest. "I'm going to have to pull it out. It's barbed, so it's going to hurt." He glanced at Owen. "I'll need you to help hold him down. He'll thrash."

Owen knelt down and braced himself against Dilan, holding him tightly in place.

"Owen," gasped Dilan. "I still need to breathe."

"Sorry." Owen loosened his grip.

"You seem to know your way around wounds, Father," Dilan said.

"I was with Duke Stron and his army, although I was very young."

"Father," said Owen. "We're not lying. Stron never killed her. I found his corpse—she drove his own sword through his chest. She's alive, she's free, and she's coming here next."

Father Cotlas shook his head. "I'm not going to debate this with you. The reeve is in command, and he's made his decision. You'll both stay here until we can confirm what's happened. If you're telling the truth, then you'll be—"

"Father," said Dilan, "if we don't get ready for her—right now—we're all going to die. She's not like anything you can imagine."

Father Cotlas extended a hardened piece of leather to Dilan. "Bite down on this. I'm sorry for what comes next."

Dilan opened his mouth and bit into the leather strap.

Father Cotlas was right. Dilan did thrash.

Chapter 45

Father Cotlas

Removing the arrowhead from the young man's shoulder took Father Cotlas more than an hour. It took another half hour to clean and stitch the wound, but when he was done, he was reasonably certain the soldier would fully recover—unless Dert hanged him first. Father Cotlas then put several stitches in the young blond man's cheek before bidding good night to the prisoners. He left the gaol, utterly spent, in need of a glass of wine and a long night's sleep, although he doubted very much he'd find them that night. The young soldier needed a real physician, but if what the two men had said was true—and he was beginning to believe it—then Modwyn was a traitor.

And Serina Greywynne—the monster of my youth—is still alive.

He stared at his trembling fingers, spotted and gnarled with age. *When did I get so old?* He remembered that day forty-eight years before, when Oskaley, trembling like a terrified colt, had emerged from the catacombs. Serina was dead, he had sworn, as were Stron and all the others, buried in the destruction of Sight-Bringer. His first command had been to seal the catacombs, ordering the priests to place wards. Oskaley had been near witless with terror that day—Father Cotlas had seen it in his eyes. Everyone had seen it, but no one had gone back to check, to confirm he was telling the truth and she was truly dead.

We all wanted her to be dead. We needed her to be dead so we could go home. Now, here I am, forty-eight years later, an old man now. There's too much for this to be just a story—the red moon, Sight-Bringer, Modwyn's betrayal.

In his heart, Father Cotlas knew the two prisoners were telling the truth. He sighed, his knees aching as he climbed the stairs out of the cellar and stepped out of the tower into the cool, fresh air.

High above, the moon was burning crimson.

A cold sweat broke over his skin. Lady Danika hadn't been exaggerating. *The moon is exactly as it was before the battle at Roald's Farm all those years ago. This* is *necromancy.*

She is coming!

He turned and fled back into the tower, wincing as he climbed the stairs to Dert's chambers. Dert's office door was closed, but Father Cotlas simply barged in.

Dert, sitting behind his large wooden desk with Sight-Bringer lying across it, jerked his head up in fright, but once he saw Father Cotlas, his eyes narrowed. "What is it? What's wrong now?"

"The moon is red."

Dert scowled, rose to his feet, and rushed to look out an open window, sticking his head out and twisting it upward so he could see the moon. His body stiffened. When he turned, fear shone in his eyes, an unhealthy pallor to his skin. Dert's lips trembled. "A… a natural occurrence… a… a trick of the light. Swamp gas."

Father Cotlas shook his head. "None of those things. Necromancy."

"No, Father. This is insanity." Dert rushed toward him, gripped his priest's frock with his hands, and shook him, his eyes wild. "Can you hear what you're saying? If it's necromancy, then—"

"Then those two men are telling the truth, and Serina Greywynne *is* alive." Father Cotlas gripped Dert's hands but couldn't move them. He cast a glance at Sight-Bringer. "Think about it. No one has ever gone back there. Then, Lord Palin reopens the catacombs, digs out the Great Crypt. Now, we hear of Modwyn's betrayal, Serina's return, red moons, and there—right before your eyes—is Sight-Bringer! We need to rouse the men, get ready to defend—"

"Enough!" Dert shoved him, sending him stumbling backward.

Father Cotlas fell hard and landed on his wrist. Sharp, stabbing pain ran up his arm, and he cried out in agony.

Dert, his face flushed, stepped closer, raised a fist, and shook it down at him. "You're an old fool." Spittle flew from his mouth. "I command here until Lord Palin returns, and I will decide what we do and don't do, not some senile old priest. Serina Greywynne is dead, has been dust since before I was born. I won't have you frightening my men with ghost stories. If I hear one more word about this from you, I will put you in the gaol with those deserters—now get out!"

With great difficulty, Father Cotlas climbed to his trembling feet, clutching his wrist. At best, it was sprained—at worst, broken. With the stabs of pain shooting up his arm, it was almost certainly the latter. He shook his head at Dert. *He's afraid, and his fear is going to get us all killed.*

He stumbled out, and Dert slammed the door behind him. Father Cotlas leaned against the wall and closed his eyes, concentrating on breathing. Tears ran down his cheeks from the pain. *What can I do now? No one will listen…*

No. There is one who might listen.

Chapter 46

Owen

Owen watched Dilan sleep. He needed to do something, to convince someone they were in danger, but Sayer and Dert were in charge, and neither man believed them.

The gaol door opened, and Father Cotlas entered with Lady Danika just behind him. The guard, looking uncertain, stood just behind them. Owen jumped to his feet and lowered his head in respect. Lady Danika's eyes were bloodshot, her face white. Clearly, she was in mourning for her brother, but hidden beneath the sorrow was a hint of steel, a resolve that Owen wouldn't have thought a pampered noblewoman would possess. She followed Father Cotlas into the cell, smoothed her dress, and then sat down on a wooden crate, her hands folded in her lap. Father Cotlas closed the door in the guard's face. The old man looked like he was in pain, and a sling was fastened around his arm.

Lady Danika looked upon the sleeping Dilan and then at Owen, her brown eyes filled with sorrow. "You will tell me everything that happened. Leave nothing out, no matter how…" Her voice broke.

"No matter how much pain you think it will cause me. I need to know everything."

"I only saw a part of it all, my lady. I'll need to wake up my friend."

She nodded and then sat patiently while Owen shook Dilan awake. Despite clearly still being in pain, Dilan sat up, listened to what Owen was asking, and then proceeded to explain the events of the previous night: the moon, the ghouls, then—faltering—he told of Serina's entrance and how she had torn apart the soldiers. When Dilan explained that he had fled in terror, he was unable to meet her eyes.

"It was the same with me," said Owen. "It's hard to describe. All I could think of was to run away, to flee."

"The Dread," said Father Cotlas.

Then, Owen proceeded to tell his part of the tale. When he described the murder of Lord Palin, Lady Danika's eyes filled with tears, but her gaze remained locked on his, listening carefully to every word.

Pampered noblewoman or not, there's a steel core to her. She's far tougher than anyone realizes.

"And..." She paused, looking away from him. "Captain Awde... You did not see his death?"

"No, my lady," said Owen softly. "I... I ran away."

"Then... then he may still be alive."

"My lady," said Father Cotlas. "Serina never spared anyone. Best not to have false hope. We need to survive this night so that we can escape, warn the king."

"I... yes, of course." She glanced down at her hands and wiped the tears from her cheek. "We have a duty." She closed her eyes and remained like that for long moments. When her brown eyes finally snapped open again, her pain was still there, but so was resolve, that core of steel, like a sword blade. She rose and called for the guard, who opened the door quickly. "I am releasing these men."

The guard's gaze darted from her to Owen and Dilan, and then to Father Cotlas. "My lady, I… I have to check with—"

She glared at him, seeming to stand taller. "I am Lady Danika Dain, daughter of Duke Oskaley and last member of the Dain family. You have sworn an oath to serve my family, which is now *me*. Free these heroes immediately."

The guardsman jerked back and then nodded quickly, licking his lips. "Yes, my lady. Apologies."

She stormed past him without another word. Father Cotlas, a tepid smile on his features, followed her, as did Owen and Dilan. She left the tower, stepping out into the courtyard. Several guardsmen standing nearby turned and watched her. When they saw Owen and Dilan, their faces went hard, their hands drifting to their swords.

"You men," she called out to them.

"Yes, my lady," one answered.

"Rouse the fort. I want every man on the walls—every single man. Is that understood?"

"My lady, Reeve Dert—"

Owen heard running footsteps behind them and turned to see the reeve rushing out of the tower, still holding Sight-Bringer, confusion on his features. Dert stumbled to a halt behind her, his mouth open.

Lady Danika addressed the growing group of soldiers, drawn by all the excitement. "I am Danika Dain, daughter of Duke Oskaley and now heir to the Wolfrey lands—including this island. This is *my* fort, and I command here."

"My lady," stammered Dert, looking about himself in fear. "What is it you think you are doing?"

"I think, Master Dert, that you will obey me, or I will have *you* locked in a cell." She pointed to the red moon. "Look about yourself.

We are all of us in grave danger. This is necromancy. Serina Greywynne is alive, and you all act as if nothing has changed. *Everything* has changed."

A murmuring of fear rippled through the men. They cast nervous glances at the moon then Lady Danika. In the distance, a dog howled, followed by the cries of others.

Lieutenant Sayer pushed through the men, his hair disheveled and his eyes wild. "My lady," he asked, "what if these men are lying?"

"Yes." Dert looked from face to face, addressing the men. "What if they *are* lying?"

She stepped up to Dert and took the longsword from him. Just for a moment, he hesitated, as though he didn't want to give it up, but then he relented. She held it point down between her legs, resting against the stones of the courtyard. The hilt of the sword—the strange beast-like woman—reached her chest. In the moonlight, the flawless blade shimmered like fire.

"I believe these men," she said, looking at Owen and Dilan. "I believe they're telling the truth. We've been betrayed, and we're in great danger."

"I..." Dert looked at Sayer for help, but Sayer shook his head and turned to address Lady Danika. "What command, my lady?"

"Stand to the fort. Death is coming."

"A rider!" a sentry atop the gatehouse yelled, pointing at the twisting trail that led up the hill to the fort.

Owen and the others rushed to the gatehouse to see better. He stared through the gates of the lowered portcullis. The guard was right. A man was riding up to the gatehouse. Suddenly, cold anger swept through him—it was Modwyn! The physician, seemingly unconcerned at the stares directed at him through the portcullis bars, dismounted and approached the gate.

"Open the gate," Modwyn called out.

"You!" Lady Danika spat, moving up beside Owen. "What have you done?"

"Open the gate, fools," Dert ordered the sentries. "This is the physician."

"Don't open the gates," said Owen. "He's a traitor. He murdered Lord Palin."

Modwyn cocked his head and sneered at Owen. "Of course, I didn't murder Lord Palin—you did! Let me in, my lady, and I'll prove that this man betrayed his oath, murdered your brother—his own liege lord—and ran away with that sword you hold in your hands."

"He's a liar!" Owen said. "This is a trick."

Dert rounded on Owen, pointing a pudgy finger at him. "I knew it! I knew I was right about you. Guards, seize him."

Two of the guardsmen rushed in to grab Owen, but he moved first, snatching one of the men's outstretched wrists and twisting it over his head so that the first man spun about and crashed into the second. Both fell, entangled. More soldiers drew swords, and by habit, Owen's hand went for a sword that he wasn't wearing. Lieutenant Sayer, his sword drawn, stepped forward, preparing to run Owen through.

"Enough!" yelled Lady Danika, sounding nothing like a quiet young noblewoman. She rounded on Dert, pointing Sight-Bringer in his face. "I've already told you once this night not to question my orders."

Dert's face blanched. "My lady, this man—"

"I said *enough*." She stormed past him, approaching the bars of the portcullis. As she did, her face took on a puzzled look, and she stared at the sword in her hands.

Modwyn drew back, farther into the shadows.

"The sword… hums." She turned in puzzlement and looked among the others.

"It did the same thing in the Great Crypt," said Owen, "and then once again when I was searching the caves at the base of the fortress, seeking a way out."

"According to the old tales," said Father Cotlas, "it... *awakens* when needed or in the presence of great evil."

Danika, holding the sword in both hands, came right up against the bars of the portcullis.

As she did, Modwyn moved even farther back. "Open the gates," he said. "Open the gates, and I will explain everything... Please, you all know me. I'm one man, no threat."

"My lady, please," said Dert in a small, pleading voice, no longer filled with arrogance and bluster. "This is crazy, all this talk of monsters."

Danika peered through the bars, searching. "There's... *something* out there." She turned, her eyes coming to rest on Owen. She moved to a lit torch placed within a sconce on the inside wall of the gatehouse. Then she pulled it free and thrust it into Owen's hands. "Go up top and throw this as far as you can."

Owen did as he was told, running up the stairs to the gatehouse's upper battlements. The others looked about themselves in confusion.

"My lady," said Father Cotlas. "What—"

"This is crazy," said Dert. "It's just one man, a physician. We're letting fear unman us."

Atop the gatehouse, Owen drew back the lit torch and sent it flying, trailing embers as it tumbled through the air. When the torch hit the trail far behind Modwyn, it exploded into sparks, revealing scores of men hiding in the dark.

"You're going to die, cow," Modwyn snarled, baring his teeth. "But before you do, I'm going to split you open then let every single man on this island ride you."

"Kill him!" yelled Danika.

One of the guardsmen atop the gatehouse was armed with a longbow. Owen grabbed it from him, snatched at an arrow from a nearby quiver, then notched and released it at Modwyn, but the doctor—moving impossibly fast—darted aside, disappearing into the darkness.

The men who had been hiding in the dark moved forward as one, without a single word of command. Their movements were wrong—too jerky, too awkward, and then Owen saw with horror that they were not men at all but scores of ghouls, some still wearing Wolfrey armor and colors. Their own comrades—recently dead—had returned to kill them. His skin went clammy when he recognized a familiar face among the ghouls—Fin, his eyes black, his throat a gaping wound, was leading them.

Chapter 47

Owen

Yells of alarm arose throughout the fort as the small garrison rushed to the walls. Owen, remaining atop the gatehouse, loosed arrow after arrow into the ghouls, but in sinking horror, he soon realized the arrows did nothing to men already dead. Each time he struck one of the ghouls, the walking corpse would shudder under the impact but keep coming. Then, something flashed past his own head. *An arrow!* A moment later, he saw shapes behind the ghouls, living men loosing arrows from hunting bows. *The islanders!*

Owen transferred his aim to the living men. He hit at least two before the others concentrated their fire on him. He hid behind the battlements and darted out to release an arrow before ducking back behind cover just before a storm of arrows shattered against the wall. *We need more men on the walls.*

Stron's Watch sat against the edge of the cliff, built to present only a single approach for attackers. Unless they could climb a steep sea cliff, the ghouls and the islanders could only come at them from the one direction.

How many soldiers are still within the fort? Couldn't be more than thirty men. The Greywynne islanders had been kept in line with the threat of mass hangings if they rebelled, and the garrison was only ever a token presence. With Serina free, the islanders didn't care about retribution from the mainland. If the ghouls got through the gatehouse, everyone inside the fort was going to die. The islanders could attack from only one direction, but that also meant that there was no way out for the defenders.

Owen darted out and loosed another arrow. He had the satisfaction of seeing another islander fall before the volley of return arrows drove him behind cover again.

His back to the stone parapet, he drew another arrow and peered around the stone, seeking another target. An arrow shattered against the stone near his face, and he flinched back. They knew exactly where he was and were waiting for him to show himself again. He was wearing no armor—hadn't since Greywynne Fortress. Without armor, he felt particularly vulnerable.

Then, more soldiers joined him, and soon, the release of longbow strings could be heard all along the wall. Below, the ghouls massed near the portcullis, but they weren't advancing, only standing in place, many with arrows jutting from them like porcupines.

What are they waiting for? "Don't waste your arrows on the ghouls," he yelled at the newly arriving soldiers. "Aim for the men with the bows."

Soon, the islanders with the hunting bows were driven farther back, away from the greater range of the longbows. Their arrows became more erratic and less effective, but then a group of islanders charged the gatehouse bearing a wooden log between them that they had tied ropes to, creating handles. *A battering ram!*

"Get those men! Get those men!" Owen yelled, loosing an arrow, which hit one and sent him rolling.

Other defenders fired on the men carrying the ram as well, and under the hail of arrows, the islanders broke, dropping the battering ram, and retreated into the darkness. The ghouls, though, remained bunched near the portcullis. If those men had managed to breach the gatehouse…

Then, the islanders tried a new tactic. The first warning the defenders had was the sound of wagon wheels and the neighing of horses from the path leading up to the fort. Out of the darkness, a wagon barreled up the path, its two ponies whipped into a mad dash by the wagon's two riders. The men drove straight toward the fort's wall. One of the riders held a flaming torch that trailed along as the wagon—its bed stacked at least eight feet high with kindling and hay—picked up speed.

"Stop them," Owen yelled as he released an arrow at the riders.

Others also shot at the wagon, and in moments, one of the riders, struck by at least four arrows, fell off and rolled along the ground behind it. The other driver, the one with the torch, threw himself into the bed of his wagon. The hay must have been soaked in oil because it erupted into a roaring ball of fire. The two ponies, driven mad by the flames, ran faster, fanning the fire behind them. The terrified ponies never even tried to swerve away. The wagon hit the keep wall, and flames and thick black smoke poured over the defenders, obscuring all sight.

The thick smoke drove Owen back, away from the gatehouse and down the stairs onto the courtyard. Someone yelled that the islanders were going for the battering ram again.

Owen looked about, frantic. *Where is Sayer?*

The ghouls near the gatehouse parted just enough to allow the men to begin battering at the portcullis bars while still protecting the men wielding it, with their own dead bodies. Moments later, the bars began to bend inward. Owen knew if he and the others didn't do something right then, the ghouls were going to get inside. The battering ram pushed past two of the bars, creating enough space for the ghouls, one at a time, to force their way in. The first ghoul shambled toward Owen, a walking corpse in mail armor. Owen recognized him—Gastor, a tall, lanky young man with a once easygoing demeanor. His face was devoid of all emotion, his eyes dull. He carried no weapons, and one of his arms hung loosely by a piece of sinew, twisting about as he walked. Gastor reached for Owen with his one good arm. Again, Owen reached for a sword he wasn't wearing.

Father Cotlas stepped in front of Owen, holding his Craftsman's hammer before him with his one good arm, thrusting it into Gastor's face while intoning a prayer. Owen expected the ghoul to rip the old man apart, but instead Gastor halted and simply stared at the priest.

"Soldier, here," Lady Danika yelled, shoving Sight-Bringer into his grip. "Kill it quickly before it can move again."

When Owen grasped the longsword, that power again resonated through his arms, a vibration that filled him with strength. His vision, previously distorted by the darkness and the smoke, became much clearer. He rushed forward, moving from the back guard into a rising cut, slicing upward. The tip of the blade cut through Gastor's chest and up into his chin and then his head, almost splitting it in two. It had cut so effortlessly through the man's flesh that it had felt as if he were only cutting air. Gastor fell back and lay unmoving, as if he were truly dead again. Smoke rose from the gaping wound in his chest and face.

Power surged through Owen. Two more ghouls shoved their way past the bent bars and staggered toward Owen. Moving from the high guard—holding the sword above his head with both hands—Owen cut downward at the closest of the ghouls, slicing its head in two. The blade kept going, cutting deeply into the ghoul's torso before swinging free, almost singing. The ghoul fell unmoving, its wounds smoking as if Sight-Bringer were a white-hot brand. Owen stepped forward, lunging with the blade, impaling the other ghoul through the torso—punching completely through its ring mail as if it weren't even there. The third ghoul fell, also smoking and still. The blade's hum resonated through Owen's skull, driving him onward. A righteous zeal filled him, burning away his fear.

How dare Serina desecrate the corpses of these men, turning them into monsters?

Yet another ghoul was trying to force its way through the bars. Owen rushed forward and took its head off, barricading the opening with the ghoul's headless body. The other ghouls pushed against the bars, straining to reach through and grasp at Owen, but he stood his ground, lopping off arms and hands with each swing—and every cut he made killed a ghoul for good, no matter where he struck. Within minutes, the silent bodies of ghouls blocked the twisted portcullis bars. The rest of the ghouls moved back, as if sensing the danger of the longsword. The fort's defenders cheered, and men rushed to Owen, patting him on the back and hugging him.

"Well done, soldier," said Lady Danika. "You saved our lives."

Feeling fatigue for the first time, Owen stumbled and fell to his knees. Men helped him up. Sight-Bringer's magic, it seemed, had its limits.

Gasping for air, he held the hilt of Sight-Bringer out to Lady Danika. "Your sword, my lady."

She looked at the sword then at the ruined portcullis. The flames and smoke from the burning wagon still obscured the fort's walls. "You keep it for now, soldier. I don't know how to use it."

"Well done, lad," said Father Cotlas. "The Craftsman moves through you this night."

Owen coughed and gasped. "It wasn't me. It was the sword."

"Aye, lad," said Father Cotlas. "They said it was like that for Duke Stron as well. That's how we beat back Serina's undead army—with sword and prayer."

Dert, his face streaked with soot, suddenly appeared. "Where's Sayer? Who's in charge? What do we do?"

The men looked about themselves, muttering in confusion.

"The Lady Danika is in charge." Dilan stepped forward, moving stiffly, favoring his wounded shoulder. His face was pale but filled with resolve. Everyone turned to face the diminutive noblewoman.

Dert faced her as well. "What orders then, my lady?"

Just for a moment, fear and uncertainty flashed across her features, but then her eyes hardened. "We stay alive. In the morning, we look for a way off the island, to warn the kingdom."

"My lady," Dert said, looking about for support. "Perhaps we should find Lieutenant Sayer. Maybe he can—"

"She's right," said Dilan. "Serina herself will come next. We need to hold until morning, use the sword against her if we have to. We can figure out what to do then."

"You don't know that!" Dert rounded on Dilan. "All this talk of Serina—"

Owen laughed, surprising himself that despite the horror around them, he even still could. "Look about yourself. The moon is red, and there are ghouls attacking us. Of course Serina is alive."

"Someone needs to take command," said Dert.

"Someone has taken command," said Danika. "*I* have."

"No offense, my lady, but perhaps a… a man… I mean a soldier. If we can't find Sayer, then one of the sergeants, maybe."

A small crowd had gathered near the gatehouse. Most of the Greywynne garrison was composed of older men, men who had seen too many years. The younger ones had gone north to Serina's fortress.

"Whatever we're going to decide," Owen said. "We need to do it now. This gatehouse needs to be barricaded and quickly."

Lady Danika bit her upper lip and glanced about before resting her eyes on Owen. "You, soldier. If not for you, we'd already be overrun. You will be my commander here. You will direct the defense of the fort."

As their gazes swung to him, Owen's breath caught in his chest. He felt trapped, overwhelmed. "I... I can't do that. I'm not a leader. I'm just a soldier." He shook his head, seeing the surprise and disappointment in Lady Danika's face. "Dilan," he said, turning toward his friend. "Dilan was a Ram. He's been a soldier for years, fought in real battles. He was at Prophet's Bridge, the only survivor. *Dilan* should command."

Then, everyone turned toward Dilan, his left arm in a sling. Dilan frowned at Owen and then addressed Lady Danika. "If you'll have me, my lady, I know what needs to be done."

She inclined her head, casting one last glance at Owen, who looked away toward the ruined portcullis, his face burning.

We really do need to barricade the entrance, shore up the twisted portcullis.

"So be it," Lady Danika said. "You... What is your name?"

"Dilan Reese, my lady."

"You, Dilan Reese, are in command of the fort."

"Yes, my lady." Dilan raised his voice to address all the men. "Owen, stay here with the sword. Keep the ghouls from getting inside."

Owen nodded.

"You lot"—Dilan pointed at a small knot of men—"help him barricade that portcullis. Do it now!"

The men rushed to obey. As they did, one of the men who had remained on the walls despite the smoke called down to them. "They're coming again, this time with ladders."

Dilan appraised the situation. "Right, Lady Danika, I need you and Father Cotlas to stay back—the rest of you, up on the walls."

"The smoke," one of the men complained.

"The ghouls will climb the ladders. If we let them have the walls, we're as good as dead. Get your asses up there. A little smoke won't kill you." Dilan sheathed his sword, grabbed the closest soldier, and propelled him toward the stairs leading up to the walls. "Hurry, damn you." He then turned to Dert. "The supplies that didn't go north, the extra oil and firepots for the marsh ticks, where are they?"

Dert's face demonstrated his confusion. "What? Why?"

"Because while ghouls don't die, they can still burn."

Understanding finally registered on the other man's face. "Down below, in a storeroom next to the gaol, but there aren't that many left, maybe a dozen."

"They'll do," Dilan said. He pointed at two of the men. "You come with me." He stopped and stared at Owen. "Why aren't you barricading the gate?"

Owen opened his mouth but then ran to follow orders.

#

When the attack began again, it was double-pronged, coming at the walls and the gatehouse. Once again, the undead soldiers threw themselves in frenzy against the partially destroyed bars of the portcullis and the barricade that Owen and the others had piled before it. When the attack came, Owen had been helping to push a wagon they were intending to prop up against the barricade. As the first walking dead man pushed through the barricade, Owen wasn't close enough to stop it. Despite their efforts, the barricade hadn't even slowed it down. In moments, the ghoul was shambling toward the closest soldiers, another of the monsters coming through the bars just behind it.

"Wait," Owen yelled to the soldiers, who ignored him and rushed at the ghouls.

They struck down at the creature with sword blows that would have killed a living man, but the walking corpse ignored the wounds, instead grabbing the closest of the men and pulling him down. The second soldier stared in horror, frozen, as the next ghoul through the barricade reached him. He went down as well. Then, more undead warriors pushed through, piling atop him.

Owen got there just as the ghouls ripped the soldier's ring-mail coat apart with their bare hands, the rings popping and flying through the air. Then, they ripped out his intestines. Sight-Bringer thrumming in his ears, Owen attacked from the back stance, swinging the longsword up over his head to cut down, splitting a ghoul's head in two. As another ghoul reached out for him, he dodged backward, taking off the ghoul's outstretched hands with a reverse cut. The ghoul stared at its severed wrists, which smoked, then fell forward atop the first, unmoving.

More ghouls climbed past the barricade, and Owen launched himself into them, dispatching one with a rising diagonal cut that took its head off, then killing the next with the reverse swing. The remaining ghouls fell back, and the surviving soldiers rushed forward to restack the barricade.

Exhausted, Owen turned and stared toward the east. *Is that a red glow on the horizon or just a trick of the moonlight?*

Chapter 48

Dilan

Dilan climbed the stairs to the fort's walls. The smoke from the burning wagon still obscured visibility and brought tears to his eyes, but it wasn't as bad as it had been at first. He held a lit torch in one hand and used his bandaged arm to hold one of the firepots against his chest. The two men behind him also held armloads of firepots. Dilan paused as a spasm of pain lanced down his back. *Come on, man, you once fought for an entire day with a broken foot. You can do this—you have to do this!* Leaning over the top of the wall, Dilan assessed the situation. The islanders had brought at least six wooden ladders forward and set them against the base of the wall. Small groups of ghouls were already atop the walls, attacking the soldiers. If they didn't do something quickly, in minutes, more would climb up and overrun them. Owen wouldn't be able to take them all on, even with Sight-Bringer. The ghouls would surround and overwhelm him.

Using the burning wagon to drive the defenders from the walls had been a good trick, but it was quickly becoming less effective. If they could just deal with the ghouls, they could use the greater range of their longbows to pick off the islanders. Even then, the approach to the fort was littered with dead men. All of Port Eaton seemed to have risen in arms against them. From that height, Dilan could see at least three score more ghouls milling about the ladders, waiting for a chance to climb up. If they didn't take back the walls right then and destroy those ladders, they were going to die that night.

To his left, not ten paces away, a Wolfrey soldier flailed away with his sword, desperately trying to keep back three ghouls, their backs to Dilan. He dropped the torch onto the wall's landing and threw the firepot he had been holding. It hit the stones beneath the closest ghoul, shattering and throwing oil. Dilan picked up the torch again and sent it tumbling through the air. The moment it hit, the oil ignited in a blast, setting two of the ghouls aflame. Dilan took another firepot from the men behind him and tossed it at the final ghoul, hitting it square in the back, enveloping it in flames. The burning ghoul, ignoring the flames, rushed at the soldier and wrapped its arms around him. Together, they fell, burning, to the courtyard below. The other two ghouls, engulfed in flames, stumbled about blindly atop the wall. Dilan approached them warily before kicking one into the other. Both went tumbling over the wall. Not one of them made a sound.

More ghouls were climbing up the ladder, and Dilan, taking another firepot, threw it in the face of the closest monster. As the ghoul climbed onto the wall, the nearby flames ignited the oil, setting it and the upper half of the ladder on fire. The burning ghoul fell from the wall as well. The fire forced Dilan and the two others away, but the ladder burned and, with it, several of the ghouls that had been climbing.

When the flames receded, Dilan and the two guards moved farther down the wall, setting other ladders afire and burning three more groups of ghouls that had reached the battlements.

Wiping dirt and smoke from his eyes, Dilan looked to the east and saw a red glow along the horizon. *How long until sunrise?*

Will they even stop at sunrise?

#

Later, Dilan found Lieutenant Sayer atop one of the battlements, sitting propped up against the wall, the shaft of an arrow jutting from his chest. Kneeling next to him, Dilan reached out and felt a faint pulse in the man's throat. Sayer opened his eyes at the touch and moaned. Only one guardsman remained with Dilan, the other having died after helping Dilan clear the last of the ghouls.

How many of us are still alive? Dilan pointed with his chin farther down the wall and ordered the guard, "Check the others. Tell the men that dawn is almost here."

The man looked from Sayer to Dilan, nodded, and moved away. Examining Sayer's wound, Dilan saw right away it was a mortal wound. In truth, he was amazed Sayer was still alive.

Sayer tried to speak, and Dilan put his ear near the man's mouth. "Still… stand?"

Dilan squeezed his hand. "We're not dead yet."

Sayer closed his eyes and grimaced, coughing up a bubble of spit and blood.

"Hang on, Lieutenant. We're all going to survive this night—you, too."

Sayer grimaced and shook his head. "Liar."

Dilan sat back against the battlements next to Sayer, holding his hand and waiting. The fighting had almost stopped, meaning the islanders either had run out of ladders or hadn't realized how close the fight had been. Arrows continued to fly only intermittently against the fort's defenders. Sayer's breathing became more irregular, the pauses lasting longer.

"You know," Dilan said softly, almost in a whisper. "I need to tell you something I haven't told anybody else. That night at the inn, when we first met, you weren't wrong about me. Prophet's Bridge, the battle… It wasn't what everyone believes it was. We weren't being brave. We simply couldn't get away. My brother Artur and I were the last, the others all dead. Something hit me in the head, a rock maybe. I stumbled and fell off the side of the bridge, over the gorge and the river below. Artur caught me—just barely—but the rebels were still coming. I told him to let me go, let me fall, and save his own life. He… he wouldn't, so one of the bastards ran a spear through the back of his neck—that's the only reason he let me go. I hit the rapids below, certain I'd drown, but I didn't." He snorted and smiled, though he really felt like crying. "I washed ashore farther up the river, sodden and clinging to life, but alive. That's when my courage failed, and I ran for my life. For two days, I evaded their hunters, finally making my way back to our lines."

The wind picked up, gusting across the battlements, chasing away the stench of burned wood and charred flesh, replacing it for a few moments with the fresh smell of the sea.

"No one believed I had fallen into the water. They were all certain I had abandoned the others, but no one wanted to tarnish the image of the Rams. The tale of how a few had died holding back so many was already becoming a legend. Instead, they just… released me. So you see, you were right that day we met at the inn. I did run."

Sayer said nothing, making Dilan wonder if he was already gone, but then, Sayer's bloody lips parted, and his eyes focused on Dilan. "Don't… run… this time."

Then he died.

Chapter 49

Modwyn

Modwyn fumed. He stood on the twisting trail that led to the fort, far out of longbow range. Several of the more influential islanders, their leaders, stood beside him. They all watched the fort, highlighted against the early-morning sky. He paced in short steps, his posture stiff, his jaw clenched. He needed to take that fort soon. *If she arrives before then...*

"We need to build more ladders," said Galvin, the large bearded man the others deferred to. The man stood with his hands on his hips, surveying the fort. Unlike the others, Galvin wore a sword and was protected by a worn but still-functional leather coat. He, at least, looked like a warrior. The others, though, were clearly farmers and fishermen, armed with whatever tool they could lay hands on that would double as a weapon, axes mostly.

"So? Go get them already," Modwyn snapped.

Galvin shook his head. "I said *build* more ladders. Those they burned were what were already in town, from the larger barns. We need to make more and then hit them again."

"They'll burn them again," Modwyn said.

"How much oil can they have in there?" Galvin asked. "If we pull the ghouls back, leave men with bows to keep them locked up in there, we can spend a day just building ladders, enough to overwhelm them. We've already sent riders to the other villages. More men will come—a *lot* more men."

Modwyn shook his head. "We'd have had them already if not for that damned sword. She was right to be concerned about it. Who would have thought that some idiot guardsman would bring it all the way across the island and use it to defend that stupid little fort?"

"They can't go anywhere. We'll finish them tomorrow," Galvin said.

Modwyn felt his frustration grow. He knew nothing of siege warfare. The glow of the sun was rising over the hills to the east, and he turned toward it. She would be angry at the delay… angry with *him*—again.

"No," Modwyn said. "We can't wait. We need to attack once more."

"Man," said Galvin, irritation in his voice. "We have no ladders. We can't—"

Modwyn spun on him, moving so quickly that the other man had no chance to react. With one hand, he lifted the large islander into the air by the throat, his booted feet dangling, kicking helplessly while Modwyn glared at him. "Don't you see? I can't fail her. I can feel her. She's coming, getting closer. We must take that fort!"

Galvin's ruddy face turned red as Modwyn choked him with one hand. His eyes were wide, beseeching.

Then, Modwyn realized he had already run out of time. *She is here.* He dropped Galvin to the ground, forgotten.

Serina stood, not a dozen paces away, watching him with her new childe standing next to her, his all-red eyes filled with malice. She was dressed as before, naked but for the torn, ancient ring-mail coat.

Yet still she looks the queen she is.

Modwyn dropped to his knees, and a moment later, the others did the same. The morning was cold, and a chill wind carried the promise of fall, but it wasn't the cold that caused him to shiver so violently.

I've failed her again.

She approached, but he kept his eyes on the ground, seeing only her bare feet before him, crusted in dried blood and dirt.

"The sword?" she asked, simply, quietly.

"Still… still in the fort, my queen… with them," Modwyn said, the words burning his throat.

She was silent for several long, heavy moments. "And the Dain girl?"

"In… in the fort also, my queen."

The wind gusted again, bringing with it the acrid stench of smoke. Modwyn coughed, as did the islanders. Serina and her childe didn't. "Well, I guess that means I'll need a different place to sleep—before the sun rises," she said. "Someplace large, secure."

"Yes, yes, my queen," answered Modwyn. "The alehouse, I think."

He risked a glance at her and saw that she was staring at the fort, her eyes tight. "I will need the ghouls. Leave the townsfolk to watch the fort."

"Yes, my queen."

"It… it would be our honor… for our dead to lie with you as well, my queen, as they did in the old days," stammered Galvin, stepping closer, wringing his hands before him.

Modwyn glared at the man. *How dare he address her directly?*

But instead of admonishing him for speaking out of turn, Serina approached him and ran her fingers through his hair, as if he were some kind of dog. The man actually whimpered.

"Don't worry. I don't blame you for this failure," she said as her gaze fell upon Modwyn.

Modwyn shivered. "I'm… I'm sorry, my queen, but we can still take them. One more assault, and they'll break."

She watched the fort for long moments, staring at it silently. The only sound was the crashing of the waves, the howling of the wind.

"No," she finally said. "There have been enough of my people killed this night. I will need them all for what is to come."

"Yes, my queen," Modwyn said.

She turned away, and Modwyn watched her back as she approached her childe and ran her fingers over his cheeks and down the scar on his neck.

"You will go forward, kill whoever holds Sight-Bringer, and then bring it to me," she said. "If you would sleep with me this day, you must pay for your boarding with the sword. Do you understand?"

Brice Awde smiled, exposing his fangs.

Chapter 50

Brice

As he sprinted toward the wall of the fort, Brice saw that the sun had yet to rise, but its glow was clearly visible just below the tree line. In less than half an hour, it would break the horizon. He knew he needed to take the sword back and bring it to the queen before that happened, or he would die. He didn't understand how he knew that, but he was certain of it just the same.

A great deal had changed since the night before, when the queen had forced him to drink her blood. The world seemed completely different, as if he were seeing it as it truly was for the first time. The people moved sluggishly, as if they were all underwater. His sight, his sense of smell, and his strength and speed—all were vastly more powerful. He had become akin to a god.

But with the gifts had come needs as well. The first was the mandate to obey Serina, to please her and make her proud. That urge filled the core of his being. She was with him always, a part of him. He felt her, watching over him, within him, confident he would make her happy—and he would! She had become his entire world.

All that had come before her was unimportant, like a distant memory that had quickly faded and would soon disappear entirely. He remembered the others, especially Danika, but she seemed so… far away now, as if his love for her had never been more than an odd infatuation.

His most powerful urge, however, the one that drove him nearly mad, was his hunger, his ravenous thirst for blood. Blood had become like air to him. He could smell it now, flowing through the veins of others. His sense of belonging with the rest of humanity was gone. People were only prey, nothing more. The warrior called Brice Awde was only a memory. After a day or two at most, even that memory would be nothing more than a smoky dream, he was certain. All that would remain would be Serina's new childe, the first of her battle captains—and he would make her proud. He would drown the world in blood for her.

But first, the sword.

He picked up speed, sprinting full out toward the far end of the wall, near the cliff face. He ran so quickly that the air around him blurred. He jumped halfway up the fort's wall in a single bound. His fingernails, stronger than steel, ripped into the stone, giving him purchase. In seconds, he was over its side and onto the battlements.

One of the guardsmen stood before him, a look of disbelief on his face, his hands still gripping his longbow and arrow. Before the man could move, Brice reached out and gripped his face with one hand, driving his fingernails deep into his eye sockets, and then—with one quick jerk—ripped most of his face free. The man, making mewling, animallike noises, spun about, thrashing as he fell. Brice had already moved on, leaping down into the courtyard.

Another guardsman charged at him with a sword raised above his head but moving far too slowly. Brice sidestepped around him, ripping his throat out as he did. The man, unaware of what had just happened, ran three more paces forward then fell forward into the dirt.

Brice was already gone, moving on toward the tower.

He didn't know where the sword was, but a location within the fort's tower was most likely, perhaps in the reeve's chambers. No one else challenged him. With all that had happened that night, and with the speed at which he had been moving, the fort's defenders probably hadn't even seen him approach. With luck, he'd kill whoever had the sword and be back over the wall on his way to Serina within minutes.

As expected, the tower was empty. Anyone who could fight was already on the walls or congregating in a small group atop the gatehouse. Brice swept through the tower's chambers like a shadow, moving quickly up the stairs. The reeve's chambers were empty. Wendel Dert must have joined the fighting himself. *How surprising.* Brice had expected to find the man cowering beneath his desk. The chambers appropriated by the Dain siblings were just above him. Perhaps Danika had Sight-Bringer.

Danika.

He paused, staring at his blood-soaked fingernails.

What is this I feel… love? No—someone else had loved Danika. The only person he loved was Serina, and she was counting on him to bring her the sword.

He ran up the stairs, coming out onto the landing before Danika's quarters. He heard her moving about on the other side of her wooden door and smelled the blood pumping through her veins. His thirst coursed through him, washing away everything else. His need to feed was overpowering, irresistible. In a moment, he was through her door, his fangs bared.

When Danika's young handmaiden, Wren, saw him, she stared, openmouthed in abject horror. A moment later, Brice was on her, driving his fangs deeply into her neck, ripping through her veins. Hot blood poured down his throat, driving him on. She beat at him futilely with her small fists, but he kept drinking, feeling the giddy joy of her blood flowing down his parched throat as he consumed her. In seconds, her heart slowed then stopped.

Letting her corpse fall, he wiped the back of his hand across his mouth, smearing the blood over his face. As his blood-need subsided, he could think clearly again. *Danika isn't here, nor is the sword.* He swept through her chambers, stepping over the white-faced corpse of Wren.

Where would Danika be, then? He paused by her window, staring down at the people standing atop the gatehouse.

Their attention was on the islanders and Serina, which meant they still didn't know he was here.

Good.

His vision tunneled in upon a small figure with long dark hair standing beside an elderly man—Danika, and in her hands, she held a longsword.

Brice smiled.

Chapter 51

Owen

Owen stood atop the gatehouse with Lady Danika, Dilan, and Father Cotlas. "They pulled everyone back," Owen said, "including the ghouls."

Dilan leaned out past one of the gatehouse's stone merlons, peering at the besieging force, out of longbow range. "Something's happening. They're all on their knees."

Lady Danika moved past him to peer around the stone.

"My lady," said Dilan, "I don't think that's—"

"I can't see," she said then turned to face Owen. "Give me Sight-Bringer."

After he handed it to her, she held the sword point down, resting against the stones, while she peered around the merlon again. As she did, her body went rigid. "May the Craftsman save us. There's a woman with them, and she's covered in blood."

"Tall?" Owen asked. "With long blond hair tied in braids, tattoos covering her face?"

She nodded, handing the sword back to him. Once again, he was amazed at the rush of energy that coursed through him when his fingers touched its hilt.

"What do we do now?" Lady Danika asked.

"The sun will be over the horizon soon," said Father Cotlas. "She'll need to find somewhere to sleep. Then, we can—"

Without warning, Keep-Captain Brice Awde swept up the stairs of the gatehouse coming from the courtyard, trapping them against the battlements. Fresh blood streaked his face, and he grinned at them, exposing two long fangs. "Hello, friends."

"Blood fiend!" yelled Father Cotlas.

Lady Danika screamed.

Awde took a step toward her, but Father Cotlas darted before him, holding his Craftsman's hammer and intoning a prayer. Awde glared at him but then faltered, his face registering his distaste.

"Back, demon," Father Cotlas commanded, thrusting his hammer forward.

Awde stumbled back, his eyes darting away from the priest, as if he couldn't look at him. Father Cotlas advanced again, looking tall and proud despite his age. Awde stumbled back farther, cowering before him, holding his forearm across his face.

"Now! Use the sword," Father Cotlas yelled. "Drive it through his heart!"

Owen raised Sight-Bringer, holding it two-handed and aiming its point at the keep-captain's heart. He was about to thrust forward when Lady Danika grabbed at him, knocking him off balance.

"No, don't!" she yelled.

Owen stumbled into Father Cotlas, knocking him forward. The spell broken, Awde moved impossibly quickly, spinning the elderly priest about and ripping most of his throat out with his talon-like fingers. The priest's blood sprayed over them, interfering with Owen's thrust. Awde threw the dying priest into Owen, knocking him down. As Owen tried to untangle himself, Dilan charged, swinging a sword with his good arm, but Awde caught the weapon's blade in his bare hand and ripped it from Dilan's grip. He kicked Dilan in the chest, sending him flying back down the stairs. Owen staggered to his feet as Awde tossed the sword away.

"Give me Sight-Bringer, lad," Awde said. "I'll let you live. She doesn't care about you."

Owen struck, aiming a downward cut at Awde's head. Once again, Awde swept out of the way while lashing out at Owen with the back of his hand. The jarring blow sent Owen reeling back once again into the battlements, knocking him down. Sight-Bringer fell from his fingers to clatter against the stones of the gatehouse.

"Wrong choice, Toscovar." Awde shook his head as he bent down to pick up the longsword.

"Brice, no!" screamed Lady Danika as she rushed forward, throwing herself over Owen and covering him with her own body. "Please don't do this."

Owen tried to push Lady Danika away, certain the creature who had once been the keep-captain would cut them both down with Sight-Bringer, but when Awde grasped the longsword, he froze, his eyes widening in shock. He stiffened, standing tall before them, holding the Illthori longsword before him, staring at it in abject wonder.

His gaze—sorrowful, agonizing—went to Lady Danika, and he reached for her with one of his blood-soaked, talon-like hands. "Danika… what… How?"

"Brice." She reached out for him. "My love."

His gaze went from her to his bloody hand to the longsword he held. Once again, he met her eyes. "I'm sorry, my love. I failed you. I failed your brother. I've failed everyone." He spun from her, placing the hilt of the longsword against the battlements, positioning its point against his chest.

"Brice, no!" she screamed, reaching out for him.

A moment later, he drove himself forward onto the longsword. In one clean movement, it punched all the way through both sides of his ring-mail armor, the blood-covered blade extending a foot out of his back. Lady Danika screamed.

Keep-Captain Brice Awde fell forward onto his knees, his head resting against the stones of the battlement. Then, his body fell to one side and deflated, shrinking upon itself. In moments, nothing was left but his clothing and a foul, stinking shell of flesh that had once been a great man—a hero of the north. Moments later, even the skin dried up and blew away, leaving only armor and clothing.

Far away, where the rebels were congregating, a woman screamed in unholy rage.

And the edge of the sun broke over the horizon.

Chapter 52

Danika

With the sun's rise, Danika stumbled away from the battlement and entered the fort's tower, heading for the small armory. Little of use remained there as most items of value had gone north with her brother, but she found a leather jerkin that, although large, would fit her. She then took a leather half-helm with a broken nose guard, a hand axe, and a long dagger and carried them up to her chambers. When she saw Wren's corpse, something inside her snapped, and she fell to her knees beside the young woman, letting the tears flow, releasing the sorrow she had been holding within her. She gasped and sobbed, moaning like an animal.

Palin, Wren, Brice... Too much death.

She didn't know how long she remained like that, perhaps minutes, perhaps an hour. Eventually, she dragged herself to her feet. Glancing at her bed, she considered climbing into it, pulling the covers over her head, and finding solace in sleep. *No. I'm a Dain—the last Dain. I can't quit. Brice would never have quit. He wouldn't want me to. I'll live for him. I'll live for you, my love.*

Removing her dress, she pulled on a pair of thick hunting pants, a heavy wool sweater, and a pair of short riding boots. As expected, the half-helm was too large, but she stuffed a wad of cloth into it and tied it in place with the chin straps.

Attaching the dagger and hand axe to her belt, she went back outside into the courtyard.

The surviving members of the garrison were stacking the dead in two long rows. The fort's garrison had consisted of thirty guardsmen. Thirteen had died the night before, and three more would likely die of their injuries that day—that left fourteen men, none of whom were in their prime. With Dert and the two young soldiers who had done most of the fighting the previous night—Owen and Dilan—that made a total force of seventeen warriors... and her. *Not much of an army, really,* she mused. *Certainly not enough to hold out for another night, let alone the week or more it might take before another ship arrives in the harbor on its way to Port Ollechta.*

Owen and Dilan stood separate from the other soldiers, talking together beside the rows of Wolfrey dead. She joined them, noting that they too had equipped themselves with new gear following the battle. The two men wore ring-mail coats and carried half-helms under their arms. Owen wore Sight-Bringer on a makeshift cloth sheath over his back.

Both men nodded in respect at her approach. "My lady," they said.

"Have you eaten?" she asked them.

"A quick bite," answered Dilan. He looked exhausted, ready to fall down, but he had carried himself admirably the night before.

I don't know him. How long has he been in our service? "You did well last night—Dilan, is it?"

He inclined his head. His left arm was still in a sling, but if he was in pain, he didn't show it.

"We still need to figure out what to do with the dead," the other man, Owen, said.

She remembered Owen then, the young troublemaker her father had sentenced to service as a guardsman—the one Brice had thought had leadership potential. She considered him critically. He was a large man, muscular, with wide shoulders—but he was clearly not the dumb, violent brute her father had thought him. Her father had often been a very poor judge of character.

"What do you mean?" she asked. "What about the dead?"

Owen frowned, biting his upper lip. "It's just… well, Serina."

"We're afraid she'll turn them to ghouls tonight," answered Dilan. "If they're inside the keep when that happens…"

Sudden understanding made her sway. *Father Craftsman, help us.* "Can we burn them?"

Neither man met her eye.

"No, my lady," Dilan said. "Most of the firepots went north. We only have two bombs left. We'll be in trouble if they come again."

"*When* they come again," she said.

Dilan nodded.

Owen looked very uncomfortable but inclined his head as well. "When they come again."

The reeve, Wendel Dert, joined them, looking pale and exhausted, his face covered in soot. "My lady." He inclined his head, finally demonstrating respect.

Another man accompanied Dert, one of the older guardsmen, a weathered sergeant named Tosk.

Where was he last night, when we needed an experienced leader? No matter—Dilan Reese has proved his leadership. "Master Dert," she said. "Where have you been?"

"Inventorying the fort's supplies," Dert answered, glancing at Tosk, who nodded.

"And?" Danika waited.

Dert looked ill, as though he was ready to fall down.

Tosk answered for him. "Not good, my lady. We've plenty enough of food and water, but it's arrows we need." His eyes swept the dead soldiers. "And hands to shoot them."

"We can't defend," said Dilan.

Dert's eyes grew wide. "Will Serina even take prisoners?"

"No, of course she won't," said Danika.

"Actually," said Dilan, "I was thinking of attacking."

"You're crazy," said Dert, staring at him in disbelief. "We're outnumbered—the islanders, the ghouls… Serina herself. We might as well cut our own throats. We can't—"

Danika raised her hand, cutting him off. "What are you suggesting?"

"They won't expect us to come out," said Dilan. "We have Sight-Bringer. Serina will be asleep. We kill her, and this is all over."

"Master Dert isn't wrong about the odds," she said.

"The odds will only get worse if we wait. She'll sleep during the day. That gives us a chance."

"My father said Serina was still awake, waiting for them in the Great Crypt when Stron confronted her—during the day."

"Maybe, my lady," said Dilan. "But what other choice do we have? I don't know if ghouls sleep during the day, but we can't see any from the walls, just the bowmen they left to watch us, but when the sun sets again, they'll definitely return, as will Serina. They'll come with more ladders and more ghouls. We no longer have the firebombs to burn the ladders. The only weapon we still have is Sight-Bringer, and only one man at a time can use it."

"Keep going."

"The islanders have left only a handful of men to watch us."

"They'll attack us the moment we come out the gate," she said.

"They'll kill us before we can get near them, let alone near the alehouse."

He shook his head. "No, they won't. Because we're going to form a shield wall. If we're fast, we'll be on them before they can do anything. These men aren't warriors—they're farmers and fishermen." He pointed toward the dead. "There's plenty of armor now, enough for all of us. We make straight for the alehouse. That's where she'll be. If she's asleep—and I pray she is—we fight our way inside and drive Sight-Bringer through her heart. If she's awake, we may still get lucky."

"Dilan," Owen said, concern in his voice. "She's... she's far more powerful, more frightening than you realize. In the Great Crypt, running away was all I could think of doing. To go against her... I'm... I'm not sure—"

Dilan reached out with his good arm, gripped the back of Owen's neck, and pulled him in closer. "I know. I know what she's like. I watched her rip apart our ranks in the fortress, but I believe we're alive for a reason, that we have Sight-Bringer for a reason. You were meant to find that sword, to bring it all the way here. Now, we're *meant* to go in there and finish her."

"You're all insane," said Dert, his frightened eyes going from Dilan to Owen to Tosk and finally to her. "No. We run and hide, in the interior."

"No," said Danika. "They'd pull us from the woods one by one, bring us before her to be drained and discarded. And she'll take the sword back so that no one can ever use it against her again. Then, she'll raise her army once more from among the other clans. By the time the rest of the kingdom even realizes she's alive, she'll be unstoppable." She pulled her shoulders back, feeling small and insignificant and utterly incapable of confronting such a demon, but she knew she had to try. "No. We attack. We kill her today, while we still have a chance."

Owen, Dilan, and Tosk, their faces grim, nodded in agreement.

Dert, looking like a trapped animal, glanced away at the rows of dead soldiers, wringing his hands. Then he also nodded.

Chapter 53

Fioni

Fioni dropped the last several feet from *Fen Wolf*'s large single mast onto the deck of the longship. Vory and Kora were waiting for her, anticipation on their faces. Many of the crew were sitting back against the hull of the ship, watching her as well. The black smoke rising from the northerner's fort was clearly visible to all of them, even that far out to sea.

Earlier, she had had every intention of sailing past the island and its deep-water port. They had only been out to sea for a few days, and *Fen Wolf* was still fully provisioned, negating any need to visit Port Eaton. Besides, she really didn't like the Greywynne islanders. They had forgotten what it meant to be Fenyir, giving up a life of raiding for fishing and pig farming. Still, they did act as a focal point for shipping, which made raiding those vessels that much easier for people like Fioni—who hadn't forgotten what it meant to be Fenyir.

"Well?" asked Vory.

"Nothing," said Fioni. "There was clearly a large fire, but there's no smoke over the town, just the fort."

"Just a fire, then," said Kora. "Not so strange."

Fioni stared at the island, hazy in the morning light. Something was not right there. She couldn't put her finger on it, but her intuition was warning her that whatever had happened was not "just a fire." She paused, biting her lower lip and thrumming her fingers over the hilt of her sword.

"What are you thinking, skipper?" Kora asked, a hint of amused anticipation in her voice.

Fioni gripped Kora's bare bicep and squeezed it. "I'm thinking of sailing into the bay after all."

"We're docking?" Vory asked.

"I didn't say that," answered Fioni. "I said we're sailing into the bay. I want to see that fort a bit closer."

"Aye, skipper." Vory shuffled back through the tightly packed crew toward the rear of the ship and the steering board.

"Something is going on here," said Fioni, mostly to herself, though Kora was still at her elbow. "Something that we may yet profit from."

"Your father wouldn't like this," Kora said.

"My father's not here," snapped Fioni. "Besides, we're not docking, just sailing past, and we're all friends in these islands, aren't we?"

Kora snorted and spat over the side of *Fen Wolf* into the water.

Fioni smiled. Kora liked the Greywynne islanders less than she did.

Chapter 54

Owen

When Owen handed Sight-Bringer to Dilan, he did so grudgingly. It wasn't his, he knew. If it belonged to anyone, it belonged to the king and, in his absence, Lady Danika, but Lady Danika couldn't wield it. And though Dilan was injured, he was in command—the plan was his. Therefore, the responsibility to kill Serina was his. However, the power that ran through the longsword had given Owen the strength to hold off the ghouls. Without it, he was just another soldier. Dilan couldn't carry a shield with his injured shoulder, so he couldn't stand in the shield wall, and Owen, who could add his considerable strength to the older men's, couldn't carry a shield *and* Sight-Bringer—the weapon was too large to properly use one-handed, not in the press of a shield wall. Dilan's decision to take the weapon just made the most sense… as much as Owen wished it didn't.

Dilan hefted the longsword.

Owen squeezed Dilan's good shoulder. "Luck, my friend," he said then moved to join the others, milling about near the gatehouse.

Tosk, the grizzled older veteran, winked at Owen. The man had seen better years, but he seemed solid enough. All of the men—including Dert, whose presence among the soldiers surprised Owen—wore mail armor and helmets and carried wooden round shields and swords. Several had also slung long-handled axes over their backs, just in case they ran into ghouls. Five of the men, the best shots, carried longbows with the few arrows that remained. When the fighting started, Owen, in the center of the shield wall, would hold the line with ten other men while those with the bows would stand behind with Dilan and Lady Danika, killing as many islanders as they could, especially any trying to get around the sides of the shield wall.

"Don't worry yourself, Horse-boy," said Tosk with a grin. "I know these men. They're not the youngest, not the strongest—and they're certainly not the brightest—but they know how to hold a shield wall, especially against a gang of farmers and fishermen."

Owen looked away, toward the twisted portcullis, from which the obstructions had recently been removed. "My name is Owen."

"No offense meant, lad. I heard some of the others call you that, figured it was a nickname."

"Are we ready?" Dilan called out from behind them.

Standing beside Dilan was Lady Danika, looking small in her armor, with a hand axe in one hand and a wooden shield in the other.

Owen sighed. *This is what it's come to. How desperate we've become.*

The men, silent and grim, nodded, hefting their swords. Tosk rapped his blade against his metal shield boss. The others followed his example, the clanging of metal upon metal echoing from the keep's walls.

Dilan pointed with Sight-Bringer out past the gate. "Those men out there are traitors. There will be no quarter today, no prisoners. Have no doubt—if they get their hands on you, they will skin you alive, but without Serina, they stand no chance. If we kill her, we end this rebellion. Here. Today."

The men muttered angrily, their faces hard, frightened perhaps, but resolute.

"There is a reason why this sword came to us. Father Craftsman wants us to finish her."

The men nodded, their eyes determined.

"Too many good men have died already. What she did to them, the way she sent our own dead brothers back after us..." Dilan shook his head and lifted the longsword high, where the sun glittered off its point. "We end her today, or we die."

Owen threw his shoulders back and thrust his chin high. He found himself nodding at Dilan's words. His lungs expanded as he took in deep breaths, preparing himself for the bloodshed to come. *We can do this. All we need is courage and the Craftsman's blessing.*

"So what are we waiting for?" Dilan yelled, pointing at the portcullis. "There's a monster that needs killing, and no shit-streaked, inbred island scum is going to stop us!"

The men cheered. Then, they raised the damaged portcullis gate. It jerked as the chains screeched, but it still went up. Owen and the others poured out the gate, forming a shield wall on the other side, Owen in the center, providing the anchor for the others. He used his shield to cover the man on his left as he was covered by the man on his right, all their shields overlapping. His heart pounded in his chest, and he roared in anger with the others, smashing his sword against his metal boss.

Scores of paces away, stunned islanders stood and stared openmouthed at the soldiers, pointing at them and calling out to one another in confusion. At a glance, Owen counted at least twenty, maybe thirty of them, all with hunting bows.

"Forward!" Dilan yelled.

The men stepped off, stomping with their left feet, smashing their shields and screaming as they marched toward the stunned islanders. Taken by surprise, the islanders hesitated, waiting too long to use their bows. By the time the first halfhearted arrows thudded into their shields, the wall of warriors was on top of them.

Most of the islanders turned and bolted, having no heart for standing against a shield wall, but a handful remained, dropping bows and thrusting out at the men with boar spears. Owen, protecting the man on his left, caught one of the spears against his shield and then lashed out with his sword, cutting at the man's arm. His foe howled in pain and dropped his spear, staring wide-eyed at the stump of his arm. A moment later, Owen struck him again, this time hacking down at the top of his head, splitting it open all the way to the neck, as if it were a melon.

The men stomped forward, moving as a single unit. The men with the longbows loosed arrow after arrow at the islanders. From that close, the arrows flew straight and fast, punching all the way through one man and spinning him about with the force.

The men cheered as the last of the islanders, a grouping of about eight men, broke and ran. The archers still loosed arrows after them, killing at least two more, before Dilan ordered them to stop, to conserve their arrows.

"Break the wall," yelled Dilan. "Form two ranks and prepare to run."

The men did as he instructed, and Owen put himself near the front of the left-side rank, with one man in front of him. Tosk was at his right, grinning through a mouth long missing several teeth.

"Forward!" Dilan yelled.

The men broke into a trot, keeping in ranks as they ran down the dirt path leading to the town. Several more islanders were ahead of them, hiding behind bushes and halfheartedly loosing arrows at them before breaking and running. The arrows flashed overhead—the men were too frightened or excited to aim properly.

At the bottom of the hill, the path skirted the pier and the bay, moving inland toward the town. Scores of small fishing boats remained in harbor—the islanders were too busy with rebellion to fish that day. The ranks of soldiers ran past the bay, heading for Port Eaton.

Owen gasped for air. A man could run in mail, but doing so was never easy, and one could only do it for a short while. He glanced at Tosk. The man was twice Owen's age, perhaps even a grandfather—far too old to run and fight in armor, as were most of the others, but none of them faltered. Tosk's face was ashen and strained, but he stayed in rank.

The wattle-and-daub buildings of Port Eaton drew closer. The dirt path was worn, lined on one side by a short rock wall. Farmers' fields sat on either side, some fallow, some yet to be harvested. Owen smelled the livestock—the pigs, cows, sheep, and chickens. Dogs barked madly, chasing along beside them, snapping at them and risking shield blows. Owen heard the cries of alarm rising before them, and someone pounded on a metal object, the ringing echoing across the town. As they reached the first of the town's outlying huts and farms, men with bows—hiding behind walls—loosed arrows at them. One of the warriors behind Owen screamed and fell.

Owen wondered how many soldiers remained. Fewer than a dozen, he guessed. A quick glance showed Dilan and Lady Danika running between the two ranks. More arrows whipped past, and one of them hit his helmet and went winging off in another direction, leaving him with a ringing in his ears. Then, they were past the first of the town's buildings. More homes surrounded them, providing more cover for the islanders, but the resistance was paltry, unorganized—they were moving too quickly, having taken their enemy by surprise. Dilan's plan, audacious, bold—more than a little stupid—was working. Owen thought they might really reach the alehouse. He knew dealing with Serina, however, would be an entirely different matter.

Father Craftsman, please make her sleep.

They passed a blacksmith's forge, his tools hanging from the open rafters of his work area, his forge still burning, the stench thick in the air. Children peered at them from behind buildings, and terrified women chased after them, screaming at them to come away.

One little boy, no more than ten, stood his ground in the middle of the path and glared at the quickly approaching warriors. Owen's heart leapt into his throat, but at the last moment, the ranks just split, moving around the boy as if he were a rock in a stream, leaving him untouched. Behind them, a woman picked him up in her arms and bolted away.

Islanders screamed obscenities. Some of the women and children threw rocks. One hit Owen in the cheek near his stitched-up cut, and fresh pain lanced through his face as his blood flowed again. They passed the communal bakery, smelling the aroma of fresh-baked bread mixing with that of pig shit. Then they were into the town center, the village green. Just across the open festivity space lay the two-story stone alehouse that dominated all the other, much smaller, town buildings.

The Wolfrey soldiers stumbled to a halt as they saw a line of Greywynne islanders formed up before the alehouse in their own shield wall, at least thirty men, maybe more—two-to-one odds against them.

"Shield wall!" Dilan yelled. "Re-form the shield wall."

The men stumbled stupidly, tired, as they too slowly formed ranks again.

"Move it, you useless dead men," Tosk yelled, spittle flying from his mouth as he grabbed men and threw them into line.

Owen took the center again, his heart pounding.

"Where did pig farmers get shields?" one of the men asked.

"They're ours," another answered.

He was right. The islanders held shields bearing the Lion of Wolfrey. They must have taken them from the ghouls. They carried axes and castle-forged swords. Some of the islanders even wore mail armor, likewise stripped from Owen's friends.

Angry heat flushed through Owen. "Doesn't matter," he yelled. "Dress pig farmers in armor, and they're still pig farmers."

Bracing himself, Owen set his shield before him, and the men closed ranks. Only eight garrison soldiers remained to stand beside him, for a total of nine, not much of a wall. In surprise, he noted the man on his right was Wendel Dert, the reeve. Pale faced and gasping for air, the overweight Dert had somehow kept up.

Three men with longbows remained, clustered around Lady Danika, trying to protect her with their own bodies while at the same time loosing arrows at the islanders. Dilan stood beside her, a shield he couldn't use hanging from his injured arm, the long blade of Sight-Bringer held one-handed above his head, gleaming in the early-morning sunshine.

Behind the islanders' shield wall, a tall, thin man with long dark hair dashed into the alehouse. *Modwyn!* Owen prayed he'd get the chance to cut the traitor down. A flurry of arrows came at them, and Owen caught two on his shield. He cut their shafts free with one swing of his sword. Behind him, one of the archers bent down on one knee, striking flint to stone, trying to set a torch ablaze.

"Forward," yelled Dilan, and Owen focused on the threat before them.

Once again, the Wolfrey soldiers—exhausted, bleeding, and outnumbered—stamped forward, no longer surprising Owen with their spirit. Those warriors might have been past their prime, but they were still men of the north. He would happily die amongst them if he had to.

He roared in challenge, tired but wanting nothing more than to close with the enemy and cleave them, to feel their blood dripping down his blade and onto his hand. About ten paces away from the islanders' shield wall, a firepot—one of the last they had—flew through the air and hit the ground in front of the enemy line, splashing oil over their feet. The islanders, focusing on the advancing Wolfrey soldiers, didn't pay any attention until a lit torch flew through the air, igniting the oil. Several islanders broke ranks and ran screaming as they tried to wipe the burning oil from their shins.

Then, the Wolfrey shield wall struck against the distracted foe. Because of Keep-Captain Awde, Owen and the others had long trained for that moment and were ready—their foes weren't. The soldiers held their ground, shoving back against the farmers and fishermen, men with no training and no understanding of battle, but the more numerous foes found their courage and pushed back. The islanders' enraged faces screamed at them from over round shields, yelling and shoving. Just for a moment, the Wolfrey line wavered, then Dilan—screaming in fury—rushed forward and shoved Sight-Bringer over Owen's shoulder, point-first into the face of the man across from him. Taking advantage of the opening before him, Owen put his shoulder into his shield and shoved forward, throwing another islander back. He then lashed out with his sword, cutting another man's hand off at the wrist. In that moment, the islanders' courage broke, and panic swept through them like an unstoppable wave. The strength of a shield wall was in its cohesiveness, he knew, and when one side broke, the battle became a slaughter.

He cut out with his sword, keeping pace with the men on either side of him, keeping Dert defended. Dert, clearly more competent with a sword than anyone would have thought, cut down his opponent.

In moments, the last islander fighter was either dead or running away. The soldiers cheered. The alehouse lay undefended before them. A quick glance showed Owen that four more soldiers had fallen, including the grizzled Tosk, which left Owen, Dilan, Lady Danika, Dert, and three other men. Some of those who had fallen must still have been alive, he knew, but for the time being, they were on their own.

"Owen," Dilan called out from beside the wooden door of the alehouse. "You and two others go in first. We'll follow behind you. Watch yourself."

Owen, gasping and bloody, nodded. He was exhausted, but they were almost inside the alehouse. *I'll do my part.* Grabbing two others, Eggers and Lowry, Owen told them they were going in with him. He saw the fear in their eyes, but they prepared themselves.

Owen readied his shield and braced himself in front of the door, with his sword held before him. "Ready?" he asked the two men.

When they nodded, Owen kicked the door. It must have been bolted because it cracked but held. He kicked it again and then again, putting all of his weight into it. On the fourth kick, the door shattered inward, and Owen moved forward. Before his eyes could adjust to the darkness, a man rushed him from his left, screaming incoherently. Owen had only a moment to react, spinning and thrusting with his shield. The man's cry became a strangled grunt as he hit the shield, but the impact still knocked Owen back, and as his attacker fell, he pulled Owen's shield free with him. Owen kicked out, smashing a boot into the man and knocking him farther back. He then gripped his sword with both hands and cut down from the high guard, feeling the satisfying crunch of bone and flesh. His attacker fell with a squeal.

Eggers and Lowry rushed in behind Owen, moving past him to

confront other foes. From Owen's left, a woman screamed in rage, and he spun to face an obese woman charging at him with a cleaver raised high above her head. As she brought the cleaver down, aiming for his head, he used a hanging guard to catch it on the flat of his blade. As she raised her weapon to strike again, he reacted instinctively, stepping forward and thrusting his sword point into her face. To his horror, the blade went all the way through, with at least a foot of it coming out the back of her head.

I've just murdered a woman.

More screams erupted around him, and he heard the flurry of combat. With no time to think about what he had just done, he placed a booted foot against the falling woman's face and yanked his blade free. Eggers was on his knees, with two islanders hacking down on him with hand axes. Lowry hacked down his own opponent then spun about and killed one of the islanders attacking Eggers. Owen rushed forward and cut through the neck of the other islander. *Too late.* Eggers was clearly already dead.

No one else came at them. As his eyes adjusted to the darkness, he saw he and Lowry were alone in the common room of the alehouse. The stench of corruption, of rotting flesh, washed over him, almost making him gag.

"Owen?" Dilan called out from the doorway.

"Come in," Owen answered, stepping farther into the darkness.

All the windows had been shuttered or sealed, but from the light of the open doorway, Owen could make out a mountain of corpses piled in the center of the common room. Flies buzzed madly. The eyes of the dead seemed to stare accusingly at him.

"Father Craftsman, help us—what is that stench?" Dilan asked. He had either lost or dropped the shield he'd been wearing. He was gripping Sight-Bringer's hilt with both hands, still clearly favoring his wounded shoulder.

Lady Danika and Dert followed Dilan inside, their faces pale.

"We need a torch," said Owen.

Lady Danika nodded, dropped her shield, pulled out a torch and flint, and struck spark to stone. "One of the archers dropped it. I thought it might come in useful."

"Bless you, my lady," said Dilan.

The spark caught and ignited the oil-soaked rag. She held the torch high, illuminating the scene of horror before them. Owen swallowed hard, his stomach rising into his throat. Most of the dead men had been Wolfrey men, the surviving ghouls from the previous night. One of them was Fin, his thin body discolored, purplish and green.

A wave of revulsion and anger washed through Owen. *Damn Serina Greywynne and her foul necromancy!*

Dilan stepped forward and, with one swing from Sight-Bringer, severed Fin's head from his corpse. He stared down at the headless body. "Good-bye, Fin." Then, he looked about the common room. "Where is she?"

Owen sighed, glaring at the corpse pile. "She's beneath—"

A blur of movement was the only warning they had before a form leaped from the stairs, landing atop Lowry and smashing him to the rush-covered floor. Owen heard the man's neck snap.

Modwyn, still kneeling atop Lowry's body, let go of his head and grinned wolfishly at Owen. "Still alive, Horse-boy?"

Rage gripped Owen, and he rushed forward to kill the bastard, but before he could take two steps, Modwyn was back on his feet. Impossibly fast, he darted out of the way, leaving Owen to swing his sword at empty air. Then, rushing forward in a blur, Modwyn grabbed Owen in a vice-like grip, lifting him above his head and throwing him through the air. Owen's helmet hit the wall with a resounding crack and fell free.

Shaking his head, Owen climbed clumsily to his feet just in time to see Modwyn advancing on Lady Danika, grinning like a fiend, but rather than back up, she shoved the lit torch into his face. He screamed in pain, holding his face and stumbling backward as Dilan advanced on him with Sight-Bringer.

Owen rushed to Dilan's side, arriving at the same time as Dert. Together, the three men advanced on Modwyn, standing between him and Lady Danika. Owen had dropped his sword when he hit the wall, but he held up his fighting dagger. Modwyn's feral eyes went from Sight-Bringer's gleaming blade to the faces of the three men. He moved farther back, toward the rear of the common room. They had him trapped, but then Modwyn grinned and, in one impossible leap, jumped straight up into the rafters above—a distance of at least fifteen feet. As the men stared up at him, their mouths open, Modwyn disappeared through the roof, pushing his way through the thatch. Sunlight poured in through the opening he had made, and straw fell to the floor.

"He's gone," said Dert, breathless.

"We'll deal with Modwyn later," said Dilan. "We need to find Serina."

"Hurry," said Lady Danika, rushing to the corpse pile. She grabbed one of the corpses and grimaced as she yanked the body free onto the floor.

The three men rushed to help her, unceremoniously throwing corpses away from the pile—except for Fin's.

Owen gently lay his friend's headless corpse on the floor. "I'll do you better later," he whispered before rushing back to help. Then, as he pulled free another corpse, he flinched, his breath catching in his throat.

Serina Greywynne lay on her back before them, sleeping as if the corpses had been a macabre blanket. She was naked, her arms folded across her small white breasts, her skin glistening in congealing blood. The stench of corruption hit Owen like a wall, and he backed away, gagging.

"Craftsman, save us," said Lady Danika in a small voice.

Once again, Owen felt the stirrings of the same panic he had felt in the Great Crypt—the Dread. He knew they needed to act immediately, while they still could. If she awoke, she'd kill them all—he was certain of that. "Do it, Dilan!"

Dilan braced himself. Where Serina lay atop the corpses, she was perfectly positioned for a killing blow from Sight-Bringer.

"Hurry," said Lady Danika, pleading.

"Father Craftsman, grant me strength," said Dilan. Holding Sight-Bringer upside down—using both hands despite his wounded shoulder—Dilan positioned the sword's point over her naked chest, just above her heart.

Time slowed to a crawl. Owen watched Sight-Bringer's perfect steel blade gleaming in the torchlight over Serina's dead white flesh. Her long, braided hair, drenched in blood, was almost unrecognizable as blond. The bizarre tattoos on her face seemed to writhe and move, like the patterns on the stones of the landing before her Great Crypt.

"Die, monster!" Dilan rammed Sight-Bringer through her heart. The perfect blade went right through her flesh, driving down into her, leaving only a foot of gleaming steel and the elaborate carved white hilt jutting above her breasts.

When Serina's red eyes snapped open, Dilan fell back, letting go of the sword. She stared in confusion at the sword impaling her. At any moment, Owen knew, she'd shrivel and curl up into herself, like a dead spider—just as Keep-Captain Awde had.

But she didn't.

Her eyes narrowed in rage, and she shrieked, smashing a fist against the blade jutting from her chest. The Illthori longsword shattered, pieces flying everywhere.

Serina sat up, pulled the remnants of Sight-Bringer's blade from her back, and glared at Dilan and the others. "How dare you!"

Owen moved first, rushing forward with his dagger. Without even turning to face him, she backhanded him, sending him flying again. That time, he hit the far wall hard, and his vision erupted into bright light.

Vaguely, he became aware of screaming, of the sounds of battle. He shook his bleary head and saw that the remaining Wolfrey soldiers were inside the alehouse, battling Serina. Heat and light blanketed him—*The alehouse is on fire.*

Serina stood engulfed by flames, but they seemed to have no effect, and she lashed out at the warriors, shredding their bodies whenever they dared come near. Dilan, sword in hand, was among those fighting her.

Owen had to help. He rose but immediately fell to his knees. Then, someone grabbed him, yanking him to his feet. Wendel Dert was before him, shaking him, screaming at him to do something. Lady Danika stood just behind Dert, disbelief on her features.

Dert turned and thrust her at Owen. "Get her out of here, fool!" Then Dert spun away, sword held high as he charged at Serina.

Owen staggered toward the alehouse's door, half carried by Lady Danika. He felt his terror—the Dread—spike at that moment, and looking over his shoulder, he saw Serina rip Dert's head clear from his body in a shower of blood.

She turned and glared at Owen and Danika, her red eyes locked upon the two of them. "Now you die, niece of Stron," she hissed.

One of the surviving guardsmen attacked her, but she disappeared in a blur, moving around the man, who was already falling, his throat ripped out.

She's too fast. We'll never make the door.

But then she must have stepped into the beam of sunlight stabbing through the opening Modwyn had made in the roof because she screamed in pain and spun away, her skin burning, and fell to her knees.

Before she could rise again, Dilan leaped upon her back, his arms wrapped around her neck. "Run, Owen!"

Then, Lady Danika dragged him away, out into the sunlight. Stumbling, they left the carnage behind.

"Where are we going?" he gasped, light-headed and disoriented.

"The bay," she said. "We're leaving this damned island."

"But—"

"The kingdom needs to be warned. Serina is coming."

THIS CONCLUDES BOOK ONE OF THE VAMPIRE QUEEN SAGA. THE STORY CONTINUES IN BOOK TWO, *THE SHIELD OF SERL RAVEN-EYE.*

<<<<>>>>

About the Author

William Stacey is a former Canadian army intelligence officer who served his country for more than thirty years with operational tours in Bosnia and Afghanistan. He is a husband, father, and avid reader, with a love for the macabre.

For those who want their fantasy laced with heroic adventure.
Visit him online at http://williamstaceyauthor.com
Words of Dark Adventure

Previous Works

Black Monastery

An outlaw Viking clashes with a demon that flays and wears the skins of its victims...

Viking warband leader Asgrim has been banned from his homeland. His only hope of redemption is to raise a princely blood debt. When he learns of a great treasure hidden away on a Frankish Island, he thinks fate has given him one more chance. But Asgrim has been tricked.

Deep beneath the stones of the mysterious Black Monastery, an unearthly evil has been set free. Asgrim must team with a suspected Frankish witch to stop a demonic force before it's unleashed upon the world.

Black Monastery is a dark fantasy horror novel that features compelling characters, raw and vivid imagery, and graphic fight scenes. If you like explosive action that mixes the paranormal and historical, then you'll love this award-winning book!

Starlight: Book 1 of the Dark Elf War

A secret power. The revival of magic. An ancient evil stirs.

Twenty-year-old university dropout Cassie Rogan has returned to her small British Columbia home. Tortured by an accident that killed her parents, she drifts, failing life at every turn. When an impossibly localized lightning storm hits the surrounding forest, Cassie discovers her supernatural side.

After centuries of atrophy, the forces of magic are flowing back into our world, and Cassie can wield arcane powers. Her life seems destined to turn around, until the downside of magic brings everything to a screeching halt. Horrifying mythical beasts now prowl the northern wilderness—including the Basilisk—an enormous eight-legged lizard that can turn its prey to stone.

Recruited by a secretive agency, Cassie must quickly master her powers to protect mankind. As she develops her skills, a dark power secretly watches from the shadows. The Fae Seelie (a.k.a. the Dark Elves)—humanity's ancient enemy—have returned to settle the score.

Starlight is the first book in the Dark Elf War series, an epic urban fantasy and coming of age series that features fast-paced action, mysterious creatures, careful world-building, and breathless pacing.